RUSTLERS HEIST

By Kasey Riley

ALL RIGHTS RESERVED

No part of this book may be reproduced or transmitted in any form or by any means, electronic or mechanical, including photocopying, recording, or by any information storage and retrieval system, without permission in writing from the author, except in the case of brief quotations embodied in reviews.

This is a work of fiction. All names, characters, places, and events are the work of the author's imagination.

Any resemblance to real persons, places, companies, or events is coincidental.

Copyright 2022 – Kasey Riley

Table of Contents

Chapter One _____ 1

Chapter Two _____ 9

Chapter Three _____ 22

Chapter Four _____ 32

Chapter Five _____ 45

Chapter Six _____ 58

Chapter Seven _____ 68

Chapter Eight _____ 81

Chapter Nine _____ 94

Chapter Ten _____ 108

Chapter Eleven _____ 121

Chapter Twelve _____ 133

Chapter Thirteen _____ 145

Chapter Fourteen _____ 162

Chapter Fifteen _____ 170

Chapter Sixteen _____ 184

Chapter Seventeen _____ 197

Chapter Eighteen _____ 211

Chapter Nineteen _____ 218

Chapter Twenty _____ 241

Chapter One

"Sheena, are all the riders accounted for? We need to start back to the R-bar-B if we expect to get there before sundown." Bethany's red gelding, Coup, danced a circle as she spoke. He was more than ready to hit the trail again. Thirteen miles back home would be a cakewalk for the retired endurance horse.

Sheena side-stepped out of Coup's path and laughed. "Yep. I got three horses in the trailer and their riders in the truck, and you've got the other twenty-two riders to lead back. I'm surprised they all look energetic at this point of the day. We've had a great fund-raiser for Betty's Animal Rescue. Suzie will bring up the rear on Gypsy so there won't be any stragglers." She waved the group off onto the trail down into the canyon before returning to the guests in the truck.

The scattered white clouds caused the late afternoon sun to play hide-and-seek on the trail into the canyon. The rising breeze felt chilly, as expected for the second Saturday in May at this elevation. The riders, filled with the tasty food from the picnic and relaxed from the music, held random conversations as their horses moseyed down the trail to the crossing of Blue Creek close to the Gunnison River. The horses knew they were heading back, and the pace picked up wherever the track allowed. Bethany chuckled at Coup, who knew this trail, day or night, sun or rain, and seemed to feel the pace was slower than needed. She drew him in more than once when he tried to shift gears.

"How's everyone doing? Anyone need to stop for anything?" Bethany yelled the question to the riders behind her by turning in her saddle. When the query reached the last rider, Suzie waved to show no one had needed to stop. Now came the fun part. It was quite a climb up out of this gorge.

A whinny off to her right made Bethany swing her whole body in that direction. It was doubtful that there would be stray riders in the gorge today. Her skin goose-bumped, remembering the last time she heard a horse but didn't see it. The day they found Gypsy without Suzie. It couldn't be Gypsy today. She and Suzie were at the back of the group. Having stopped Coup, blocking the other riders, Bethany turned to the group.

"Take a minute. There's possibly a horse and rider over that rise. I'll be right back," Bethany warned the group of the approaching rider. She directed her horse up the trail toward the river. This side was the tougher of the two ways down to the Gunnison, and she hoped it was mustangs over the rise. The whinny sounded again, closer. Coup responded and picked up his pace.

At the top of the rise, Bethany saw a saddled but riderless horse limping toward her. She recognized the horse. What in hell was Buster doing out here? More importantly, where was his rider? Oh, crap! Bethany jumped off Coup and started walking down to the injured animal.

Buster's shoulder was bleeding from what looked to be rock scrapings with a deep gash on his right side, and the saddle horn laid over to the left. If Bethany guessed, she would think the horse had fallen off the trail to the right and rolled over on the saddle and possibly his rider. Unless the rider dived off to the left as the horse went down. She said a silent prayer for that to be the case. The fall had been a steep one, from the looks of the lacerations. Blood covered Buster's golden buckskin coat, and more red showed in the black of his lower back right leg. Neither injury was spurting, but both had shed quite a bit of blood. Judging by the dried and fresh blood, Bethany felt the accident had happened hours ago. The animal must have been wandering ever since, too sore to make it back to the ranch.

Hearing an approaching animal, Bethany grabbed the rein hanging from Buster's bit to keep him from moving. The horse behind Coup stopped, and Bethany turned to see Suzie climbing off of Gypsy.

"Holy cow! Poor Buster! What happened, ma'am?"

"Looks like he fell off the trail and rolled at least once down the embankment." After judging the teen, Bethany came to a decision. "I need you to lead the group back to camp. As soon as you reach the top of the ravine, call 911. Tell the operator we have a lost and possibly injured rider on this trail. You're going slow, so you get to lead Buster. He's sore, but it doesn't look like anything is dangerously hurt. Call Roger and have him meet you to get these people back to their rigs. Okay? Think you can do this?" Bethany watched Suzie straighten her shoulders, accepting the weight of this new responsibility.

"Yes, ma'am. I'll make sure everyone gets back to camp, and I'll call as soon as I have a signal. I'll text Roger right now, so he'll get that before I can get to the top of the canyon. Buster has a halter and lead rope tied to his saddle. I think he was supposed to be rented out for this event." Suzie pointed to the items tied to the back of the saddle.

Bethany quickly switched the horse's bridle to his halter. She was glad to see the attached rope was one of the twelve-foot variety. She managed to get Buster past Coup, who mildly pinned his ears at the other gelding because it was close to Bethany. In Coup's mind, Bethany was in his herd, and other horses were *not* supposed to be close to her.

"Here you go. If it starts getting dark, send the riders up the trail. The worst that would happen is they would make the R-bar-M's gate and not know which direction to take. You've got another hour before the sun sets. You'll be riding in twilight once it goes behind the mountain." Bethany gave directions to Suzie's retreating back before turning back to Coup. "Okay, Bud. It's just you and me. Let's see if we can find the scene of the wreck before dark. The full moon is still several days off, but it should be bright enough for us to retrace our steps—if the clouds stay away."

Stepping up onto a boulder, Bethany swung herself on Coup and moved down the trail toward the river. She'd taken this trail before, but the storms last spring had caused a lot of the river bank to be washed out. She hoped that wasn't what happened to Buster. Obviously, the rider had missed the turn down to the Blue Creek crossing and, as a result, ended up on this nasty trail toward the Gunnison. A blood trail weaved from one side of the path to the other, where the horse had grazed his way back from the accident site.

Twenty minutes down the trail from where they had found Buster, Bethany found the spot of the disaster. At this point, what there was of the path was more of a deer track than a horse trail. She jumped off Coup and threw his reins over a nearby sagebrush. Coup was well trained. He'd wait for her unless something like a bear or cougar jumped out—

then, it would be every creature for themselves in horse logic.

On foot, she stepped cautiously along the track's narrow ledge to the spot where a recent slide from erosion had taken out the entire path. She stopped and peered over the edge, whistling at the drop and the scramble marks in the loose soil. Yikes! Buster was lucky nothing had broken. The tracks below showed where the horse had regained his feet. The rider had either stumbled or slid down the long embankment, and it looked like he had possibly ended up in the river. Bethany shivered. That wasn't a good sign. She looked over at Coup, who appeared to be napping. "You wait here, boy. I'll be back." Bethany spoke mostly to hear her own voice.

She walked back to the horse almost as an afterthought and pulled the first aid kit and a rope from her saddle. R-bar-B wranglers tried to be prepared for the unexpected when leading a group. Patting Coup's shoulder, she stuck the kit in her baggy jacket pocket and slung the rope over her shoulder. She began the long descent to the edge of the river. A little way down the bank, she looked back up at the slide. Something didn't look right; the river couldn't have eroded this high up the hill, and there were no drainage grooves above it where water would have rushed to the river. There were too many wide-open spots above and below this location. The river would naturally lower and slow its flow in the broad basins, even in floods.

Bethany found blood where the horse had come to rest. The rider's canteen and cell phone lay nearby. The loose dirt showed an impression of what might be an elbow or knee and about a yard farther, the depression caused by a body. She could envision a rider landing hard and scooting out from under the horse before possibly passing out. That would account for the "dirt angel" impression. Just below this spot, she saw where the likely injured rider had rolled over, possibly trying to stand, and then rolled head over heels down the remainder of the slide. At the river's edge, only one bootprint remained inches from the water. *SHIT!* From this angle, it looked like the rider had gone into the river.

Bethany moved to the side of the slide. No sense in messing up the tracks that Search and Rescue would need to track the unfortunate rider. She took photos with her phone in each part of the scene. Where the horse had rolled, and the rider had lain. Bethany followed down one side where the person had tumbled down to the river. There, she examined the bootprint, trying to tell if the rider was a man or a woman, and realized the bootprint was toe-heavy. The person had been off-balance, and from the proximity to the water, he must have fallen into the river. Even during the dry spells of summer, the Gunnison was never a slow-moving lazy river. A groggy, off-balance, possibly injured rider stood little chance against that current.

Bethany worked her way back up the slide, keeping out of the tracks made by the falling horse and rider until she was at eye level with the trail.

"Sonofabitch." Bethany muttered when she saw what looked to be shovel marks or pickaxe grooves eating into the soil and rocks under the trail. This wasn't a total accident. Someone had worked to destroy the track. Quickly, since the light was fading, she got photos of the bank under the trail. She was careful to get extra pictures of the bank before the wreck site and beyond where the track had broken off and slid down to the river.

With a heavy heart, worried the rider had been washed downriver, Bethany got back to Coup, turned him toward home, and mounted. She hadn't gone a half-mile before meeting riders and a person on a four-wheeler from the R-bar-M. Roger was leading them, and all Bethany wanted to do was fall into his arms and cry. The day had not turned out as she had planned. Not. At. All.

"Hey, babe. I saw Buster. What did you find?" Roger rode up to Bethany before asking.

"It doesn't look good—about a half-mile behind me. Buster got caught up where the trail gave way under him. He rolled. The rider managed to scramble out from under and might have laid there a few minutes or hours. Who knows? When the rider tried to stand, he must have been dizzy and tumbled head over heels down to the river. One clear bootprint is on the bank. It's toe-heavy, like the wearer still might have been out of control. Do you know who was riding Buster?" Bethany's voice cracked despite her resolve not to get emotional.

"Yeah, it was that guy who reserved a horse last week. He's making a place out on the southwest corner of the 3Cs. Bought about fifteen acres and built a cabin. I don't think he's got any stock yet, but I sent one of the hands over to make sure. No sense in letting animals go hungry while we search for their owner." Roger reached for Bethany's hand and squeezed it to comfort her.

"I took photos of everything. This was no accident. Someone worked under the trail with a shovel or something. That trail didn't just get eroded. I can't think of anyone who would want to shut down this trail, can you?"

"No. There were some disagreements about kayakers and canoeists pulling out at Blue Creek to rest. Still, I don't see where destroying this trail would resolve that argument." Roger turned to the men behind him.

"We don't have much daylight left. I want everyone to dismount at the wreck site down to the river. Search the bank for any tracks of a person coming out of the water. Look for anything in the eddies and back-wash areas. Take at most half an hour, and then start back to the ranch. We don't need to have you injured trying to locate the rider. Spread out and good hunting." Roger turned back to Bethany.

"I'm going home. Megan and the Search and Rescue team can't really get started until the morning, and I want her to see these photos before they begin. I'll see you when you get home. I love you. Be careful." Bethany squeezed Roger's hand before pulling hers free and continuing up the trail.

Chapter Two

At the R-bar-B Campground and Lodge, Sheena watched while the riders she'd brought back from town offloaded horses and meandered back to their rigs. With all the fundraiser's excitement, it didn't seem probable anyone would want to stay for dinner. Betty's Diner had provided the food in town, but Sheena had helped spread it among the riders. She'd made a big pot of chili in case returning riders were hungry, but now, she knew it would keep. Tomorrow she would freeze half and use the other half for herself, wrangler Mike, and his daughter. As soon as the riders got back and all the guests cleared the parking lot, Sheena wanted to head to the "A Bad Idea Bar and Grill" to let someone else cook her a burger. Betty's Diner would be closed when she could get to town, so the bar would get her business. Besides, a beer would go down well after the long day of fundraising for Betty's Animal Rescue. While Bethany shepherded the donors to town and back on horses along the river trail, Sheena had fed them goodies while they saddled and registered. She'd left for Riverview within an hour of the group on horseback so she could help Betty set up the event in the park.

Sheena waved the first group off and went inside the lodge. Her room was behind the kitchen, and right now, she felt the need for a hot shower. From cooking breakfast early to feed the volunteers checking in the riders this morning, she'd been going all day.

Before the first rig pulled in, Sheena had made fresh baked sweet rolls and coffee. Once all the riders were out of camp—including the fool who had shown up half an hour late, she had cleaned the kitchen and driven the truck with the four-horse trailer into town. She spent most of the afternoon with the Search and Rescue Squad feeding the riders and volunteers. The free concert had been great, but now, Sheena was ready for a hamburger, fries, and an icy brew.

She found herself humming a Willie Nelson tune that had something about "beer for my horses" and laughed. This was only her second year working with the R-bar-B, and she felt like it was her home. Last summer, she'd changed her style from leggings to jeans because jeans were more substantial. Besides, with all the cookouts, she needed more durable clothes that looked the part. The same reason could be used for switching to boots, but in reality, she loved her cowboy boots and wouldn't give them up for any fashion choice or trend. Stephanie's Closet sold jeans with glass gems down the seams and across the pockets, making them prettier. Stephanie had helped her choose the style and colors for her new look. Sheena had gone from an urbanite to a cowgirl. The R-bar-B wrangler, Mike, was teaching her how to ride, and while she found it a little scary, she loved the horses.

Sheena looked at her watch. It was just after seven. The riders should be straggling into camp any time now. The ride back from town took almost three hours, and they had left Riverview about four. She dressed quickly after her shower; it felt good to be clean and not smell like grilled food. She peeked out her window just in time to see a rider at the edge of the campground, riding in from the Blue Creek Trail.

"Yikes!" Sheena squealed softly. The sight of another rider behind the first put spurs to her movements around her room. By the time Suzie led the riders into the parking area where they would dismount, Sheena met them there in her best jeans and a snug tee-shirt advertising the R-bar-B. "Hi! Glad to see everyone made it. Where's Bethany? Did she pull out at the ranch?"

"No. We left Bethany out on the trail. She's looking for Buster's rider. I left the horse with Dad. Buster's pretty beat up. He looks like he fell off a cliff or something. Poor fella." Suzie dismounted and began relating the excitement to Sheena.

"*WHAT??* Buster fell? Was his rider hurt? Do you need me to call for the helicopter?" Sheena's thoughts of her dinner and beer flew out of her mind.

"No. We found Buster without his rider. The horse was limping along on a side trail to the Gunnison. The horse and rider must have gotten lost and then fallen off the trail," Suzie explained.

"Let me find the name of the rider. We had one who showed up after you guys left this morning. He was given Buster. That trail is so obvious; we never thought he could get lost. *Crap*. This is all we need. I hope the rider is okay." Sheena worried that a rider could manage to get lost. While she was concerned over the man's condition, she worried about any liability the R-bar-B might suffer if the man sued. *Shit*.

She ran inside, found the liability release, yanked the man's name and cell number from it, and returned to Suzie as Roger pulled up.

"Do you have the name of the rider on Buster?"

"Yes, I've got it right here, Nicholas Davis." Sheena handed the paper to Roger instead of Suzie.

"You two have this? I'll go help Dad with Buster." Suzie remounted and rode Gypsy toward the barn.

"I'll call Search and Rescue. Give Sheriff Megan the details too. Was this rider with the group?" Roger turned to get back into his pickup.

"No, he was about a half-hour behind them. He insisted he could catch up and wanted to ride the trail, so we let him follow. We wouldn't have let him go if we had known he had no experience following trails. He seemed experienced. Mike felt it was safe," Sheena clarified.

"I'm riding out to find my wife. With any luck, she's located this yo-yo, and all is well. Otherwise, we'll be mounting a search in the morning." The truck spewed gravel into the air as Roger left the campground, and Sheena shuddered at the thought of a lost and possibly hurt rider, alone in the dark.

Well, there was nothing she could do at this juncture. Tomorrow might be another long day, but first, she had to make sure all these friendly people left for their respective homes. While some had spent last night camping here, none had reserved a site for tonight.

Sheena strolled out to where riders were untacking and grooming horses. She spoke with several she recognized. "Hey, Robert. I hope you don't have to come back here tomorrow morning to be part of the search team."

"Yeah. I saw that horse. I only hope the rider came off before the animal rolled. I wonder what happened out there?" Robert Pearson replied.

"I spoke with the guy before he left camp. He had a map and seemed to be experienced on a horse. Confident around Buster and balanced when he mounted. Something had to have gone seriously wrong. Maybe he had some sort of medical issue. We won't know until we find him," Sheena said.

"I'm going straight home. I'd planned on spending some time at the bar, but now, I'll get a good night's sleep and be ready to ride again tomorrow. Tell Bethany this was a great event, even with this disaster. People had fun, and Betty can use the money for all her rescues. She really gave us a ton of food while we listened to the bands. I hope there are more fundraisers out here. This camp is a great staging area." Robert pointed his paint at the open trailer door, and the trail horse loaded without any further urging. Robert swung the door closed and dropped the pin to secure the latch. "I hope I won't be needed in the morning. See you around."

Sheena waved at him as he drove off and at the other four rigs following him. That left six of the horse trailers still to load. Sheena hoped they would get moving so she could get to A Bad Idea for dinner. With a bar, they would be serving until midnight, so she wasn't worried about missing the meal, but she was starving.

"Does anyone need anything?" Sheena called out toward the horse owners in the process of loading animals. Several waved at her, but no one stopped to respond. She waved to them and started back to the lodge. Once there, she pulled some frozen dough out to make sweet rolls again in the morning and counted eggs to make sure she could create a hearty breakfast if needed. She had all the makings for an Amish casserole in the fridge, which would feed about a dozen hungry men. Especially if they also had sweet rolls to munch. When she was done taking inventory, she went back to the door and was amazed to see the last trailer's tail lights moving for the highway. That was fast. She was surprised to see it was almost eight when she looked at her watch. Damn, how time flies. She jumped into her truck and headed for town.

Sheena cruised around the square to see if Chris might still be working. Christopher Long owned his shop and tended to work late, and she could use some company. If Chris were with her, none of the locals would pester her for information about the lost rider. Maybe. Her heart eased at the sight of his store lights. He had to be there working on something. The store would have closed at five, six if he had an appointment. Instead of parking at the bar, Sheena pulled in front of Chris's Custom Jewelry and Gems. He was a certified gemologist and had all the equipment needed to examine and categorize gemstones.

On top of that, Chris was a mastercraftsman with gold and silver metalwork that made her drool. She stopped in front of his window, noticing the empty spaces where his current art pieces usually sat. Well, it was after hours. He most likely had put them into the safe for the night. Sheena went to the door and knocked. There was no answer. She pounded harder in case he was running a grinder and couldn't hear her. Still no answer. Maybe he just forgot to turn off his lights. She tried the door handle for some reason, expecting it to be locked. The handle turned, and the door opened smoothly, without even a squeak. This wasn't good. He wouldn't forget to lock up. Even if he were only stepping out for dinner, he would lock his door.

"Chris? Are you in here? Your door is unlocked. It's me, Sheena." Sheena called as she stepped into the shop. Once inside, she got a better look at the premises. One display was open, a chair upended, and an expensive lamp was on its side. Broken glass littered the floor around another shattered display case where Chris kept precious and semi-precious stones.

Sheena stiffened, petrified by the thought that the villain could still be in the store. This shop only had one way in or out. She reached for her cell and hit 911. Before the operator could pick up, she heard a moan in the next room. *Chris! Oh, shit!* He was still here. "Chris? It's Sheena! I'm calling for help."

"911—What's your emergency?" a calm female voice inquired.

Sheena was feeling anything but calm as she raced into the next room. "I'm at Chris's Custom Jewelry in Riverview, and there's been a robbery. Christopher Long is hurt. I don't know how badly. I need help!" Sheena's voice shook.

"I'm dispatching local assistance and calling in an ambulance. Please stay on the line with me until help arrives. You say there is an injured victim? Can you see him?"

Sheena knelt on shattered glass next to where Chris lay on the floor, ignoring the sting of shards biting through her jeans. He put his hand up to his head and moaned again.

"Chris. Can you hear me? Do you know where you are and what happened?" Sheena pulled his hand down to get a better look at his face. His eyes appeared glazed and vague in his pale face. Sheena realized she hadn't ever seen him without a smile.

"I was working, and someone hit me from behind. God, my head hurts." He put his hand back over his eyes, shielding them from the bright overhead lights of his workshop.

"Ma'am, Chris is waking up from being hit on the head. I'm not letting him move until the ambulance gets here. His face is ashen, and his eyes seem glazed and unfocused. What should I do?" Sheena spoke into her phone.

"You're correct not to move him. You can put a cold rag on his forehead, but don't let him eat or drink. Ask him his name and to count to ten, see if his cognitive powers have been altered." The emergency operator directed Sheena, and she did as told. In the middle of Chris counting to ten, Sheriff Megan Holloway burst into the shop.

"*Holy crap!* Chris, are you okay? What the hell happened here? "

"No. Chris is *not* okay. He was hit over the head and has been unconscious for heaven only knows how long." Sheena snapped at her friend.

"Sorry, that was a stupid question. Chris, do you remember what time it was when you last checked?" Megan knelt to speak with the man lying on the floor.

"I don't know, but it wasn't dark yet. I lose track of time when I'm working on a new piece." Chris moaned. He began to raise his hand, but Sheena grasped it to still his movement.

"*Shit!* I'll bet the thief took the piece on my workbench, didn't he? I've spent over a week on the filagree and settings for the seed pearls and diamond chips. That golden topaz was difficult to find in that size; I don't know where I'll find another. There were over four carats of diamonds and an ounce of gold on my bench. My insurance agent is going to have a cow." His voice cracked, and he moaned the last sentence.

"Hush. Don't worry about insurance or anything right now. Don't try to move until the paramedics get here. You might have hurt your back or neck when you fell out of your chair." Sheena brushed the hair from Chris's forehead, focusing his attention on her and not his losses.

"I'm going to get some crime scene photos before the paramedics tromp through here. You stay with Chris," Megan ordered Sheena.

"Chris, do you want me to call your mom? She might be worried." Megan offered.

"NO!" Chris tried to sit up, only to have Sheena push him back down.

From Sheena's phone, the emergency operator could be heard. "The paramedics are almost to Riverview. Did I hear a law enforcement official?"

Guiltily, Sheena remembered the woman was still on the line.

"Thank you. Yes, Sheriff Megan Holloway has arrived here and can take over until the ambulance pulls up. Thank you so much for your assistance. Do you need to stay on the line with me until the paramedics arrive?"

"So long as you are no longer alone and there is an official to assist you, we can end this call. I hope everything works out for both you and the victim." She rambled off some call data for the record and disconnected the call.

"I'll call Thelma." Sheena offered. "Chris can talk to her until the medics arrive." Sheena put her phone onto speakerphone and dialed his house.

"Hello? Sheena? Chris isn't here; I think he should be at the shop." Thelma Long answered the phone with an explanation.

"Thelma. Hi. I'm here at the shop with Chris and Sheriff Megan. Chris will be alright, don't worry, but there's been a robbery, and the thief hit Chris over the head. He wants to talk to you." Sheena explained the situation in one breath and held the phone in front of Chris.

"I'm okay, Momma. Sheena will come to get you as soon as the medics are done with me. Momma, they got everything. My safe was open because I was working from it, and the display pieces were still in the window. The new piece, the makings for the next piece, all the stones I keep in the floor displays—the shop has been cleaned out. That filagree and pearl pendant Roger ordered—I was almost half done with it. Roger wanted something special for Bethany as an anniversary gift." Chris finally broke down as he spoke to his mother. A few tears leaked from the corner of his eyes.

"Listen to me, young man. Those are just things. <u>YOU</u> are all that matters, and if you can talk and worry about things—then everything else *does not* matter. We carry insurance and have paid for years to cover something like this. Now, put Sheena back on the phone." Thelma's voice had strengthened to a command.

"Yes, ma'am." Chris made eye contact with Sheena as she pulled the phone back to her body. "She's pissed," he whispered.

"You bet your bottom dollar that I'm pissed. For years, I've warned you that working in that shop alone after dark wasn't safe." Thelma responded to the whisper.

"Yes, ma'am. You won't get any argument from me on that point. I saw his lights on, stopped to pull him away for dinner, and found him on the floor. Scared the crap out of me." Sheena spoke with conviction to Thelma and Chris.

"Tell me the truth. How bad is Chris banged up? Is he bleeding?"

"I can't see any blood. If the hit to his head cut the scalp, it's not bleeding now," Sheena said. "He's kind of dizzy like his eyes are crossed, or he's had a few beers too many. But he's making sense when he talks. That's a good sign in my book. We aren't letting him move around." Sheena paused, listening. "I think I hear the paramedics; I think they're here. I'll be there as soon as they take him away. Don't you look at me like that, Christopher M Long—*you are going to the hospital.*" Sheena cut the connection without letting Thelma or Chris respond. Thelma had all the information she needed for now.

Sheriff Megan met the paramedics at the door and led them to Chris in the back room. "I need you two to be careful what you touch. Move what you need to move very carefully. I've got photos of the scene, but the less disturbed we can keep it, the better." She stepped aside, allowing them to get to their patient. Megan grabbed Sheena and pulled her out of the medics' way so they could work.

"Come on. We're no help here. Let's walk outside, and you can tell me what you know." Together, the women walked through the disaster of the showroom floor, out into the chill night air.

"You heard me tell Thelma. I was on my way to A Bad Idea when I saw the lights on in the shop. I swung by here, and the rest is history. I knocked, and there was no answer. I knocked a second time and tried the door handle. It was unlocked, so I called for Chris, and that's when I noticed the mess in the showroom. That was sinking in when

I heard Chris moan. I called 911, and you showed up. There's not much else to tell." Sheena rubbed her eyes and shook her head. This day had already been too long.

"Are you okay? Do you need me to dispatch a deputy to collect Thelma?" Megan's voice reflected worry and caring for her friend.

"No, thanks. It's just been a long day, and now it looks to be a long night. Have you heard anything about the lost rider? Have they found him yet?" Sheena asked.

"No. Search and Rescue can't start until the morning. They are bringing boats to comb the river while riders search the land. If he rolled down into the water, he either drowned or floated down the river before getting out. If that's the case, he could be trying to get up the canyon walls anywhere. He's new and doesn't really know that staying on the river would be his best chance." Megan explained the situation as she saw it.

"You would think that some of the river rafters would have seen him," Sheena responded.

"This time of year? Even on a Saturday, there can be hours between rafts on the river. A month from now, there will hardly be space for another raft, but it's still cold, and that water is almost freezing."

"You've got a point there. If S&R uses the R-bar-B as a staging ground, I'll be fixing food for them." Sheena cringed at the thought of dozens of sandwiches.

"I expect they'll want to stage across the highway at the R-bar-M. If the helicopter's called into the hunt, it can stage in the closest pasture."

"I just hope they find him trying to scale a canyon wall and not floating down the river," Sheena said, adding a silent prayer for the rider's safe recovery.

The women turned and watched the paramedics coming out with Chris on the gurney. They stopped when Chris raised his hand, motioning for attention.

"Sheriff. My keys are on the desk. Would you lock up and keep them until I get home? Not that there are many portable items still left, but my gemology equipment is pricey, and I'd hate to lose that machine too." His hand fell back to his chest, and his eyes closed.

One medic looked at the BP reader on his arm and used his chin to direct his partner to get the gurney into the ambulance. Chris never stirred when the stretcher bumped the bed of the ambulance as it slid into place.

"Did he pass out?" Sheena demanded.

"Yes, but that's to be expected with a head injury. He'll likely be in and out of it the entire ride to Montrose." One medic climbed into the back with Chris, and the other entered the front of the vehicle after closing and latching the doors.

"I don't know if following the ambulance will get you any more data, but you lock up here, and I'll take Thelma to the hospital in Montrose." Sheena started for her vehicle at a trot.

"I'll see you tomorrow. Tell Thelma everything here is locked up, and I've got the keys." Megan waved to Sheena and the ambulance as both vehicles spun gravel, starting their separate journeys.

Chapter Three

Megan watched them out of sight before turning back to the store. The crime scene unit would arrive tomorrow. Her role was to keep everyone from disturbing the evidence, but she wanted to look around. Her job was to find the criminal who committed this assault and robbery. She might as well get started. Tomorrow would be consumed with searching for the missing rider, so tonight might be her only chance to examine the scene. She pulled on the latex gloves from her evidence kit.

The shop was a disaster. Shattered display cases, the front window showcase emptied, naked, and messy. It appeared like someone snatched exhibited items, taking parts of the display. The display mountings were scattered on the floor. A black velvet cloth was partially covering them. The fabric could be the backing of the window setting. One spot to the left of the mess on the floor was neat and clean—no pieces of glass or scattered rocks, just a bare floor tile.

Megan squatted next to this spot and looked at it more closely. It looked like something had been sitting here when the cases were ransacked, or something had fallen, and the mess cleaned up very carefully. A square trash bin sat along the wall. Megan looked into the trash can and found it empty. She lifted it and found shards of glass under the container. The robber had used this can. She made a note for the CSI team tomorrow. Most likely, there wouldn't be prints, but it didn't hurt to check.

She returned to the mess in the middle of the shop. Megan knelt to lift the corner of the black cloth, trying not to disturb any evidence under it. Nothing was there except some broken glass, and a few river rocks tumbled to a sleek shine. She had no idea what she expected to find. Some sand was scattered around the shop, but no more than might be tracked in by some desert rock hound on any given workday. From her spot sitting back on her heels, she noticed one clump of what looked to be mud. It almost looked like a boot print. She moved to stand and froze. There was a small gold nugget tucked inconspicuously behind the leg of the display case.

"Well, what have we here? Were you so small the thief didn't feel it worth the effort to pick you up?" Megan questioned the small nugget and carefully picked it off the ground. She rolled it on her rubber-encased palm and found dried glue on one side. Maybe the thief didn't drop the nugget from the goods he was stealing. It could have fallen from Chris's workbench anytime. Megan slid the stone into an evidence baggie from her pocket. This stone would go to the evidence safe located in her office. Chris would remember if he'd dropped a nugget and not been able to spot it.

She stood, placed a dollar bill next to the glob that might be a boot print, and took three more photos. She made a second note to the CSI team, asking them to put this glob into an evidence baggie before vacuuming the shop. If it was a boot print, the soil's composition could help locate the person who made it. Satisfied with her findings, she locked the store and took the key back to her office, putting it and the nugget into the evidence safe. These items might not be the highest dollar pieces of evidence she had ever found—still, they could be critical in prosecuting the crook who attacked Chris and ransacked his store.

Megan whirled from the open safe at the sound of her office door opening.

"Sheriff, Roger Meadows called. He asked what time the searchers needed to start tomorrow? He's setting up two teams for ground search and pulling one volunteer water rescue squad from the next county to search the river," Her receptionist, Shirley, asked from the open door.

"*Crap!* You startled me. Better to start the search as close to daybreak as we can. There's rain predicted for tomorrow afternoon and evening. I pray we can find this guy before the weather turns." May was an unpredictable month at this elevation. Rain could turn to snow, and anyone lost on foot could suffer hypothermia without the temperature dropping below thirty. Not to mention what rain would do to any tracks out there.

"I'm pretty sure Roger would expect that timetable, but I'll call him and confirm. Joe's on duty tonight. You should head home and get some sleep. Tomorrow looks to be a long day. Longer now that we're also expecting the CSI unit. I can let them into the jewelry store if you like. That way, you can stay with the search crews," Shirley offered, extending her hand for the key Megan was about to lock in the safe.

Megan retrieved it and pitched it to Shirley. From long practice, Shirley caught the keyring in mid-air. She wasn't a catcher on the local softball team for nothing.

"Thanks. That's one less thing I have to worry about. Here are the two notes I made for the CSI crew chief. I'll need this data specifically as soon as they can get it done. I'll upload my photos to their data page in my case report. I can do that from my computer at home. I'm bushed. See you tomorrow. I'll be with the search crews early in the day and later with Chris if you need me. I've got a couple more questions for him."

"Oh, Aaron called too. He said he's cooking steaks, and I have to call him when you get into your car. He's not heating the grill until he knows you're on your way. He muttered something about having had burnt dinners before." Shirley laughed and continued, "I think it's sweet that he comes over and cooks for you."

"Well, we had a date tonight, but that went out the window when Sheena called in the robbery. I'm thrilled that he forgives me when work causes me to cancel. But then, come calving season, our dates will be few and far between, so I guess we both have careers that make dating difficult."

"You two need to get married and not worry about dating and getting together." Shirley saw Megan's expression and backtracked, "all things in their own time, I guess. You get out of here so I can call Aaron."

"Okay, okay. I'm out of here." Megan shut the safe, spun the dial, and grabbed her hat. As the station door closed behind her when she heard, "Aaron, she's on her way."

The Colorado sky was alight with stars once she cleared town. The moon was half-full, so the heavens were pitch black around the twinkling lights above. Megan drove slower than her usual pace, enjoying the night and the peace on her small ranch. Shirley had startled her with the statement about marriage. Aaron had asked, and she had said 'later,' refusing to commit.

She loved Aaron and knew he loved her. However, she still had occasional nightmares and flashbacks to her time in the military. Some nights she'd wake up in a cold sweat, swearing she could hear Pashto voices outside her window. Sparkles would be nudging her hand, letting her know that she wasn't in Afghanistan but safe at home in her own bed. So long as she still suffered from her past, she didn't feel ready for a secure future.

Aaron was her mentor with her PTSD problems, but she didn't want him to witness *every* flashback and nightmare. She would ask Aaron to marry her when she could go a month without a breakdown. That was the deal they had made the night he proposed. He, above all others, understood her desire to be self-reliant and in control of her emotions before getting married. He'd also suffered when he returned to civilian life. Yeah, he understood her. Hopefully, they would be married and have a family in the not-too-distant future. But not just yet.

Megan almost missed her driveway between being deep in thought and admiring the stars. She was happy this road had so little traffic as she slammed on her breaks. She twisted the wheel to make the left turn. Thankfulness filled her that the county supplied the sheriff's vehicle with excellent brakes and tires. The SUV's stability kept her safe when she made such a quick move.

On the half-mile driveway to her house, she drove much slower. The last quarter mile was through a pasture, and speed could prove deadly for her and her livestock. She smiled at one of her momma cows, nudging her calf away from the oncoming vehicle. The SUV clattered over the final cattle guard and into the yard. No one could drive up to the house without making a racket that set Sparkle, her Great Pyrenees, to barking and the watch donkey in the paddock to braying. It was no wonder she felt secure living alone out in the middle of a cow pasture, miles from town. It would take a well-trained assassin to reach her without setting off all her rural alarms. Being Sheriff did have a few drawbacks, including the possibility of making serious, vindictive enemies.

The porch light was on, and through the kitchen window, she saw Aaron waving at her. He opened the door before she reached the porch, holding two steaks for the grill.

"Hi, babe. I held off putting the steaks on, but the baked potatoes are done, and if you toss the salad, these will be ready shortly." He brushed a soft kiss on her forehead as they passed each other.

"Sure thing. Need a beer? I'm grabbing one." Megan wished the kiss had been to her lips with more passion, but then again, she was more hungry for food than his touch at the moment.

"Yeah, set one out for me...it'll give me the incentive to have these steaks ready quicker." Aaron's laugh followed Megan inside the house.

Ten minutes later, he walked into the house with two medium-rare New York strip steaks. Megan wasn't sure which had her drooling the most—the smell of the perfectly cooked steaks or the sight of the man she loved holding them. A wistful sigh escaped her when he put the steaks on the table and swept in to give her the passionate kiss she had missed earlier. Now *that's* what she had been longing for, his lips on hers, possessive and strong. His lips released hers, and he chuckled.

"I don't know if I want to eat or go upstairs. You get to choose." Aaron whispered in her ear.

Chills raised goose-bumps on her arms. "I think we better eat these yummy steaks. I hate to waste good beef, *and* we're going to need energy when we go upstairs," Megan slid her lips against his throat as she replied.

"Hmmm...I like your reasoning." Aaron pulled away from her and moved to sit down across the table. For a time, only the sounds of cutting and chewing were heard in the room. Aaron paused to look closely at Megan when her steak was almost half gone.

"I heard about all the excitement. You look tired. Are you okay?"

"I'm fine. Tomorrow will be a bitch, but maybe the rider will hike out, and the crooks will break down along the highway with the stones hanging out of the car—solving all my problems at once." Megan wished with a smile.

"What color is the sky in *that* perfect world? Oh, Bethany gave me the rider's cell phone she picked up below the trail. You might want to put it in a safe place."

"Thanks. I'll stick it in the SUV tomorrow." She slipped the phone into her pocket. "I know neither scenario is likely to happen, but a girl can dream, right?" Megan stuck another bite of the juicy meat into her mouth and hummed her approval. "You make the best steaks. I might need to keep you around for a while."

"Is that a proposal?" Aaron's eyes lit up at the hope.

"Almost. I think if the current stress doesn't trigger any flashbacks, we might want to revisit your proposal. I love that you understand me so well that my hesitation doesn't threaten our relationship. It doesn't, does it?" Megan didn't want the question to be answered, but her conscience needed to ask it from time to time.

"Most of the time, waiting doesn't bother me. Only, when I know you need my support, I wish we were married, and I could be here all the time for you," Aaron answered the question honestly.

"Funny, but it's because there are times I need your support that I don't feel comfortable getting married. I need to stand on my own and face my demons without backup. I'd love to lean all over you and let you carry me, but I think that sooner or later, you would resent it." The steak tasted like ash in Megan's mouth at the thought of losing Aaron because he was tired of her issues.

"Babe, there's *no way* I'd ever get tired of backing you up. Not emotionally or physically. All I want is to be there for you when you need me. It kills me when you have nightmares or flashbacks." He extended his hand to cover hers where it lay on the table. "You fought and suffered enough for your country, the same as I have. You don't deserve to continue fighting that war in your mind and emotions now that you've come home and healed your physical wounds."

"I honestly love you. Maybe it's time we became engaged. We can set a date for months from now. A Thanksgiving wedding would be easy to remember for us in our old age. What do you think?" Megan turned her hand to clasp his to keep from trembling. This decision was a gigantic step for her—for them.

"Seriously? Thanksgiving? Day or weekend? Oh, crap, either would be fantastic. I love you. I'll be right back." Aaron jumped up like he'd been hit with a cattle prod and ran for his truck. Minutes later, he was back at the table and down on one knee. "Megan Holloway, will you marry me? You name it, any day, any time, or any place, and I'll be there." Out of breath, he pulled Megan's left hand forward and slid a ring onto the third finger before she had a chance to answer.

Tears welled in Megan's eyes. He must have been holding onto this ring for months. The thought that he carried it in his truck gave her a watery smile as she turned her hand in his to examine the beautiful ring. Western floral tooling was etched into the gold band with a diamond inset at the center of an intricate flower. "Oh My God, this is gorgeous. Did Chris make it?"

"Yep. Chris is a true artist. He even put an inscription inside. 'With you, I belong,' and he'll add the date of our wedding and our initials later." Aaron couldn't let go of Megan's hand. "My band will say, 'To you, I belong.' Unless you can think of something else you would prefer." Aaron was watching Megan closely. Clearly worried about how she would accept all the preparations he'd made.

"I *love* it. The inscription is perfect in mine. I like yours, but I've got months to decide if I love it." Megan leaned down to kiss the frown from Aaron's brow. "You did good. I doubt I'll change the wording on yours. I just want to keep the option open."

"So long as you like the ring I chose, I'm walking on air. I knew the minute I saw that design that it was the perfect one for you. Western but girly at the same time." Aaron stood and drew Megan into his arms, sealing his proposal with a passionate kiss. Now that he knew she accepted him, the ring and his choice of inscription on hers could all be changed as needed.

"Why don't you run upstairs while I clear off the table. I'd carry you up there, but then Sparkle would clear the table, and I'm pretty sure that wouldn't end well." Aaron released her and pointed her toward the stairs.

"We could toss Sparkle outside for a while—then you could come upstairs with me. I think that's the best idea yet." Megan took Aaron's hand and began to pull him toward the stairs. "Sparkle. Outside, baby." The big dog headed for the oversized doggy door in the laundry room at a trot. As soon as she cleared the laundry room door, Megan shut the door until she heard it click. "Race ya!" Before she could turn to run, Aaron picked her up and threw her over his shoulder in a fireman's carry.

She couldn't help her excited squeal of surprise as he started for the stairs.

"Oh, no, you don't. I'm not letting you win, and this way, I can tickle you all the way up the stairs." His hands started roaming over her body, poking and tickling while Megan began to howl in laughter.

The laughter continued until after the bedroom door closed. That's when the laughter evolved into soft moans and heavy breathing.

Chapter Four

"Oh. My. God!" Bethany grabbed at Megan's left hand. *"When did you get this?"* she shrieked.

"Aaron gave it to me last night. Isn't it fabulous?"

"Chris had to have made it. I love that the band looks like floral tooling on a saddle with the center flower created to hold a diamond. I'm almost green with envy." Bethany let go of Megan's hand and stood back.

"Okay, spill. Do you have a date? What brought on this decision? I thought you didn't feel ready to commit to marriage." Bethany waved to a group of horsemen and women gathering to search for the missing rider. Roger was in charge, so she had a few minutes to grill her friend.

"I don't know exactly how it came about. We were talking, and somehow I realized I had just told Aaron that maybe we needed to set a date." Megan fiddled with the ring for a moment and then turned it to admire the diamond. "I hardly had the words out before he's on one knee and pushing this ring onto my finger. What could I do but say yes?"

"What date did you choose?"

"We're still discussing it, but either Thanksgiving or Thanksgiving weekend. I think the Friday of Thanksgiving weekend is an excellent choice." Megan realized she actually *did* think the Friday after Thanksgiving would make a fantastic wedding day. It might be fun to celebrate that day, no matter what date it fell on the calendar. She would bring it up to Aaron tonight. Meanwhile, she needed to talk to the man in charge of the water rescue crew.

"Can I use one of your four-wheelers to run down to the river and talk to the Water Rescue team? If I start now, I'll be ahead of the riders," Megan stated.

"Take one. The one over by the barn has gas. I filled it yesterday, so I *know* it does." Bethany pointed to the quad parked next to the big barn.

"Thanks. I shouldn't be more than an hour—if that long. We can have a 'girl's night,' and I'll give you all the details when this is over. By then, the date and time might be set." Megan waved at Bethany and trotted over to the quad. The key was in it, and the machine started smoothly. Got to hand it to Roger. He kept the R-bar-M running smoothly down to the littlest detail.

Fifteen minutes later, Megan stopped at the spot the crew had blocked off with surveyor's tape last night. She could see the river below and a boat pulling up to the bank. Megan waved to the man operating the craft. He waved back before jumping to the shore. There were two choices on how to get down to the water from this point. Park and hike down from here or go back to the trail's fork and take the easier route from the town side of Blue Creek.

While cussing under her breath, Megan left the quad at the blocked trail and began hiking down to the river. A couple of spots were slick with loose dirt and sand, forcing Megan to sit and slide until the ground let her stand and hike.

"Hi, Sheriff. I didn't expect to see you down here. Where's Roger and the team of searchers?" The rangy man in khaki shorts and hiking boots reached forward to shake Megan's hand.

"They're on their way, Don. I just wanted to touch base with you. This search possibly could be part of a crime, so take photos of anything you find. The trail above looks like it was undermined intentionally, creating the rider's fall. If he isn't found alive, it will be listed as murder and prosecuted accordingly. We'll need lots of documentation. If you see anything on the shore, come in below it and hike back. Just get photos before anyone else trashes the evidence."

"Wow. Someone *wanted* this guy to fall into the river?" Don's face reflected his amazement. The idea of sabotaging a trail as a murder attempt had obviously never occurred to him.

"We don't know. It seems far-fetched, but until the rider is found safe and sound, this is all we have to go on: someone used a shovel or pickaxe to undermine the trail, and the horse fell." Megan looked around the site, trying to feel how the rider could have ended up this far down from where the horse rolled.

"Bethany got photos last night, and from the angle she viewed them, it looks like the rider lay unconscious and then tumbled down into the river when he tried to stand up. Maybe the saboteur wasn't aiming to kill this rider, but that's possibly what happened. Any rate, be careful, photograph everything, and look for anything unusual. Say a prayer for that rider while you search."

"Okay, Sheriff. I've got chains to drag, but first, I'll cruise both sides of the river. I expect Johnny to be here shortly with his boat, and I'll read him into the situation. We'll be careful and thorough." Don turned back to his boat, closing the conversation.

Megan began her slow climb back up to the trail and the quad. She noted a few tracks along the way, uncertain if they belonged to Bethany or any other searcher. She photographed the tracks in case they didn't. Just below the path, she stopped to closely examine the ground next to the section which had given way under Buster. There were unmistakable marks of both a pickaxe *and* a shovel with the morning sun hitting the spot. Yeah, somebody sabotaged this trail. No doubt. She photographed the evidence and walked below the slide until she reached a place the track continued without problems. At this end, she found where a shovel had left slices into the ground to loosen the packed earth of the trail. Megan took more photos from above and below the path.

From her photographic perspective, Megan noticed a footprint next to the trail. Climbing around the slide, she managed to get above it. When she looked down from this angle, she could see a clear set of prints leading from this far edge of the slide down toward the Gunnison. Damn, these could be the tracks of the saboteur. Megan walked carefully beside the tracks, flagging them as she went. She followed the bootprints to the river about fifteen yards downstream and around the point from where the boat waited for Roger.

On the shore were several marks where a kayak had landed—sharp end into the bank. Boot prints led up the hill to go with the trail down from the damaged spot. Hmmm, this was odd. There were different sole patterns to the tracks around the boat and then away from the kayak upriver. Megan detailed the footprints leaving upriver before turning back to the trail she'd followed down from the sabotaged path. Those prints told a story of a person returning to the kayak from his or her sabotage work above. A single footprint came out of the river next to where the boat's tail had rested. This print looked the same size but had a different shoe sole than the pattern walking upriver. How many people were involved in this? Or, how long was the boat here, and how many times was it visited?

Megan pulled a small tape measure from her pocket and photographed all the prints. They seemed to all be the same measurement. Odd but not necessarily unusual. It might be a typical size for men. It was improbable that a woman had this size foot, but she wouldn't rule it out. Not impossible. In fact, from the tracks and prints, the possibility existed that the river's single footprint could be the injured rider. Again very unlikely. She noted the final photograph of the foot pushing the boat into the water. This shoe's sole pattern was a diamond grid. From the indications left in the sand, she would guess the boat was a fishing kayak with a sharp hull, flat bottom, and a wider tracking skeg for ease of steering. There were hundreds of this type of kayak in the area. Tourists loved them, fishermen swore by them, and the kids loved to float down the river with several tied together to share the beer in the summer months.

Megan noticed her little camera's memory card was almost full. Crap. She hadn't grabbed an extra card. If any of this was evidence, she would be spending hours going through the data, but better have it and not need it than the other way around. Pulling a cell phone from her pocket, she realized, from the screenshot, it wasn't her cell phone. This screenshot showed a man's hand wearing a gold nugget embellished jade pinky ring. She'd pulled out the missing man's cell phone and not her own. Crap. Megan remembered she'd stuck hers in her inner jacket pocket for safety. She replaced the stranger's phone into her zippered thigh pocket, hoping she would have a chance to return it to him.

Megan decided to follow the tracks upriver. They might lead her to the saboteurs while the searchers looked for the victim. The tracks looked to be hiking boots from the deep pattern of the soles. The criss-cross grid pattern would work well to keep a hiker from sliding forward or back. Some athletic shoes might have similar, but hiking boots were more common than Nikes around here. The prints led along the water—the person walked up the hill to stay out of the water in a few spots. She waved when she rounded the bend to see Don talking to Roger.

"Hey, I found a spot just downriver where a kayak put in, and it looks like the owner took a hike. Keep your eyes open for a fisherman's kayak. Like that will help. Ninety-five out of a hundred people on this river use fishing kayaks," Megan chuckled.

"You think the kayaker had something to do with this, Sheriff?" Don asked.

"Well, there were tracks from the slide that led down to the boat. Could mean anything or nothing. You know how it is at this point; photograph everything, and review it later. I need to finish this and get over to talk with Chris about the robbery last night." Megan waved and moved off from the men. She lost the trail where all the searchers had trampled the ground but found it again, and it was still heading up the Blue Creek toward the path down from town.

At the hiking and equestrian trail, she lost the specific boot tracks. This close to town, she had to assume the kayaker went up that direction. But when did he come back, and *how* did he get back to his boat. Maybe he over-heated and swam back to the kayak. Swimming downriver was a snap, and that water was cool enough to relieve any heatstroke. Megan decided to stay on the trail back to the quad. It might be just a little farther, but the good ground would increase her speed, making the walk easier. Retracing the up and down of the tracks she had just followed would be slower than following the main trail.

The riders who were searching for the lost equestrian had spread out. Some riders followed Roger down to the river's edge, and some riders searched above the track. Once all the horses were well beyond the quad, Megan started it, managing to back it until she could turn around.

Once at her SUV, Megan headed for the hospital in Montrose, where Chris had spent the night. Thelma had left a message this morning that Chris would be okay and was expected to be released before noon. Megan had a few hours to reach the hospital to question him. Experience taught her that interrogating a person in the hospital resulted in clearer memories without the distractions of home or the discomfort of the police station. When he was home, his mind would be full of the shop's condition and what was missing. Right now, he should be able to remember more details of the attack. Anything would help.

She made the drive in almost record time. She stayed close to the speed limit, glad she was driving in that magic hour—after the morning workers' commute and before the tourists finished their breakfasts. Another few hours and traffic would pick up, slowing her down. She loved this time of day, especially driving west, away from the rising sun. Today's sky was that crystal blue only the high desert ever enjoyed. The sun reflected on the green of the cultivated lands and the grays and tans of the desert mountains. She felt she could never tire of living anywhere along Highway 50 in

Colorado. Stark contrasts, beautiful skies, incredible vistas, all within an hour of her home. These things made living through the harsh winters worth it.

The hospital in Montrose wasn't huge, so Megan found Chris quickly. When Megan entered the room, she nodded a greeting to Chris's mother, Thelma, who stood by the window. "Good morning, Thelma. Did you sleep here?"

"Yes, that chair is quite comfortable. I knew Chris wouldn't need me, but I couldn't just go home. I wouldn't have slept there either." Thelma indicated the chair in the corner. It almost looked like a recliner, with thickly padded arms and back.

"Is Sheena coming back for you?"

"Yes, she had to get some food together for the searchers and said she would be here by about eleven," Chris spoke up from where he sat on the bed. His face was pale, with a bandage around his head, but otherwise, he looked much better than last night.

"Chris, I know you were knocked out quickly, but I need you to think back to the evening and what was going on up to the minute of your last memory. Just use a few moments to think back over the day. Did any strangers come in? Anybody stand staring in your window at the display?" Megan watched Chris concentrate on her questions. While he thought, she pulled her recorder from her pocket.

"You don't mind if I tape this do you? It helps to get inflections and thoughts exactly as they are told to me," Megan explained.

"No problem, Sheriff," Chris and Thelma both nodded their assent. "Well, it was Saturday, so some tourists were drifting around the square. Nobody looked out of place once I remembered it was Saturday. A couple of cowboys stopped and looked in the window. One pointed to that buckle I put out there last week. He looked closer and saw the price, and his face fell. I could tell he really wanted that thing. He didn't come inside, though. I would have put it on lay-a-way for him and even given him a rancher's discount. I could tell he was a working man, not just a flash wannabe cowboy." Chris stopped and made eye contact with Megan. "He couldn't be the thief. I think he works for the 3C's; I've seen him in church on Sunday."

"Can you pick him or his buddy out of a crowd?"

"Sure. Like I said, I've seen the man in church. I just don't know his name."

"Okay, what else do you remember? Was the day busy or quiet?"

"Besides the two cowboys, there were some tourists who gazed in the window, and one couple came in to look at rings. They were so caught up in each other; I could have been a robot showing them the rings. Tourists love those Black Hills Gold sets. After lunch, the square quieted down, and the town emptied. I left the shop open in case there were any stragglers, but I moved to my workbench. I've got—or at least I *had*—two pieces I needed to finish for the next craft night in Gunnison. My gallery there does well on those nights. These pieces were replacements for items I sold last month. Now, I'm gonna' have to start over after getting more stones and gold to use. Shit. This is a disaster."

"Christopher. You watch your mouth. You know I disapprove of such language." Thelma didn't turn away from the window, but her voice alone would stop an errant child. Chris ducked his head and wrung his hands.

"Sorry, mom. But you know how hard I've been working, and from what I could see from the stretcher, this crook took everything." His shoulders slumped under the weight of his loss.

"You can make more. Things are only things. Yes, they are hard work, but they are still just things. *You* are all that matters to me. You are safe, and I don't care about objects we can replace. Ah! There's Sheena. She's parking the car." Thelma waved.

Megan wanted Chris to finish before Sheena arrived and distracted him. "Continue. The couple were tourists, not from here, and you moved to your workbench. What happened after that?"

"I guess it was about four or so when I pulled the stuff from the safe and began working on my pieces for Gunnison. I needed both the gold and the diamonds for these items. I've been layering the gold into another flower for days. Now, I've got to start over."

"Maybe you can make it even better. Do something you've been thinking of and haven't tried?" Megan tried to encourage the depressed man.

"Not a bad idea. I've got my drawings, and there was something I wanted to try. But, back to what happened. I noticed the light changing and moved my spot around as the sun lowered. I should have locked up then, but I was so involved, and the metal was hot, and this is Riverview—not New York. Things don't happen around here. I hardly ever lock up at home, and my shop lights were still on, so anyone coming in would be walking into a lit store." Chris justified his actions to himself as well as to his audience.

"Anyway. I had just laid on the hammered gold leaf that would camouflage the diamond's setting when I felt movement behind me. I saw men's boots and tried to turn just as something hit my head. Man, I must have dropped like a brick. I don't remember anything else until Sheena was calling my name and not letting me get up." Chris looked up at Megan. His eyes slid past her to a figure entering the room.

"Chris. I'm so glad to see you sitting up. You're still too pale. Have you been released?" Sheena walked past Megan to Chris.

"Not yet. I expect the doctor any minute now. If they wait too long, they'll have to feed me again." Chris chuckled, reaching out to put his arm around Sheena's waist. "Thanks for coming to get us."

"I had to, silly. I brought Thelma to town, and you were brought by ambulance, so it was either I come to get you, or you would have to pay a fortune in cab fare back to Riverview." Sheena leaned into his arm and gave him a peck on the cheek.

"I hate to break this up, but I need to talk to Chris for a few minutes alone. Thelma, why don't you and Sheena go see what time the doctor will be coming by?" Megan worked to keep her voice from reflecting her irritation at Sheena's interruption. She knew her friend didn't even realize she had interrupted and that knowledge was the only thing that kept Megan from snarling.

"Good idea, Sheriff. I could use another cup of coffee too. It's been a long night." Thelma took Sheena's elbow and steered her out of the room.

"What did you have to ask that you wanted my mother and Sheena gone?" Chris grinned as he quietly inquired.

"Caught that action, did you? I have a few more questions and need all your attention. I didn't want the distraction of their presence. I need you to think about and concentrate on what happened last night. You said you saw boots. Men's, women's? Color? Cowboy, hiking, GI, motorcycle? Concentrate." Megan commanded and waited while Chris spent a few moments trying to remember.

"I think they had to have been men's. If they were women's, that woman had a gigantic foot. The boots had that harness leather strap across the top of the front, and the one I saw, the strap was almost cut through on top. It was pretty scuffed up and water-stained. They could have been cowboy, but they looked kind of motorcycle style; the toe was squared." He paused and rubbed his forehead like a headache was bothering him. "Really, Sheriff. I can't remember much else. The boot had a square toe with scuffs, and the strap was almost gone. Did I tell you they were brown with stains?" Chris laid back on the pillow, his voice fading and face paler than before.

"You did fine. Thanks. Why don't you rest until Sheena and your mother get back? I've got to get back to town. I'll keep you in the loop. Do you ever use glue on a gold nugget?" Megan asked.

Chris shook his head. "Only time you do that is if you're attaching a nugget to a stone too fragile to drill. I've done it in the past, but not since I got back from my last gemology course. Why?"

"I found a nugget on the floor behind something, and it looks like it has glue residue. Sound like something from your stock?"

"Not in this shop. I used to decorate some of the native stones from my tumbler with gold nuggets when I first started, but I haven't done that in years. I haven't made that style of jewelry since I moved into the store and put my workbench in the rear."

"Okay. You rest. I'll touch base with you if I hear anything." Megan closed the door behind her and looked around. No sign of Sheena or Thelma. The hallway was quiet. Megan was thankful she didn't need to make small talk or explain herself, so she hurried to the door leading downstairs.

Chapter Five

On the way back to Riverview, Megan snagged a burger at a place along the highway and mulled over her discoveries. Megan's cell rang as she approached the turn into the R-bar-M ranch. Pulling off the road, she answered it. "Sheriff Megan Holloway."

"Sheriff! Sheriff. Guess what? One of the search parties just spotted a man wandering about a quarter-mile from their location. They think it's the lost rider. He seems to be disoriented." Deputy Joseph Kaleo sounded like he was bouncing out of his boots.

In the distance, Megan heard the report of a rifle. A single shot would signal the man to wait for the search party. It also notified other searching groups that the search was over.

"I just heard the shot. I'm turning into the R-bar-M now. Have the party call me using the satellite phone as soon as they make contact." Standing on the gas, making the SUV kick dust into the air, all reflections of the robbery flew out of her brain. She slid into the ranch yard next to the quad at the barn. Her only thought was that the lost rider would be okay. All she wanted to do was get out there and join the group.

Megan jumped at the vibration in her pocket. "Yeah. What's the news? Do we need a medical evacuation helicopter?"

"Sheriff, this is Roger. Yes, the rider has been found. While he's limping, scratched up, hungry, and dehydrated, he seems in good spirits. You're at my place, right? Bring the quad like you're going to the Blue Creek trail, but turn left before going through the gate and follow the fenceline. I think he came out of the river close to that field's northeast corner and followed the fence. That probably kept him from falling off a cliff. I'll stay with him and send the other searchers back. You should be able to reach us within thirty minutes. Be careful of the big boulders and holes along the fence. You'll see the riders before you get to me."

"Be there as quick as I can." Megan slipped her phone into her inner jacket pocket, where it wouldn't bounce out, before mounting the quad and taking off to find Roger and the lost rider. As the quad bucked under her, Megan bashed her memory, trying to come up with the rider's name. Just as she topped a rise and dodged a huge boulder, it flashed into her thoughts. Nicholas Davis. That was it, Nicholas Davis.

The search party, minus Roger, was in a basin below her, so she slowed to a stop and let them approach. Best to let the horses adjust and come to her than to approach them on the noisy machine. "Hi, guys. Congratulations, you found Nicholas. It's a relief to locate him walking and not floating." She kept her voice even so the horses could realize she was human and not a monster. Most animals around here were used to ATVs and such, but it was where they saw it, not what they saw, that could often spook even the most sound-minded horse.

"Sheriff. That guy looks good enough to ride out with you on the quad. He's not much hurt, considering how bad that fall looked. I think his adrenaline was running high after he saw us coming. He was grinning ear-to-ear and almost dancing when we rode up," Doyle, leading the group, said.

"Good to hear that he doesn't need to be air-lifted. One less expense for this rescue. Oh, call Don on the satellite phone and let him know the man's been found, would you? I still want any photos or reports on anything he found on the river. Maybe we can track the person who sabotaged the trail. I think they came and left by kayak." Megan waved the men off, knowing Doyle would call Don for her while she collected the missing rider.

After topping the third or fourth rise, Megan could see a horse with two men. One man was standing, and the other was sitting, slump-shouldered, on a boulder. Megan smiled at the scene. Standing next to the boulder, Roger was well-muscled from long hours in the saddle and working around the ranch. Her friend Bethany had a good, reliable husband. Riverview was lucky to have him too. She waved and stood on the gas, bouncing and shimmying down the slope to the pair.

"Hey, you two waiting for a taxi?" Megan cut the motor, letting the machine under her roll to a stop next to the men.

"Glad you got here so fast. My cell got lost somewhere so that I couldn't call—not that there's a signal out here," the seated man responded, trying to muster up a smile and failing. "I tried to keep that mountain on my left as I walked away from the river. Figured sooner or later, I'd come to a road or a cabin." Nicholas tipped his dented dusty black Stetson.

"You're Nicholas Davis, right? I'm Sheriff Megan Holloway. We thought you were drowned when we found the footprint at the edge of the Gunnison." Removing her gloves, Megan walked over to the man and shook his hand. His grasp was firm and dry. Not bad for a man who'd been wandering in the high desert for the last twenty-four hours. This guy was fortunate; he could have broken his leg or neck when Buster rolled.

"Glad to meet you, Sheriff. Just call me Nick. I've seen you in town but never had a chance to stop and say hello."

Megan pulled her hand back. Something scratched her third finger when they shook hands. "Well, this isn't exactly the welcome we give most new residents. Can you get on the quad, or do you need our help?" Megan sucked on her injured digit, tasting blood.

"I think I can get on. You hop on, and I'll slip in behind you." Nick stood while Megan remounted the machine; he limped to the quad and slid on behind her.

"I'll see you two back at the ranch. There're a couple of things I need to check out here. We lost a couple of heifers last week in this area." Roger stood holding his horse and watching as Megan turned the quad to head up the incline toward the R-bar-M. She gave Roger a questioning glance before waving over her shoulder.

"Hang on. It's going to be a rough ride." With her gloves back on, Megan gunned the four-wheeler up the trail. Nick grabbed her waist as the machine lept forward. Megan could feel his right hand snagging against the leather of her jacket. Whatever had scratched her hand was now marking her coat. She stopped at the top of the hill.

"You've got something on your hand that's scratching my sleeve. Would you mind removing it? The township issued this coat, and I don't want it damaged more than it already is." She turned to watch him as he examined his hands.

"Aww, *shit*. The gold nugget came off my ring. I'll bet I never see it again. *Sonofabitch.*" Nick pulled a jade ring off his right pinky, turning it to examine the glue residue that had been snagging Megan's sleeve. "Wow, I can see where this could do some damage. Sorry, Sheriff." He stuck the offending piece of jewelry into his pocket and again grabbed her belt loops for the ride back to the ranch.

Once the man settled, Megan started out again. She kept a good pace the entire distance, only slowing if she felt his grip slip on her waist. She stopped the quad next to her SUV, waiting for him to dismount from behind her before she stood. "Your truck is over at the R-bar-B. I can take you over there unless you need to see a doctor. I *do* suggest you get yourself checked out. That fall could have done more damage than you realize. I'd be more than happy to take you to the ER in Montrose," Megan offered.

"I did hit my head, but the headache is gone now. I twisted my knee when I was hiking. I guess I'm okay. I might have cracked a rib, but there's nothing a doctor can do for that except tell me to take it easy." Nick limped toward Megan's SUV as she followed.

"Okay, to your truck, it is. Oh, I just remembered, I've got your phone. Bethany found it near where you came off the horse." Megan fished into her thigh pocket and pulled out the phone. She started to pass it to Nick, let go of it, and caught it again while watching his eyes follow the phone. It wasn't much of a test, but she thought if he had a brain injury, his eyes wouldn't respond too fast to the change in the object's movement. Not only did his eyes follow, but his hand reached out to catch the falling phone almost before Megan could grasp it again. Reflexes were working just fine.

"You should have mentioned your rib. I could have taken it slower on the ride back. That bouncing must have hurt like an S.O.B." Megan used her fob to unlock the vehicle while Nick went to the passenger side.

"I got a pang or two, but honestly, I just wanted to get back here. I'm tired and hungry. Roger had extra water, but I haven't had a thing to eat since yesterday morning." Nick gingerly climbed into the cab.

"I'll bet there's food at the lodge of the R-bar-B. I saw the cook earlier, and she mentioned she had food ready to feed the searchers. I'll drive to the door, and you can eat whatever's prepared. Save you from driving home starved. Not safe to be distracted while behind the wheel." Megan spoke as she crossed the highway and started up the long drive to the R-bar-B compound. Searchers were unsaddling, and some were eating at the pavilion. Megan changed her course, aiming toward the edge of that structure so Nick could climb off and reach a table only steps away.

Two searchers jumped up from their meals, and each took an elbow to help the man to a seat. Once he was seated, they asked him about the wreck and how he'd spent the night. Nick told his story between bites of a salami and cheese sandwich.

"Sheriff, everything is under control here. I've heard you've got some issues in town that need your attention. I can drive Nick home if he needs it," Deputy Joseph Kaleo suggested.

Megan took a double swig of her iced tea. Yeah, she had several things to do in town, all right. "Thanks, I'll leave you to see Nick gets safely home. If he shows up, tell Aaron I'll see him tomorrow. I'm going to be working the rest of today with this and the robbery." She stood and waved to the group before snagging her tea and strolling back to her SUV.

During the drive into Riverview, she couldn't keep a grin from forming and reforming on her mouth. Damn, *every* successful rescue made her feel this way. It had to be the relief of the stress of worrying about the missing person; she knew that, but the lift of her spirits would keep her happy for days. Or until life once more interfered.

Still grinning like a fool, Megan entered the building that housed her office, the jail, and the volunteer fire department. She was sauntering past Shirley, the receptionist, when Shirley motioned her to stop. Megan could hear the woman talking and heaved a sigh. Crap. Not Henry. Not today. Shucks.

"She just walked in the door, Henry. I'm going to put you on hold to give her a chance to reach her desk. Right, good talking with you. I always appreciate it when you spot things. Hold on now; the Sheriff will be right with you." Shirley keyed her desk unit to hold the call.

"Sheriff, as if you didn't hear—Henry has a clue that might help in one of your current cases—or so he thinks. Line one is all yours. I'll bring in the notes from the CSI crew." Shirley waved Megan toward the closed door to her office.

Just what she needed today—nosy Henry, throwing his vague and mysterious clues at her. He sometimes *did* see more than others. But, Henry read far too many mysteries while working at the library. As a result, everything he saw out his window was a clue he needed to pass on to Megan. Sheesh.

Megan fought to control her frustration at his call before picking up her phone and hitting the blinking line one.

"Hi, Henry. What can I do for you today? You do realize it's Sunday, right? You should be giving your information to Officer Kaleo."

"Sheriff, that man never really *listens* to me. He just keeps saying things like 'yeah, un-huh, you don't say' and then cuts me off. I *know* when I'm getting the brush off." Henry grumbled about Megan's deputy.

"I'm sorry you feel that way. I'll speak to him. What can I help you with?"

"It's how I can help you, Sheriff. I think Billy's loaner truck has been stolen."

Henry's voice dropped when he said *stolen*. Megan couldn't resist rolling her eyes, but she controlled her voice when she replied.

"Henry, it's a loaner truck. Billy gives it out to anyone who leaves a car with him to be fixed. What did you see that makes you think it was stolen, and have you spoken with Billy?" She wished the man had called Billy first.

"That's just it, Sheriff. Billy is on vacation. Took his wife on a cruise. They left out last Wednesday and won't be back for another week. His loaner was sitting behind his shop as usual when he left. It's not there now. I saw it twice in town, but only from the back. Couldn't see who was driving." Henry's voice almost whined with sincerity.

"Okay. Okay. Give me what you saw, and I'll try to find the truck. I still think Billy probably loaned to one of his customers, but I'll check." Megan picked up her pen and flipped her notepad to a fresh sheet. Knowing Henry, this would be a long tale. And here, she thought the rest of her day would be paperwork. Drat.

"Friday, I went over to Betty's Diner because I forgot to take out anything for dinner. The loaner was sitting behind Billy's Garage when I left the library. I gazed out the window a while later and saw it driving out of town toward the highway. I thought it was strange but figured Billy must have left someone the key. I had some new books to check in on Saturday, so I stayed after I closed to work in peace. It must have been six-thirty or seven by the time I locked up. I was getting into my car when I heard tires squeal like someone hit the gas too hard. I looked up, and there went the truck again, kind of fish-tailed around the corner onto Main Street. It slowed a bit like the fish-tail might have spooked the driver, and then it followed the road out of town. I wondered about who was driving when I heard later about Christopher getting robbed. I'll bet there's a connection—whatcha think?" Excitement brimmed in the question.

"I doubt it. I'll let you know what I find out. If you see the truck, call me. Don't you go trying to stop it or causing any ruckus, you hear?" Her primary fear was that the old man would "try to help" and end up either getting shot or wind up in jail on assault charges. It would likely be the latter at his age, but then, his girlfriend *did* shoot that woman last year, so guns weren't out of the question. Megan couldn't picture him or Ida Mae in any real gun battle.

"All righty, Sheriff. If'n I see the truck, I'll call you. I think it's gone out of the county by now. Blasted kids will joy ride anything, and we both know that old truck is barely worth the duct tape holding it together. I gotta' go. Ida Mae is waving me over to the dinner table. That woman makes a mean fried chicken." The connection died before Megan could tell him not to let Ida Mae cause a stir, either. Those two were a pair to contend with in this town.

A knock distracted Megan from the information Henry had just revealed. She scribbled a note about the truck and glanced up as Shirley came in the door without waiting for Megan to invite her.

"Here are the preliminary notes from the CSI crew. They told me they would put what they found in a case file for you by Wednesday. The crew leader, Sammy Lake, said he didn't expect much, but he'll run that soil through the machine and tell you if it has any properties that would localize the dirt. He doesn't hold out much hope." Shirley set a thin folder on the corner of Megan's desk.

"Thanks for letting them in and locking up after them. I'll take the keys back." Extending her hand, she caught the perfect pitch of the jewelry shop keys. "Were you just waiting for me to get back? Doesn't Krystal take over at four?"

"Krys called and asked me to work until five for her. Her boy is sick. She has to wait for her sister to come over to sit with him. She should be here any minute now."

"Keep track of time exchanges and make sure you don't get short-changed. Krystal seems to use the goodness of those around her more than I like to see," Megan warned her dispatcher. "Besides the search and the robbery, I take it the town's been quiet here today?"

"Sheriff, there is nothing as peaceful as a ranching town on a Sunday. All the cowboys are hung-over, and everyone else has gone to church." Shirley turned to leave the office. "Oh, besides Henry's call, Betty called. She wants to buy your dinner. She seemed pretty determined. You might want to consider eating there tonight and letting everyone know Roger located the lost rider and that Christopher will be fine."

"I hear Krystal. Take the desk for a few minutes and send her in here to me."

"Will do, but take it easy on her, okay?"

Megan went back to sorting through the evidence from the robbery. She pulled the photos she took up on her computer and compared them to the file's data. The crew had found the things she circled as possible evidence. Megan smiled, pleased at how well they got the job done. A soft knock sounded on her office door. "Come in."

"Sheriff, Shirley said you wanted to see me?" Krystal strolled into the office with no sign of worry. Her uniform shirt was too tight, and she had the top two buttons open.

"Sit down." Megan waited for the woman to sit. She noted Krystal's makeup had been heavily applied to accentuate her mascaraed eyes. "This discussion is being recorded." Megan hit the record button on her desk equipment.

"I'll come right to the point. You've been missing work lately. Coming in late or simply calling in for family leave. I understand you have a sickly child, but you also have a job. I won't deny family leave when needed, but I won't tolerate abuse of our leave policies either. Next time you need to call in late or absent, I'll need a written excuse from a medical office." Megan noted Krystal's expression turning into a scowl instead of repentance for her absenteeism. Clenched fists rested in Krystal's lap.

"I'm sorry, Sheriff. I can't help it if Jason has asthma. We don't know what sets it off, he just has attacks, and I have to stay with him until the inhaler takes effect." Krystal didn't look up as she made her excuse.

"I'm keeping track of the hours you owe to Shirley and even those you owe to Billy. If you don't make up those hours during the week they occur, we'll be forced to dock your paycheck. You understand that if you don't repay the hour Shirley stayed for you, the department is forced to pay her overtime. *That's* not acceptable. This discussion is going into your record as a warning. I'll have the tape printed out so you can sign it on Monday afternoon."

"If that's how you want to be. I'll try to have my sister be able to take care of Jason, arriving early every day in case he has an attack." Krystal stood, her fists still clenched.

"Thank you. Have you looked into allergy shots? I understand they're doing great things nowadays for those with allergies." Megan suggested. She tried to sound helpful, but since she had it from Jason's teacher that the boy seldom missed school and hardly ever used his inhaler, she doubted if Krystal was needed at home. Her calls into work were very suspicious.

"The allergist thinks Jason will grow out of the worst of his allergies over the next year or so. She didn't want to put him on shots yet. I hope she's right. I hate to see my boy suffering. Is this all you wanted with me?" Krystal moved toward the door.

"Yes. Your work up until about six months ago has been great. It is only your attendance that has caused concern. I'll make sure that's in the report for your file as well. I do appreciate the job you're doing." Megan smiled and waved the woman out of the office. She reached into her desk for aspirin to soothe her pounding head.

She *hated* office discipline. An officer in the field was easier to correct. More dangerous in some respects but more quickly handled. She'd given Krystal every chance she could. Krystal had been an efficient and reliable employee during the first year of her employment. Over the past six months, the quality of her work had gone down the tubes and her attendance with it. The hour today was just the final straw. Maybe now, Krystal would realize the fine line she was walking and decide to mend her behavior. Megan had doubts that things would change. There was no repentance or shame in her demeanor from Krystal's scowl and clenched fists.

Krystal stomped to the front desk. "You can leave now. What did you do, cry on Sheriff Megan's shoulder because I asked you to stay an hour? You could have refused," she snarled at Shirley's back.

"I didn't do any such thing, but when Sheriff Megan commented that she thought I was off duty, what was I to do? I won't lie for you or anyone else. If you want to be nasty about it, I'll take my hour tomorrow. You'll need to be here at three instead of four."

"*What?* I can't do that. I have to pick up Jason after school."

"They have a vehicle called a 'school bus.' I think Jason can take number twenty-two and get off right in front of your house. It's free. I don't know why you insist on picking him up from school when there's a bus." Shirley didn't turn to look at Krystal; she kept walking out of the building.

Chapter Six

Krystal fumed. First, Sheriff Megan writes her up, and then *Shirley* wants her hour back. Tomorrow of all days! Nick said he'd take her shopping in Gunnison tomorrow. *Damn it all to hell!* He was going to be pissed. She had already set up her sister to collect Jason. She had planned on calling in from the highway to say her car had given up. They had it all figured out. A day in Gunnison, maybe even overnight at a hotel, Krystal felt her face pink at the memory of their last night out of town.

From what the sheriff had said, if she called in tomorrow, she might as well turn in her uniform. *Shit!* As much as she enjoyed Nick's company, she needed this job. With her thumb, she texted Nick: "*Can we go to G on Tu? Have to b here at 3 M.*"

Her cell jumped in her hand with the reply bare seconds after her text.

"*F no. U cnt go – tuff – I'll find someone who cn.*"

Krystal panicked. Nick was her rent money. If he found someone else, her budget would be shot. Besides, she *liked* being on his payroll. It made her feel decadent and naughty whenever they made love.

"*I'll lose my jb. Can you afford me?*" She needed to know before she risked the job she'd had for almost two years.

"*Move to rnch, ful mstrss? I can afford that just fine. You cook+clean++.*"

Krystal thought about the offer. Jason was only eight. He wouldn't know what she was doing for Nick. His room could be on the other side of the house. She squirmed at the thought of more time in Nick's bed. Yeah, that could work.

"*K. If I get fired, we move to your place. 9 tmorow?*"

"*C U*" was the only response she got from the man.

Nick was a no-nonsense personality. She didn't know much about his past, but he showed up in town with money to buy land and build a small ranch house. They'd met at A Bad Idea one night, and it had been fireworks from then on. From the start, Nick'd told her what he wanted and that he was willing to put her on his payroll if she was willing to please him any way he wanted. Krystal had some gaming debts, and this offer seemed harmless enough.

They set ground rules of no drugs, no non-consensual violence, and no cheating. Nick came by as often as he was in town. Mainly during the day when she was off work and Jason was in school. Krystal had called in late those times when he overstayed, or she was too worn out from their play.

Her body was humming, just thinking about being with him full time. Perhaps it was time to quit her job. Krystal knew she would only be young once, and her clock was ticking. Maybe she could get Nick to propose. He seemed to have enough money if he was willing to support her and Jason. She'd bring it up tomorrow on the way to Gunnison.

Sheriff Megan interrupted Krystal's daydream of a life of leisure. "*Krystal!* Are you going to get that call? The phone's been ringing about fifteen times!"

"Sorry, Sheriff." Krystal took the call from the emergency call center. "Riverview Sheriff's office, Krystal speaking."

"Krys, what the heck were you doing? We have a call from an offroad motorcyclist who's spotted a truck in Blue Creek. I've dispatched the VFD, but you might want to send a deputy."

"What are the coordinates?" Krystal took down the data without looking up at Megan, who had moved closer, listening to the call. "Thanks. We'll send someone out."

"What's happening?"

"Sheriff, an offroad biker spotted a truck in Blue Creek at these coordinates. VFD has been dispatched along with a tow truck from Montrose. Billy being on vacation is costing the county." Krystal passed the data to Megan as she spoke.

"Contact Joseph. He's possibly done driving Nick home and is watching for speeders out by the highway. He should be able to get there the quickest. It doesn't sound like it's on the freeway, so it's unlikely to be a wreck. Kids get the keys to daddy's truck and think it's fun to play out in the desert. I can't wait to hear who's little darling will be catching hell for wrecking the family truck this time." Megan handed back the paper and grabbed her hat and pistol from her office.

"I'm going home. I'll see you tomorrow at four." Megan glared at Krystal before leaving the office for the day.

"Bitch." Krystal muttered at the closing door. It would serve the sheriff right if she simply quit without resigning or even calling. "Hmph, wonder how *she'd* like that? Maybe the sheriff would learn not to be so picky. Every time I've called in, they've had lots of time to cover my shift." Sniffing in disdain, she picked her crossword book from her bag.

The office had regulations about using personal electronics on the clock. Still, there was nothing about reading or playing word games. Krystal glanced at the stack of papers that needed to be filed, chuckling to herself that they weren't her problem after tonight. All she needed was to get through this shift, clear out her locker, and leave this place behind her. It was going to be nice living on Nick's ranch. Maybe, she'd get a dog for Jason. Or even a pony. In rebellion, she pulled her cell from her purse and began playing games on it. The exhilaration of breaking the rules kept her smiling for the next seven hours.

*****

The drive to her small hobby ranch soothed Megan's soul. The mountains surrounding her turned colors as the sun lowered behind them. Official sunset was at least an hour away, but the surrounding mountains hid the sun early and turned the world into a place of peaceful twilight. Yeah, this is why she was here and not in Texas with her brothers. Colorado provided her the majesty of the mountains that her spirit craved.

She fed Sparkle her dinner in the house and headed for the barn. Tired from the stressful day, she still spent time in the barn with Radar and his recently acquired buddy, Lucky. She didn't need two horses, but she couldn't turn the gelding away when Lucky's owner moved into a nursing home. At seventeen, he wasn't old, but even gaited horses lost their allure to riders once the animal was past the age of fifteen. Lucky was a fun ride and a wonderful change of pace from Radar's energy.

Radar, at age eleven, was a handful when he was fit to compete. His attitude was "come on, let's go," no matter the terrain. Radar thought his name was either "Trot, damn you," or "Whoa, dammit!" Megan knew there would come a day when he wasn't quite so forward; she hoped it would be soon.

Before she was elected sheriff, she had competed with Bethany in a couple of fifty-mile endurance events. They had placed well, and Radar's vet scorecard was a thing of pride for her. He was far from fit enough to go fifty miles right now, but he hadn't lost the forward attitude from his time competing.

Any morning Megan came to the barn in riding gear, he was first at the stall door to be saddled. If she chose to ride Lucky, Radar would pout with his head down, glaring at her. Most of the time, she would ride Radar because she hated that glare, and Lucky was happy enough to stay behind and enjoy his morning hay.

Tonight was feed, groom, pats, and cookies for both while she mulled over the last two days' events.

First, Saturday morning—sometime after nine-thirty, a rider had a wreck and rolled down into the Gunnison River. The trail had been undermined to disintegrate with the weight of a horse or ATV. Who would sabotage a singletrack desert trail? For what purpose?

Second, Saturday evening—sometime after maybe six, someone had hit Christopher Long over the head and ransacked his jewelry-making operation. Gems, gold, silver, and finished pieces had been stolen. The perpetrator had left without leaving many clues.

Third, Sunday afternoon, they located the missing rider. Quite a bit farther down the river and up a canyon. He was wandering without direction. Nick said he was trying to keep Blue Mesa over his left shoulder, hoping to reach the highway or a cabin. Lucky for all, he wasn't more than bruised from his wreck on Buster. Buster, on the other hand, was cut up and lame.

Fourth, Sunday afternoon, Henry had called to say he had seen the loaner truck from Billy's Garage and Tow service driving around town on Friday and Saturday. Billy likely loaned it to a customer—but Billy was out of town for two weeks from last Wednesday. She meant to have Joe check Billy's to see if the truck was behind his shop but had forgotten. Crap.

Too many things were happening in Riverview this weekend. Things hardly ever happened around here. Not since they caught the arsonist a year or so ago and apprehended the diamond smugglers just months after that. Things had been quiet, with only the occasional family dispute or teen joy-riding in the farm truck.

Radar nudged her, demanding more cookies. His actions indicated his jealousy about her attention to Lucky. "Easy, boy. I brushed you first. It's Lucky's turn now." Megan pushed Radar's nose out of her way and continued to run the body brush through Lucky's glistening coat. He had shed out early, but then, he had come from farther south and hadn't had much winter hair. She'd thrown a blanket on his shivering body more than once while Radar munched his hay without showing signs of chill.

"Okay, okay. I'm done here." She stepped out of the overhang and grabbed a handful of apple cookies, dividing it between the two horses. One last pat for each, a deep sigh, and Megan started for the house.

Sparkle would be done eating and wanting to play. When a dog that size wanted to play, you played. Picking up the tennis ball thrower, Megan opened the door without blocking the charging Great Pyrenees' exit path.

"You ready, girl? Okay." She arched her back and put power into the overhanded swing of the long plastic pitching tool. The ball arced through the air, barely visible in the fading light, but Sparkle chased it across the barnyard and under the pasture fence. Megan heard it hit the ground and watched Sparkle leap up to catch the ball on the second bounce. "Good girl. Bring it here."

Seconds later, the ball dropped at Megan's feet so she could pitch it a second time. Sparkle was only energetic enough to chase the ball four times, and then she would take the ball to the back door of the house and whine. That suited Megan just fine. Her shoulder would begin to ache about the third time she pitched the ball. War wounds were a bitch. They never seemed to let her forget the price she paid for serving her country. The third time Sparkle dropped the ball at Megan's feet. Megan drop-kicked it high enough to brush the oak in the front of the house. That was Sparkle's signal the game was over. Together they walked into the house a moment later.

Megan turned on the lights and began rounding up her dinner. "Crap." She needed to call her deputy and check out Henry's story about the truck behind Billy's. Deputy Joseph Kaleo picked up the phone on the second ring.

"Deputy Kaleo. What can I do for you, Sheriff?"

"I need you to take a pass of the parking lot behind Billy's Garage. Henry thinks someone was driving Billy's loaner on Friday and Saturday while Billy's gone for two weeks. If the truck's missing, we'll have to reach Billy somehow and confirm that he didn't loan the blasted thing to anyone," Megan explained.

"Good news and bad news, Sheriff. I know where Billy's truck is, and I don't think he loaned it. When I left the scene, the tow truck from Gunnison had managed to get a hook on the thing and pulled it up the bank of Blue Creek." Joseph related. "I'm halfway back to Riverview now. The tow company is putting the truck into Billy's garage. I'll go by and lock it up. I sealed the doors with evidence tape figuring you'd want prints taken for the stolen vehicle report."

"Well, I'll be. Henry may have been onto something after all," Megan muttered.

"What did Henry tell you?"

Megan relayed to her deputy what the librarian had seen and suspected. "You know Henry, everything he sees is either where it's supposed to be or part of a crime."

"You have to admit, having his eyes around town has come in handy over the years."

"What? Three times out of thousands of notes and reports? The only thing that makes Henry a reliable source is his constant reporting of what he's seen." Megan huffed at the memories of all the times she'd talked Henry down from having seen a serious crime that was nothing more than his over-active imagination.

"Boss, I'd rather have Henry around, watching things and telling what he's seen, than have the whole town ignore the unusual and make our jobs more difficult."

"Yeah, I guess you're right. But, sometimes, I wish he'd only come forward when we're asking for clues." Megan chuckled at the belly laugh, which followed her expressed wish. "I know, I know. Don't hold my breath."

"You said it, not me." Joseph continued to guffaw at the thought of Henry keeping his suspicions to himself.

"Get prints pulled on the truck. I want to know every person who's been in it that can be identified. This time the kids have gone too far. You don't steal something from a generous man and then wreck it. Damn it. I don't understand how kids today can have so little respect for the property of others." Megan knew Billy would loan that old truck out to anybody who had a license and even one or two who didn't—if they needed it for a good reason. Maybe she could get some of the local cowboys, or perhaps the shop class at the high school, to fix the truck well enough for it to be useable by the time Billy and his wife returned. Lord knew most of them owed Billy a favor from one time or another.

"Sheriff, I expect the kids who did this will come forward. They have to know we'll be able to get their prints off the truck. It wasn't sunk much above the floorboards. With all the TV shows, they must know their prints are still in that old truck," Joseph argued.

"Joseph, I think you're giving them more credit than they're due. I'll bet they were drinking out there in the desert while joy-riding that truck. *If* they remember the night at all, they might come forward; but don't hold your breath on that one either."

"Aw, Sheriff, the kids around here are better than that. Smarter too. I expect a confession by tomorrow afternoon, as soon as they can flip a coin over who will take the fall and who can't afford the penalty."

"I hope you're right. That will save us a lot of paperwork. I still want you to lift prints from the truck; just don't run them through AFIS yet." Megan decided to save her department some cash while giving her deputy something to do. Besides, if the word got out that Joseph was dusting the truck for prints, it might speed up the confession.

"Yes, Ma'am. I'll stop by Betty's and let her know I'll be busy pulling prints from the truck tomorrow morning. That'll get our confession by noon." Joseph spoke Megan's thoughts.

"Good idea. Guilty conscience works best when you *know* you're getting caught anyway. I'll be in the office by eight. Maybe we'll have our little felons by nine." Megan's spirit lifted with that thought.

"Sheriff, you're not going to send them to juvie over this, are you?" Joseph's voice sounded concerned.

"I should, but you know I likely won't. If the perps come forward and own up to what they did, I'll try to make the punishment suit the crime. We'll have to see who did it before I can commit to how to handle the situation." Megan cut the connection.

Crap. Well, at least the truck was found. There might even be a chance to catch the thieves. Well, one crime in Riverview was possibly solved. Megan took a bottle of beer from the fridge and a casserole dish of leftover spaghetti. Five minutes later, she was sitting in front of the TV, watching the news and eating out of the casserole dish. No sense dirtying a plate when it was just her. It had been a long day, and she was more than ready to call it a night. *Shoot*, she was supposed to stop at Betty's Diner and have dinner. Mentally, she kicked herself. Eating there would have been so much nicer than forking food from a casserole dish.

However, there was a rodeo on the rural network, and soon, the bronc riding and calf roping had her attention. Two hours later, the very last bull had exploded out of the chute, and the final cowgirl had turned the last barrel; Megan heaved a satisfied sigh as she put down the empty beer bottle. A perfect way to spend the evening after a rough day at work. Shortly, she had the house locked up and the lights off before going upstairs to her room with Sparkle trailing her. When she turned off the lamp, the big dog snuck up onto the bed, taking up all of what Megan was beginning to think of as 'Aaron's side' of the bed.

Chapter Seven

Luscious warmth down Megan's back brought her slowly awake. She could see her clock, and it was only six. A deep sigh blew warm air across her neck and ear, where her hair had parted to expose it. A smile twitched the corners of her mouth while she lay there, soaking up the warmth and love radiating from behind her.

"Aaron, honey, I wish you'd woke me up a little earlier. You have to be out of here in fifteen minutes. What time did you roll into bed?" Megan asked. No response. Another sigh of breath across her neck. Megan froze. This wasn't Aaron. She began reaching her hand slowly toward the drawer where she kept a pistol, trying not to alert her intruder to what she was doing.

A warm wet tongue swiped her neck, and a cold, wet nose touched her ear.

"Jesus Christ, Sparkle! You almost got yourself shot! Don't sneak up on me like that. What're you doing on the bed, anyway? Get down." Megan tried to sound stern, but a giggle worked through the command, and Sparkle rolled over to expose her belly for Megan to rub.

"Sucking up and asking for a tummy rub isn't going to save you. You woke me up early. I thought Aaron had come in late last night to surprise me. I should have known it was you. He snores, and you don't." She softly ranted at the dog, her hand rubbing the vast expanse of Great Pyrenee's tummy. "You have such a soft pink belly. Makes me wish I could spend the day in bed, just rubbing it. But not today. Come on, let's get up since I'm awake."

Megan stood and motioned the big dog off the bed. Without waiting to see if the animal obeyed, she entered the ensuite bath. A long hot shower later, she bounded down the stairs with Sparkle at her heels. Nothing like an early awakening and a long hot shower to start her day. Especially a Monday. Too bad it had been Sparkle and not Aaron who woke her, but she had a date with him tomorrow, so she'd just have to corral her libido until then.

After letting the big dog outside, she turned on the coffee pot. It was set to come on in about half an hour, but she couldn't wait until then for coffee. She left it brewing and went out to feed the horses and chickens. The brisk morning air forced her to move faster than usual until she finished the chores. Collecting a half-dozen eggs in her jacket pocket, she quick-stepped back into her warm home. Sparkle just about pushed her over when she opened the door. Oops, she hadn't fed the dog before going to the barn. Oh, well, served Sparkle right. Everything seemed to get out of sequence when she woke too early. The coffee wasn't ready this morning, causing her to forget to feed Sparkle her breakfast. Habit, she was a creature of habit, and when things happened out of order, it just threw her off course.

"Oh, no! I'm sorry, baby. Come on. I'll feed you." Sparkle nudged her hand, looking for a pet or some treat, and Megan laughed. "No treats. I'm getting your breakfast; just give me a minute."

In between scooping kibble and opening a can of dog food, Megan managed to pour herself a big travel mug of coffee. She put Sparkle's large metal dish on the screen porch, where the big dog spent her days when Megan couldn't take her to work. Megan checked the water dish once the dog was engrossed with her food. That done, she grabbed her mug and locked the door on her way out. If she moved quickly enough, she could be down the driveway before Sparkle began to whine at being left home. Many days, Megan could take her, but not today. Megan felt a twinge of guilt but knew Sparkle would be safer on the porch.

Megan sailed past Shirley at the office, afraid the woman would have pending files that needed attention. Coffee first, and then she'd go through her Inbox. Megan put an expresso pod into her coffee maker, mentally thanking Aaron for the wonderful Christmas gift. She doctored it to her specific taste before sitting down at her desk. A yellow-sticky message gently waved in her passing, bringing her eyes to her wall calendar: Call Henry. Those two words brought a frown to her forehead, and her heart sank. Not again. Shoot.

"Sheriff, Henry's on line one—for about the third time this morning. You might as well talk to him. He's not giving up," Shirley said from the doorway. Her hands held several notes. She set her load on the desk in front of Megan, turned, and left the room.

Megan scowled at the stack and reached for the phone, punching line one hard enough to move the unit on her desk three inches.

"Sheriff Megan Holloway," she growled.

"Sheriff, Sheriff. I'm so glad you made it to work safely. I've got a hunch those mobsters are back, and this time, they robbed Chris and stole Billy's truck for a getaway vehicle." Henry's voice rose as his excitement bubbled over.

"Why do you think the mobsters are back. They don't own property around here any longer. The ranch was confiscated and sold at auction last year." Megan reminded Henry.

"I can't think of anyone else around here who would hurt Chris?"

"Henry, we found the truck in Blue Creek. Most likely, joy-riding kids took it, but Deputy Joe is dusting it for prints as we speak. I expect the culprits will come in and confess by this afternoon when school lets out."

"In Blue Creek? That's the perfect place to dump it. One of the gang could pick up the thief, and they likely left the county in one of their fancy cars." Henry confidently surmised.

"Henry, the state auctioned off the fancy cars at the same time as the ranch. You know that."

"Well, folks like that always have fancy cars. Check with the Highway Patrol and see if they spotted any Saturday night. I know I'm right on this, Sheriff," Henry huffed.

"Okay, I'll talk to the officer patrolling in our zone on Saturday and see if he remembers spotting the stolen truck or any Mafia-looking cars." Megan knew if she didn't humor the man, he would keep talking until lunchtime.

"See that you do. I'll watch for 'em to come back to visit the crime scene." Henry offered.

"Good. You do that. Chris is going to the shop today, and with you watching out for him, I know he'll be safe." And Henry would be out of her hair.

Megan cut the connection. She seriously needed to get Henry into a different genre of reading material. Maybe she could find a research project for him. Something about the history of Riverview and the Gunnison River. Hmmm, that wasn't a half-bad idea. Megan scribbled a note to remind her to talk with the local newspaper. See if she could talk them into running whatever Henry could dig up as a local interest piece. It would take Henry out of the Mystery aisle of the library and maybe give her some peace.

Megan sorted through the notes on her desk. A missing dog, someone shot a coyote and left the carcass, a cut fence at the 3C's, all everyday issues for a Monday morning.

"Shirley. I'm going to the 3C's and then the jewelry store. I have some questions for both Chris and the hands of the 3C's. I should be back before lunch." Megan slipped her holster around her waist, securing her pistol after verifying the safety. She picked up her shades and hat on the way out of her office. "Check with the CHP. See if anyone reported an unusual vehicle or that old truck out on the highway on Saturday night or early Sunday morning."

Megan stopped in at Betty's Diner for breakfast. "Give me a coffee-to-go and that danish. I don't have time for a real breakfast today."

"Sheriff, Henry was in and said you thought that the Mafia guys were back in town and that they stole Billy's truck to rob Chris." Betty filled a tall insulated cup, passing it to Megan to doctor it.

"Betty, it's Henry who believes all that. I'm still investigating."

"Well, I can tell you it was a single white man who drove the truck on Saturday. I happened to glance up when it drove past the window that evening. The daylight was going, so I couldn't see who it was. But, I can say he was alone, and his skin was so white it reflected the setting sun."

Betty handed Megan the danish in a bag and took her money.

"Thanks. That kind of puts the 'joy-riding kids' theory on hold. Unless the thief was going after his buddies, you didn't see where the truck had come from, did you?"

"No, we were slammed with the dinner crowd, so I know it was between about five-thirty and six-thirty. Other than that, I'm not much help. It was traveling from the left side of the shop to the right. I think that's from the east to the west or thereabouts."

"Thanks, Betty. Call the station and tell Shirley if you think of anything else or remember anyone who might have seen more than you did. You've helped me a lot. By the way, the lost rider was found pretty much in good condition. I don't think he even went to see a doctor, but he moved pretty stiffly when I gave him a ride to his truck."

Megan took the coffee and sweet roll out the door. In her SUV, she unwrapped the treat, taking a large bite before she buckled up and started the vehicle. Once she carefully took a sip of her scalding hot coffee, she settled it into the cup holder. This sustenance would get her out to the 3C's. She could examine the cut fence while she questioned the hands who had been looking in Chris's window on Saturday.

She pulled up to the barn at the ranch rather than the house. The foreman and ranch hands would be able to show her the cut fence, and she'd ask about the trio who were in town on Saturday, window shopping. Several men could be seen working around the building, and Daniel, the foreman, waved as he approached her vehicle.

"Hey, Sheriff. Glad you could come out so quickly. We didn't lose any stock, only because the cattle were all down by the pond. If there'd been any cows grazing, I expect we would have lost them. Don't know why some darn fool would cut the fence there. We had some first-year heifers go missing last week, but I think they're just hanging in the gullies and will wander back before long. Early spring grasses can lure the young ones away from the herd."

"I think whoever stole Billy's truck and took it joyriding is your culprit. My guess would be they wanted through the fence and didn't think twice about your stock when they cut it." Megan had been thinking over the possible connection. The 3C's north fence bordered the highway, and the pickup was found in Blue Creek between the road and the Gunnison River. Just north of 3C's land.

"Damn kids! Each and every one of them comes from the ranches around here. They *know* what a cut fence can do. You catch them, and I'll work their collective asses off to pay for the damage." Daniel slapped his worn Stetson against his leg in frustration. Dust rose from the comfortable old hat.

"I'm not so sure it was kids this time. Betty saw the truck go by with only one person in the cab. Kids seldom do crap alone; they need the moral support of buddies." Megan shook her head as she spoke. "I need to talk to three of your hands that went to town on Saturday. They might have seen something."

"Sure, Sheriff. Which three?"

"I don't know their names, but Chris saw them in the late afternoon. Tell the guys I need to talk to the ones looking in the window at the belt buckle." Megan chose the buckle because they might be embarrassed to say they looked at a bracelet or ring.

"Most of them haven't left out of the barn yet. I'll be right back." Daniel walked into the barn to find his crew.

Megan waited by her SUV, looking around the ranch and admiring all the feminine touches Jessica and Angelica had added in the two years they'd owned the place. She'd only seen it once before the ranch changed hands, but the improvements were noticeable. Rose bushes lined the front porch; lilacs formed a barrier between the green grass of the yard and the parking lot's gravel. Old man Cole would never stand for such unneeded greenery. His ranch was for cows, not women.

"Sheriff, this is George. He was one of the three hands who went to town on Saturday. Max and Josh are out fixing the fence. George will take you out there." Daniel interrupted Megan's thoughts.

"Thanks." Megan shook George's hand just as another man brought a side-by-side four-wheeler up and hopped out. She climbed into the rig, watching George get behind the wheel.

"Buckle-up, ma'am," was all he said before opening the throttle and tearing away from the barn.

Megan gripped the metal frame for dear life, even with her safety harness fastened. The way this guy drove, she hoped the roll cage was sturdy enough to take the flip she felt might soon happen. There was no time to ask questions between the dust, the noise, and the bouncing. In the distance along the fence they followed, she saw another rig like the one careening under her. One man was pounding in a metal t-post while the other looked to be splicing wire. Both men looked up and watched the four-wheeler's approach. George slid it to a stop about ten feet from his buddies.

"Here we are. Hey, guys. The Sheriff has some questions for us. Boss says to tell her anything she asks,"

George informed his friends. Each cowboy tipped his hat to her and gave her his name before shaking her hand.

"Max, ma'am."

"I'm Josh."

"Nice to meet all of you. I'll look over this area in a few minutes. I need you to remember anything you can about your day in town on Saturday. Somebody stole Billy's loaner truck, for one thing, and then the jewelry store was robbed. I'm sure you've heard of both by now." Megan watched the three men, looking for any tells that they might be feeling guilty or worried.

"We spent the day in town, waiting to go to the seven o'clock movie. It was the latest action film with Tom Cruise. Those are always a hoot, the stuff that guy gets into and out of with hardly a scratch," Max offered.

"You looked in the jewelry store window but left before Chris could tell you about the discounts he offers locals and his layaway plan. Do you remember what time that was?"

"It had to be right around five, maybe five-thirty at the latest. We were heading for Betty's. Saturday is Chicken Fried Steak night. We try to catch that as often as we can." George gave up this tidbit of information.

"Did you see any strangers who looked suspicious? You know, hanging around, looking in other stores. Likely by himself. Did you happen to see Billy's old loaner truck?" Megan asked, point-blank.

"Isn't that the truck with a different color fender and another color truck bed?" Josh asked.

"Yep. It's not like that truck can be mistaken for any other. Do you recall seeing it?"

"Not before dinner, but when we came out of Betty's, I saw it in front of the jewelry shop. I couldn't figure a reason anyone would want to drive that hunk of rust," Max said.

"Did you see who parked it?" Megan's pulse sped up. This might be a break.

"We were walking to the theater when a guy came out with a shopping bag. He was limpin' like his knee or ankle was stiff, but not like he had a serious injury. He didn't have any problem climbing into the truck." Josh rubbed his chin, frowning in concentration. "I think I've seen him before, but I don't know where."

"Could you pick him out of a line-up or photographs?"

"His hat hid most his face. I'm not sure I could be positive if I tried to identify him." Josh hedged his testimony about seeing the driver.

"Yeah, I remember now. You wondered if that guy had bought that set of earrings you wanted for your girl." This came from Max. "I'm not sure I could pick out the guy—but his hat was unique. You could tell it used to be black, but one side was scuffed with the crown kind of mashed in. You know, George, like yours was the time that stud dropped you over the fence," Max finished.

"You're right, I remember. One side of that hat was black, all clean and proper, and the other was dirty and crunched," George agreed with Max. "I remember he threw the bag into the truck cab and climbed in without taking off his hat. The crown looked to rub the headliner, so I don't know why he didn't take it off," George said.

"This was close to six?" Megan asked.

"Closer to six-thirty. We didn't have time to go to A Bad Idea and still make the movie. Good movie, but would have been more fun to watch after a beer or two." Max looked pained at the memory of missing his chance to have a beer before seeing the show.

"Sheriff, did the thief make off with *all* the jewelry in the window? Even that set of Black Hills Gold earrings?" Josh asked.

"Sorry, but Chris's shop was cleaned out. I didn't see any earrings left in the mess. I'm sure he can make you a set; just ask him. Maybe he has another pair at his gallery in Gunnison." Megan suggested. She looked at the fence being repaired and could see a vehicle's tracks approach it from one side and continue on the other. "Did you boys follow those tracks to see where they led?"

"No, ma'am. This fence only keeps the cattle from getting down to the Blue Creek. We don't have to follow them, but we plan to backtrack to see where they came onto the ranch. I would guess from the highway, but maybe from one of the Bureau of Land Management, BLM, roads. We'll likely need to mend the fence there too." Max responded.

"Tell you what. George, I need to follow those tracks to see where they came from or go along the Blue Creek. Do you want to drive me, or can I take the four-wheeler?"

"I'll take you. We can go through here. George hopped into the machine and waited for Megan to get in and buckle up.

"Can you guys follow the tracks back to where this vehicle entered the ranch and take pictures of any other fence cut by the trespassers? Send them to me along with coordinates of where the fencing is cut."

"Sure, Sheriff. A couple of BLM dirt roads enter the ranch over cattle guards. We might not find any cut wire," Josh told Megan.

"If that's the case, let me know what road you find at the end of those tracks. I want to know who, what, and how a vehicle got here and why they cut the fencing." Megan called the last over her shoulder as George gunned the ATV through the partially mended fence and began to follow the bent grasses and traces of a recent incursion by a wheeled vehicle.

Twenty minutes later, the four-wheeler sat at the edge of an embankment overlooking Blue Creek. Megan climbed out and walked around, examining all the assorted tracks. This had to be the spot where the biker found the stolen truck in the creek. The tire tracks they'd been following had broken off a small ledge of dirt, and there were tracks down the steep wall of the creekbed. On the left of where she stood, Megan saw the traces of a larger vehicle pulling something out of the creek and towing it away. Megan guessed if she wanted to follow that trail, it would take her to Billy's garage, where the truck now sat.

"Looks like there was a lot of cars and trucks here recently, ma'am. What do you think happened?" George scratched his head and looked from one set of tracks to another.

"I know what happened. A biker found Billy's loaner in Blue Creek earlier today. Looks like whoever cut the fence lost control of the truck, and it went into the creek. The other tracks are Deputy Kaleo, the tow truck, and maybe the biker too."

"Ma'am, I don't think anyone lost control of the truck. I think they ditched it in the creek. Look at the trail we followed. The driver had to pull to the left and make a sharp right turn to put the truck into the creek without rolling over. If he'd lost control, the truck would have had one wheel go off the bank and been sucked down and rolled. No ma'am. I think the truck was driven into the creek on purpose."

"Why would someone do that? What would they gain from driving the truck into the creek?" Megan wondered aloud.

"Maybe they did it for giggles, or maybe they were trying to get rid of the truck. You know, hide the evidence, so to speak," George suggested.

"You have a point. Let's get back to the ranch. I need to go look at the truck." Megan climbed in and buckled up, barely finishing before George put the ATV into high gear. He followed the tracks of the other vehicles leading away from Blue Creek.

"I take it you know a faster way back to the barn than following the creek?"

"Yep. We'll cross a BLM track and turn onto it. That track will come out on one of the county ranch roads, which will take us to the highway. Lots smoother and faster even if it adds a couple of miles." George put his foot harder on the accelerator. The ATV jumped forward, bouncing across the high desert, creating a cloud of dust.

Chapter Eight

"Krystal! Get your butt out here if you're coming to Gunnison with me!" Nick's voice boomed from inside his Ford Explorer XLT. The Explorer's rich deep copper color looked almost burgundy in the bright sun.

Krystal grabbed her overnight bag and locked the house behind her. Her sister had a key and would bring Jason home from school. If Nick wanted a sleepover in the city, Krystal had arranged for Mary to spend the night. She fully expected to spend the night in Gunnison. They usually enjoyed a night of fun whenever they went on a road trip. This time should be no different. She climbed into the SUV, reaching across the center console to kiss Nick.

"I got us a room. I've got a couple of meetings this afternoon. We'll go out on the town when I get back," Nick promised.

"Great. While you're busy, I'll visit the spa. That'll be fun." Krystal had a minor twinge of conscience about her job but nothing serious enough to tell Nick to go to town without her.

The hour drive passed quickly. Soon, Nick signed them into the nice resort hotel. It wasn't ski season, so the prices were lower, and the hotel was less crowded.

"I'll be back about four-thirty. I expect you to be all eager for me, got it? Afterward, maybe we'll be ready to go out at about six." Nick limped over to the dresser and set down one of the room key cards before running his palm over Krystal's butt and leaving her alone in the suite.

Krystal trembled at the heat in Nick's hand. He was terrific in bed. She could spend the next two hours getting pampered while fantasizing about the rest of her day. Ohhh, maybe she'd treat herself to a few glasses of wine during her pedicure. Drinking during a massage just didn't work. She called down to the spa. They had openings in all the services she wanted. By the time Nick got back, she'd be exfoliated, waxed, and have painted nails. It all would go onto the bill. She really enjoyed coming to Gunnison with Nick.

Looking at her watch, she saw it was two. With a wicked gleam in her eye, she called Shirley at the Riverview Sheriff's office.

"Riverview Sheriff's Office, how may I assist you?"

"Shirley. This is Krystal. I can't make it in today, and if you want me there tomorrow, it will need to be a half-shift, between noon and four." Krystal kept her voice sugary-sweet as she dictated what she could and couldn't do.

"Krystal. Let me put you through to the Sheriff." Shirley's voice was tight, and Krystal laughed aloud, envisioning her scowl.

"Sheriff Holloway. How may I help you?"

"Sheriff, this is Krystal. I'm in Gunnison and won't be home until almost noon tomorrow. Sorry, I'm going to miss my shift today, and I can only work a half-shift tomorrow." Krystal didn't even try to control the sass in her voice. If Megan fired her, she could collect unemployment.

"I'm sorry to hear that. I'll have Deputy Kaleo clean out your locker for you. He'll put your things in a sealed evidence bag and leave them at the front desk. I thought I had made myself clear yesterday, when I wrote you up, that any more ditching work and you'd be fired." Megan's voice sounded more resigned than angry.

"You made it perfectly clear, Sheriff. I'm sorry we can't see eye to eye about my need for time off. I guess I'm fired? I'm willing to work until you find a replacement." Krystal knew Megan would have turned on the recorder. This offer would sound good when she applied for unemployment benefits.

"Yes, as you know, this conversation is being recorded. I accept your resignation."

"I *did not* resign. You just told me my locker would be cleaned out, and I could pick my stuff up at the desk. In my book, that means *you* fired *me*." Krystal clarified the situation. If she quit, there would be no benefits. Megan had to fire her.

"Sorry, I thought that you were resigning because you offered to continue until I found a replacement. That sounds like the two weeks' notice that most resigning employees give." Megan's voice was sugar-sweet now.

"I was offering to show my willingness to work after you told me my services were no longer needed by cleaning my locker," Krystal spoke through her teeth. Somehow, this conversation wasn't going as she had planned.

"Krystal, I've got the recording of my warning you about your attendance. The next day, you call in without reason, telling me you don't plan on being at work for two days. That gives me cause to fire you, regardless of your willingness to cover at your convenience. Yes, you are fired. A copy of this tape and the recording from Sunday will be in your file. The unemployment office will review both." A loud click sounded as Megan cut the connection.

"Bitch. Now you and that whiny bitch Shirley can cover my shift today and until you find some poor schmuck who needs to work." Krystal laughed on her way to the spa.

*****

"Shirley!" Megan's voice rang out as she stared at the phone she'd just slammed back down on her desk.

"Yeah, boss? Did you fire her? Please tell me that you did. I'm so tired of covering for her lazy ass," Shirley said. "Bethany has a friend staying with her. The lady wants a change and was asking about jobs. I can call her. One of the girls working at Betty's might want to change jobs, but I think she's too young to take on the job here. This place needs someone who has some common sense."

"Get Bethany for me. I'll talk to her and see what she thinks about her friend. If the woman isn't serious about moving here for good, we don't want to hire her." Megan knew if Bethany was willing to recommend this woman, she might be a good fit.

"Yes, Sheriff. Now that the crime scene tape is down, Chris and Sheena are cleaning up the jewelry store. Have you been over there?"

"No, I meant to stop by there earlier, but I didn't see any cars parked out front, and I needed to get here and write down what the boys at the 3C's had told me." Megan stood, walking out from behind her desk. "Can you cover until about eight? I'll have Priscilla come in early to relieve you."

"Sheriff, to be rid of Krystal, I'd stay until ten. Nothing much happening at home, and John can feed himself." Shirley passed Megan her hat. "I'll tell Bethany to send her friend by about four. That will give you an hour and a half to prep some questions. I'll have an application form on your desk when you get back." Shirley followed Megan to the door.

"Let's cross our fingers that this person can start tomorrow. Otherwise, I'll be filling in a shift or two for you and Pricilla." Megan left the building. She felt justified in firing Krystal, but she hated searching for a new employee. It had to be either a local, most of whom were working or unable to work, or someone willing to drive from the smaller outlying villages. If Bethany's friend didn't feel right, Megan knew she would start calling the employment services. She would just rather it be someone she knew or a person well known to a local. Her office handled enough sensitive data that the wrong person on the desk could get someone killed. Not often, but it could happen if the person on the phone didn't have sense, or worse yet, was a gossip.

Across the square, she could see people moving inside the jewelry shop. She counted three as she approached. Darn. She wanted to have a moment or three with Chris again to see if he remembered seeing Billy's truck or anything more.

The bell over the door jingled as she walked into the shop, stopping Megan in her tracks. "That didn't make any noise when I was here on Saturday after the robbery. Was it broken before the robber got here?"

"Oh, yeah. Krystal was in last week to look at some gold earrings and knocked the bell off the hook over the door. She tripped in the door, and the force of the door opening like that broke the arm holding the bell. Doyle made me a new one but didn't get it installed until this morning." Chris explained. "If it had only been over the door on Saturday, I would have heard the guy come into the store."

Megan looked from Chris to the door and back. "Yeah, if only. How many people would know the bell wasn't working?"

"Doyle, he likely told Stephanie. Krystal, since she broke it, and any customers from Wednesday until this morning. Lord, if Doyle mentioned it to Betty—the whole town likely knew. I didn't tell Betty because I didn't think anything of it once I turned the repair over to Doyle." Chris counted off people on his fingers until he got to Betty, and then he threw up his hands.

"I'll check with Betty and Doyle. It may mean nothing, or it may give me a new direction to follow." Megan walked over to Chris. She looked him up and down, searching for any indication that he wasn't healed from the assault. "How are you feeling?"

"I woke up today without a headache for the first time since the attack," Chris offered.

"Glad to hear it. Do you remember seeing Billy's loaner truck in town lately?" Megan asked the general question, not wanting to lead Chris but instead letting him remember what he could.

"Billy's out of town. He left on Wednesday for two weeks." Sheena offered, earning a glare from Megan.

"You know, now that I think of it, I saw it driving out of town on Friday when I was locking up. Just the back end of it, but you can't mistake that beater," Chris recalled.

"Any other time? It was spotted in town on Saturday too."

"Not that I can remember. What's this about, Sheriff?" Chris stopped sorting the pebbles and rocks the thief had left behind and looked at Megan.

"Those cowboys from the 3C's saw the truck parked in front of your store just after six. We found the truck dumped in Blue Creek this morning."

"Joy-riding kids again?" Chris mused.

"I don't think so. Both the cowboys and Betty put only one person in the cab. Mischief-making kids come in a minimum of pairs, often three or four at a time. I think the truck was stolen to commit this crime. No one in town would think twice about Billy's truck being parked on the square. A personal vehicle might raise gossip or a discussion about what the driver is doing. A loaner truck? Anyone could be driving it." Megan explained her thoughts on the truck and what was going on the past weekend.

"But who? Who would go to those lengths? I doubt they got away with more than twelve thousand dollars in goods. Breaking down the jewelry and selling stones and raw gold would bring the amount down to maybe nine thousand. Though that roll of 18k gold chain could be pieced out and marked up…" This time, Chris scratched his chin. "That one piece—the special one I've been making for Roger, that might be worth some money. It's got gold filigree work around seed pearls with a large yellow topaz cabochon in the center. I hope we can find the goods before they get a chance to melt that piece down. I've labored so many hours, and that stone was perfect."

"Maybe the thief didn't know how much was or wasn't in this shop—only that you worked with gold, diamonds, and other precious stones and metals. If this is a one-man job, the cost wouldn't be high, just labor-intensive with the danger of being discovered." Megan walked around the shop, looking at the piles Chris was stacking of tumbled stones and display case fabrics. "I need the list of missing items as soon as you've made it. I'll pass it on to your insurance company when they contact my office. I have to warn you that I don't hold much hope of recovering your lost goods. Jewelry is simply too difficult to trace and easy to change."

"I understand, Sheriff. You're doing a fine job. I'm surprised you've found out as much out as you have in such a short time. Keep me in the loop as much as you can." Chris turned to sweep up the glass while Sheena and his mother carried out the trash bins of larger pieces to the dumpster in the back.

*****

Krystal spent her day in the spa being massaged, waxed, and getting her mani-pedi. The time flew by until she looked up at the clock over the door of the hair salon. *"Holy Shit!"* It was twenty past four. Nick would be getting back to the suite any minute, and if she wasn't waiting for him, there could be hell to pay. No way could she afford to piss off the man who was now supporting her and Jason.

"I gotta go! Put this on the tab for suite 301A. Add a healthy tip, twenty percent."

"But...but, madam, I'm not done with your comb out," The stylist stammered, jumping back as Krystal exploded from the chair. The shawl protecting Krystal's clothing flew across the room.

"Good enough. It's only going to be messy in half an hour anyway." Krystal slipped her barely dried toes into her sandals and ran for the elevator.

"What was that all about?" The manicurist asked the hairstylist.

"Beats the shit out of me, but we just earned twenty percent tips." Both women laughed and added the charges and tip to the bill for 301A. One added a second glass of wine, and the pair split it. Krystal hadn't been their easiest customer.

Krystal made it back to the room, managing to be ready and willing for Nick. Later, after their shower, Nick brought out a gift—a carved filigree set of Black Hills Gold earrings.

"These are *amazing!* Are they Chris Long originals? I thought he had his jewelry store robbed?" Krystal fingered the intricate workings on the hoops.

"He did, but I got these from his gallery here in Gunnison. I was downtown and saw them in the window and remembered you wanted a pair of earrings made by him," Nick bragged.

"Oooohhh…you're so good to me. I lost my job today. Did you mean it when you said that Jason and I could move into your place?" Krystal figured she might as well get him to commit right now while he was sated and feeling generous. His mood could change in an instant.

"Sure thing, babe. We'll move you to the ranch on the first of the month. I need to finish some things before you'd be comfortable there."

"I thought your house was all finished. If I move in tomorrow, we can have more fun together. What's wrong with that?" Krystal cooed, running her hand across Nick's chest.

"It *was* all finished. But the stupid contractor didn't dig the well deep enough, so it went dry. He's going to re-drill it next week; he said it could take days to get everything hooked back up. You better stay where you are until he's done." Nick neglected to mention it was his fault a shallow well had been drilled the first time. The contractor had warned the first well was too shallow and likely wouldn't last, but Nick had seen only the money he'd save by using a ground-water well.

"Okay, baby. Let's go to eat. All this exercise had made me hungry." Krystal snuggled up to Nick, letting him get a feel of her body when he moved toward the door. She rubbed against him like a cat as they walked to the elevator, only stepping away when its door opened.

*****

Megan got back to her office in time to begin cleaning off her desk, wrapping up loose ends, and filing the notes and evidence for the stolen jewelry case.

"Sheriff, Amanda Bonneau is here. She heard you want to interview her about a job." Shirley snickered as she showed a mature woman into the office.

Megan smiled and reached for the application the woman was extending to her. "Hi, I'm Sheriff Megan Holloway. Sit down. I'm glad you were able to come by today." Megan pointed to the chair across from her desk. Both women sat down; silence reigned as Megan skimmed over the application form. At thirty-five, Amanda was in her prime, so unless there was a pre-existing condition, her health should be good. Her emergency contact was a sister in Denver; no dependents were listed on the application. That was a plus to Megan, who had just spent two years dealing with an employee who used every possible reason to miss work, mostly centered around her son.

"So, Amanda, you come to visit a friend and get sent out on a job interview. Did you come to Riverview looking to relocate?" Megan needed some feeling of the woman's commitment to the area.

"Please, call me Mandy. I came to see Bethany because I needed to get away from where I was. I recently had a small inheritance, and with that money, I was suddenly free to quit a job I hated and seek a new start. Bethany and I were close riding partners back before her marriage. She seemed happy to be here in Riverview, and I thought it would be fun to see both her and the area. A job falling at my feet just seems like fate telling me to stay put."

"What was the job you hated?"

"I was a loan officer in a small bank. That translates to I worked collections as much as handing out loans." Amanda shuddered lightly.

"I see. You're used to working with the public and dealing with stressful situations. How do you feel about law enforcement? We are a small community, and you pretty much get to know everyone and everything about them. Would you have any problems holding your tongue?"

"I understand that problem. A small-town loan officer knows more than most about the community. I've never had any problems keeping my own counsel," Mandy replied. Her warm brown eyes met Megan's with a confidence born of experience.

"Do you have any issues with working from four to midnight? Priscilla wants to work from midnight to eight because her husband does the same in Gunnison. Shirley is happy with her shift, which leaves little chance of you getting off the swing shift." Megan felt Amanda needed to know she would be working those hours indefinitely.

"Those hours are perfect. I can ride and enjoy time with Bethany during the day and work nights. By the way, would it be against the rules if I wrote when things are slow? I'm not published yet and doubt I ever will be, but I love to write short stories and essays." Mandy blushed with the confession. Her coffee-and-cream skin turned a shade darker with the blush.

"So long as it doesn't interfere with answering the phone and doing your other work—I don't see any problems with you spending idle time writing. A quiet hobby will keep you awake when things get dull. We pray for boring nights around here, as you can imagine."

A knock on the door interrupted the interview.

"What, Shirley?"

"Betty called. She'd like to speak with you if you get a chance—something about old man Stowers." Shirley smiled at Mandy.

"Is she on the phone now?"

"No, she offered you a piece of pie to come by and talk to her." Shirley ducked back out of the office, closing the door.

"Shirley takes care of many details. You'll get the hang of it. Two primary sources of information in town are Betty, who owns the diner, and Henry, our librarian. Both call often, and sometimes they have pertinent information. Sometimes all they have is speculation, but I've learned to check it out with Betty. Henry only hits on suspicious activity about every other month. Betty interacts with people more and sees a lot. I trust her judgment." Megan made a couple of notes on Amanda's paperwork.

"Does that mean you want me to work here?" Amanda questioned.

"I can't quite afford your last salary." Megan's brows had gone up when she saw what Mandy had made at the bank.

"I'll need a rental. I would prefer a place with a stall, but Bethany has room for Maximum Mayhem, my gelding. What does the job usually start at?"

Megan smiled. Since Doyle and Stephanie got married, Birgitta's guest house was empty. "I know of a rental that would be almost perfect for you. It doesn't have a stall, but there's a pool, and you can have a pet. I'll negotiate the cost into line with our starting salary," Megan offered.

"Rental fees no more than a quarter of the salary?"

"Deal. Three thousand a month is our starting salary. Rent is seven-hundred-and-fifty, including utilities. Can you start tomorrow at four?"

"I can, but I need to see the house. Where is it?" Mandy stood and shook hands with Megan.

"I've got a key. Birgitta has been looking for a new tenant and left one with me. It's just on the edge of town. If you like a hike, you can walk to work, drive, or even bicycle here. I wouldn't suggest riding Maximum Mayhem because we don't have a stall or hitching rail for him. Come on." Megan chuckled, imagining the chaos a horse could cause in the town square. She opened her top drawer and took out the key marked with the address. She tossed it to Mandy. "Welcome to Riverview." Together the women left the office, with Megan leading the way.

Chapter Nine

Twenty minutes later, Megan walked into Betty's Diner. Betty looked up from where she was talking to Sheena. She motioned Megan to join them at the counter.

"Sheriff! Did you hear the news?" Betty called. Her voice carried around the room, pausing every conversation.

"Don't know if I have. What news are you talking about?"

"Sheena was with Chris when he got a call from the Gunnison PD. His Galleria was robbed today. *In broad daylight!* The clerk was working in the back when someone stepped behind her and knocked her cold. While she was out, the thief cleaned out the shop. Everything that wasn't locked in the safe is *gone*." Betty's almost shouted the last word. Conversation in the diner began to buzz.

"Sheena? What did Chris do?" Megan turned to the fiery-haired chef.

"He left for Gunnison. I volunteered to go along, but he said he couldn't guarantee to be back tonight and didn't want me to miss work. Like I would care about that at this time of year," Sheena answered, rolling her eyes.

"Sounds like I need to go call Gunnison Police Department. Betty, why did you want to talk to me?" Megan had yet to sit down at the counter and knew she'd not get the chance today.

"I wanted to ask you to go check on Marvin Stowers. He hasn't been in for dinner for the past two days. He's either sick or having truck trouble. Either way, someone needs to drop by and see that he gets some food. I've got a sack here for him. If you can't do it, could you ask Deputy Joe?" Betty snared a sizeable white bag from behind the counter and held it out to the sheriff.

"Sure, I'll see the food gets out to him. He lives in the line shack out on the 3C's, right?" Megan confirmed where the old man lived.

"Yes. Tell Marvin to get a phone and call me. I worry about him out there all alone."

"Right. Tell an old hermit who has no concept of the electronic age to get a disposable cell phone and call you. What color *is* the sky in your world, woman?" Megan took the bag, shaking her head at Betty's pipe dream, and started for the door.

"I'll call Chris to let him know you'll be talking to the Gunnison police. I think it was Detective Turner." Sheena called after Megan's retreating back.

Megan walked to her SUV and slid the bag onto the passenger seat before heading to her office, muttering to herself the entire way. "So much for getting off early. Good thing I've got nothing better to do on a Monday night. Sheesh."

"Sheriff! Did you hear the news?" Shirley greeted Megan with a smile. "Of course you did. Otherwise, you'd be halfway home by now. I'll get Detective Turner for you. He just now left a message."

Megan had just sat down when her desk phone rang. "Sheriff Megan Holloway. How may I help you?"

"Sheriff Holloway. This is Detective Turner with the Gunnison Police Department. I understand you had a robbery of a jewelry store there on Saturday. We had a robbery of the Galleria store here in Gunnison, owned by Christopher Long, the same custom jeweler."

"I just heard. How can I help you?" Megan asked.

"What have you found out about the robbery in Riverview? Any special clues?"

"Well, we think the thief stole a truck to commit the crime and then abandoned the vehicle in Blue Creek. One man, average size, mild limp, is all the description I've gotten so far." Megan rattled off the Colorado CSI File number for the crime. "I haven't had too much time to go through all the data yet, but feel free to pull down whatever you need from the file. Just keep me in the loop if you come up with any thoughts. I think both these crimes have to be connected. Did you get any film in Gunnison? The camera in Chris's store here was out of commission."

"We got some shots, but it sounds like you already know what we found—an average-sized white man, slightly favoring his left leg. I think he's got a stiff knee," Detective Turner surmised. "The guy had a hat jammed down over his forehead, and a collar pulled up over his chin, so there are no clear shots of his face. Footage shows him stepping over the door sensor that would have notified the clerk. This guy has done this a time or two, if I'm not mistaken. Casual and brazen. Once he had the clerk down for the count, he spent his time pulling merchandise from the display cases, using gloves and putting all those pieces into a briefcase. He walked out, relaxed, and slowly turned down the block and into an alley where the street cams lost him. I had the K-9 follow the tracks, and they ended at the dumpster where the man must have entered a vehicle. Only thing of interest, and it may be nothing, was he had a 'cheaters' band on his right hand. He pulled his gloves off as he walked out of the shop.

Usually, we see those on the left ring finger. This pale band was his right pinky. Oh, well. Maybe he was robbing the store for a new ring. Who knows?" The detective's voice sounded frustrated and resigned.

"Send me a copy of the report when you've got it. Will the clerk be okay?" Megan asked.

"She's got a whopping headache, but she managed to call us as soon as she woke up. That part of downtown isn't busy during this time of year. If she hadn't come out of it, the security guard would have discovered the crime after seven when the mall closed down. Gunnison runs on tourists in the summer and the ski crowd in the winter. Spring is our slowest season," Detective Turner replied.

"I know this news had to have crushed Chis. He was planning a show in June as the tourist season starts, and now he has no product to sell. Makes me wonder if this was a motivated crime. I'll talk to him and see if I can discover any enemies." Megan made a note so she'd remember to ask him. "Look, I've got another thing or two to do today. I'll let you know if I find out anything, and you'll do the same, right? Hopefully, something will click, and we'll get this tied up by the end of the week." Megan knew that it would likely never be solved if they didn't get it figured out quickly. Small town crime worked that way more than city crime did. Residents chimed in quickly when you knew everyone. If no one came forward, it meant no one saw anything or had any thoughts on who would likely commit the crime.

Tiredly, Megan used her desk to stand. It had been a long day, and now she needed to haul food out to an old hermit too stubborn to own a cell phone—another character in a town full of unusual people. One more soul to watch over. Megan grinned. She wouldn't have it any other way.

Riverview citizens were a dying breed. Loyal to each other, protective of one another, and, for the most part, supportive of each other. Once they accepted you, you could ask almost anything of them.

"Shirley, are you okay until eight? Priscilla will relieve you. Deputy Joe can help you if you need anything. He's bringing you dinner; that's already set up." No sooner had she spoken of Deputy Joe than he entered the station carrying two bags.

"Hey, ya'll. Shirley, I didn't know if you wanted fried chicken or a burger, so I got both. Take your pick, and I'll eat the other." He set two insulated cups on the counter with both bags.

Megan left the pair splitting up the food, wondering what she would have for dinner and when. She even contemplated raiding Marvin's bags of food on the seat next to her. Naw, she had stuff at home. These bags were likely all the food the old man would have. She pointed her SUV west on the highway. She turned right at a barely marked BLM road. Chuckling, she remembered it was the same one George had used to bring her out of the desert after finding the cut fence and the spot where Billy's truck was abandoned. For all the wide-open spaces around here, there were only so many places where you could turn off the highway. She turned left onto an almost invisible track just past the cattle guard this time.

Another fifteen minutes of bouncing up, down, and sideways brought Megan to a single-room, run-down shack. She could see the rear bumper of a rusty old truck showing behind the hut. Marvin had to be home. The sun was setting, and no light was glowing from the windows. Megan hopped out of her SUV with her hand on her pistol. Cautiously, she rounded the front of her vehicle only to jump back when a shot rang out, and a plume of dust jumped up a foot from where she'd been.

"Marvin! Sheriff Megan Holloway, here. *Hold your fire!*" Megan stayed put, waiting to see what the old man would do next.

"*Sheriff?* Megan, is that you? Are ya' alone? Step out so's I can see ya." Marvin's scratchy voice called out.

"Hell no, I'm not stepping out where you can take another shot. *You* come outside where I can see *you*," Megan ordered.

"But, Sheriff. If'n I step out there, the sniper can get me."

"Sniper? What sniper? Only person with a weapon that I can sense around here is you!" Megan called, opening her vehicle door to give her body some protection if there was a sniper.

"Is this Sunday?" Marvin asked.

"Marvin, it's Monday. Sundown on Monday." Megan wondered if the old man was losing his connection with reality.

"In that case, I bin hole up in here for two days. Sniper took a shot at me on Saturday, about three, I think. You don't got any food, do ya? I ran out of water a while back too."

"Betty sent me with food, and I've got a cooler I keep with water and soda. Let me in." Megan commanded. She gave up trying to talk him out of the hut. She pulled the bags to her side while reaching for a bottle in the cooler with her other hand.

"I unlocked the door. I've got ya covered. If'n I say duck, you better either quack or hit your belly. Ya' got that?"

"Sounds like an idea. I'm coming with the food and drink; you cover me, but for God's sake, don't shoot me." Megan saw the door crack open from where she stood with her hands full. She took a deep breath and rushed toward the door, trying not to look as worried as she felt. Hopping the two steps onto the porch, she jumped into the cabin with Marvin slamming the door behind her.

"Keep down now, Sheriff. Don't want that bugger to shoot you through the window."

"Has the sniper been shooting at you through the windows?" Megan couldn't help but wonder if there really *was* a sniper or just an old man with a vivid imagination.

"Sheriff Megan, I didn't graze myself with a bullet." Marvin seemed to sense her doubt. He lifted his shirt, showing a bandage around his chest. Red had seeped out, exhibiting an extended horizontal cut under the dressing. "I even pulled the bullet out of the chair back where it went after slicing my side." He pointed to a slug on the dinner table in front of a chair with a dug-out hole.

"How bad is it?"

"It bled a bit, but I've had worse when using my ax on firewood." Marvin scoffed at his injury. "Doc might want to stitch it, but it wasn't a gusher, so I'm not worried. Not like an extra scar is going to scare off the ladies." He cackled as his joke.

"Well, I'll take you to town to get some antibiotics from the clinic. You eat some of that food and get some liquid into you. I'm going to make a quick scouting run to see if I can find where the sniper was sitting when he shot you. Put that chair where it was when you were shot so I can backtrace the bullet." Megan watched Marvin move himself and the chair. Once he was seated, she could tell the bullet had come from the side window, grazed Marvin, and lodged itself in the wooden chair.

"You think it's smart to go out there?" Marvin still had a hand on his rifle.

"I think the shooter is gone. He could have shot me when I parked out front, and he didn't. Besides, no one likes to sit all night out in the cold. He likely left on Saturday." Megan saw a large flashlight on the floor next to the door and grabbed it. "You have candles, right? I'll be back in ten minutes. If you hear any gunshots – use my phone to call 911." She showed Marvin how to press the numbers and passed the old man her office phone. It didn't need to be unlocked, so he could use it without knowing more than the keypad numbers.

"Okay, if'n I hear any gunfire, I'll call the calvary. Tell'em to get here on the double."

Megan kept a low profile as she slipped out the door into the rapidly darkening evening. The moon was a few days past full, but it would take another twenty minutes or so to clear the mountains to the east. Until then, the twilight was fading, and it would be solid dark soon. Using what light there was, Megan moved to her right, around the side of the cabin. Once she reached the window the bullet had entered, she pointed the large flashlight in the projectile's trajectory, turning it on and off. The light had shown her the most likely spot the sniper had been to take the shot. She stepped to the right, out of any glow from the candles inside. Quickly she began making her way to what likely had been the sniper's position when he was there.

Megan had excellent night vision, so she left the flashlight off until she got into the boulders and needed it to find her way. Twice, she pointed the light toward the cabin until she was lined up with the window. At that point, she began searching for any sign of passage. Very few people could pass through a spot without leaving a mark, and one playing sniper would have been in place for a while. She wished it was daylight, but maybe working with the limited light helped her focus.

"Ah, ha! So you're a gum chewer." Megan pulled out a baggie from a zippered pocket and, turning it inside out, used it to pick up a gum wrapper. Slowly she circled the spot but didn't find anything else. Looking up, she realized the wrapper might have fallen from a higher vantage spot. She clambered through the rocks until she found a wider, flat site almost directly above where she had found the gum wrapper. It was in a direct line of sight to the chair in the cabin below. "Bingo," she muttered.

It looked as though the sniper had spent several hours in this location. Another gum wrapper, this one, had a chewed wad in it. Megan gave a mental fist pump; now, she had DNA too. An empty water bottle and candy wrapper were stuck between two boulders, giving her more DNA. This guy wasn't a pro. He might have taken his shell casings, but what he'd left behind could hang him. DNA was better than a fingerprint. Once she'd managed to collect the items into evidence bags, she began her trip down from the boulders. It made no sense to look for tracks tonight. The sniper was gone, and any trail would likely only lead to a vehicle's tire marks.

Megan stubbed her toe, cussing at the sudden pain. "Sonofabitch! Ouch!" she hopped a few steps before trying the foot cautiously. It held, but her toe still stung. She moved more slowly, feeling each step until she was down by the cabin again.

"That you, Sheriff?" Marvin's voice whispered.

"Yeah. No need to whisper. I don't know how long your sniper stayed, but he's long gone now," Megan assured Marvin. "We need to take you into town. You can spend the night at the Bailey's boarding house. I'll put it on the bill as part of my investigation."

"You don't need to do that. Ida Mae and I were a thing many years ago. If you catch my drift. She'll let me have that upstairs room for a few nights." Marvin chuckled and began rounding up a few things to take with him.

"Well, I'm going to tell her to bill me. If you talk her out of it—that's between you and her. Let me take that bag. You don't need to pull your side open again and get my vehicle bloody." Megan knew the old man would fight her over the bag unless she gave him a valid, masculine reason why she should take it. His pride might let him relinquish the bag to keep her SUV clean.

"You're likely right, Sheriff. This wrap on my middle hardly holds the wound's edges together. I guess I'm glad the guy was a bad shot." Marvin stepped away from the table and shuffled out the cabin door. Leaning heavily on the railing, he managed to get down the steps.

Megan snatched the bag, a sandwich from Betty's food donation, and still managed to get around him before he reached her SUV. Opening the vehicle door, she offered him her shoulder. She felt him lean onto her as he moved. "You sure you don't want to go straight to the hospital?"

"Shit, no! People *die* in hospitals. Ol' Doc can stitch me up, and I'll be good as new in a few days. I'll feel better when that food kicks in. I think I'm mostly weak from not eating." He pushed off of her shoulder to lift himself into the vehicle. Megan staggered back a step from the force of his push. "Sorry, Sheriff. I shoulda warned you I was gonna do that."

"No problem. Get your seatbelt fastened. This drive's going to hurt. Why do you have to live way out here in the middle of nowhere?" Megan knew the washboard track and the gravel road would cause the old man pain, but short of calling in a helicopter, she had no choice. The wound wasn't severe enough to need the evacuation chopper. Megan paused to call Dr. Samuelson to let him know she was on her way to town with Marvin. She asked the doctor to meet them at his clinic.

"I'll be okay. I found my bottle of whiskey, and that should numb my pain before you get to the highway." Marvin waived a pint bottle, opened it, and downed several swallows.

"No food, dehydrated, and drinking whiskey. Doc is going to give me hell. You do know that, right?" Megan shook her head and drove slowly back the way she had come, not over an hour earlier. The moon topped the mountains, and she could almost see without the headlights, but that didn't make the road any smoother. It seemed to take an hour to reach the highway, but she knew it was only about fifteen minutes longer than it had taken to get to the cabin.

"See? I tol' you I'd be okay on tha' road. Just need a lil' more of this tonic." Marvin tipped the flask up, draining the last swallow.

Megan groaned inwardly. Yep. Doc was going to lecture her. Maybe Marvin would pass out and be easier to work on if she was lucky. She ate her sandwich as she drove the short distance along the highway slower than usual, taking the curves as straight as possible to keep Marvin comfortable. Traffic was almost non-existent, and they made the clinic just as Marvin slumped over against his seatbelt.

"Great. Just what I wanted. Deadweight into the clinic. Darn you, Marvin. Did you have to drink the whole flask?" Megan knew she was muttering to herself since the old man was unconscious. She pulled up as close to the door as possible, with the passenger door opening over the sidewalk. Megan wondered if she should go inside for a wheelchair or a gurney to haul him into the clinic. Her dilemma was solved when the doctor and his wife came out, wheeling a chair toward the passenger door.

"Hi, Dr. Samuelson, Mary. Marvin has a gash across his right side. He says he's had worse, but it was still seeping through the bandage when he got in the car. He's sleeping off a flask of whiskey now, so we should be able to get him into the clinic without worrying that we'll hurt him."

"Stubborn old fool. I bet you had to threaten him to get him to the clinic." Mary offered as they opened the door and began maneuvering the unconscious patient into the wheelchair.

"No threats needed. I just told Marvin I was bringing him here, and he gave up the argument. He might have already been working on the flask by that time." Megan pushed the chair, Dr. Samuelson helped, and Mary ran to open the door.

"If he didn't argue, he was either feeling pretty mellow, or this wound is worse than he's letting on. Here, let me take over. You have a seat while Mary helps me examine and treat the patient. I'll be out as soon as I get him stitched up." The doctor took over the handles of the wheelchair while his wife, Mary, held the door to a treatment room.

Megan sat down, dead tired, glad she'd eaten a bite, but her stomach felt in knots from the day's stress. "Ah, *crap!*" Megan reached for her phone and called Aaron. He picked up at the second ring.

"Where are you, and are you okay?" Concern emanated from his voice.

"I'm fine. I'm so sorry I didn't call earlier. I took old Marvin some food Betty made and found him in a pickle. We're at the clinic. As soon as Doc lets him go, I'll drop him over at the Bailey's and be home. I hope it doesn't take too long. I really, really need to see you. It's been a long day, and I could use a hug."

"I'll make you a plate that we can warm when you get here. I've got a cold beer for you, and my arms open wide. Let me know when you leave there, okay?"

"Will do. Love you. Bye." Megan cut the connection, not waiting to hear his response. She knew if he hesitated at all, she would work herself into a frenzy that maybe his feelings had changed. Better to say it and break the connection.

The clinic waiting room was silent and half in shadow. Megan found a light switch, and the room suddenly had a cozy warmth designed to keep patients and families from worrying. Megan began pacing. She pulled the evidence bags from her pockets and examined her trove of treasures. Possible DNA on two different items and maybe fingerprints too. The sniper had been careless. Who would want to shoot Marvin? Perhaps it wasn't shooting Marvin that was the goal; maybe they just didn't want him wandering around to become a witness—but a witness to what? What could an old hermit witness out there? Megan sat down at the reception counter and used a notepad to write several possibilities. She heard the door open behind her and stuffed the paper next to the evidence bags into her pocket.

"Sheriff, if that bullet had gone any deeper, it would have done some major damage. As it is, he's going to be in pain for a few days and needs the stitches out in a week. He's still out like a light. I want to keep him here tonight. Mary and I will alternate sitting with him in case he wakes. Do you want me to call you when he does?"

"No, not tonight. I had a chance to talk to him before he got soused, and he has no idea who was shooting or why. Can you see that he gets to the Bailey's in the morning? They have that room to rent, and I want him in town until I figure out why someone shot at him."

"Sure, I can take him over there when he's ready to be released," Mary offered.

"Thanks. If you need me, I'll be home. Thanks for meeting me here—there was no way the old fart would let me take him to a hospital." Megan waved as she left the building. Her SUV was still sitting where she left it across the sidewalk. She snickered, "Good thing no one was working traffic tonight; I could have gotten a ticket." For some reason, the thought of the sheriff's vehicle with a ticket under the wiper blade grew funnier and funnier as she climbed into the driver's seat. She had to take a few minutes to get beyond her laughter, wipe her watering eyes, and blow her nose before starting the vehicle and pointing it toward home.

Chapter Ten

"Hey, I thought I asked you to call once you were heading this way," Aaron admonished as he held his arms open to Megan.

Megan almost fell into the welcome embrace, not even stopping to take off her hat or weapon. Aaron's warmth and strength surrounded her as she let the trials of the day wash over her.

"I know, I'm sorry. I'm not even sure I'm hungry. Let me have that cold beer, and I'll think about eating. I had a snack as I drove Marvin to Dr. Samuelson's. My gut is in a knot." Megan pushed off Aaron's shoulder, moved to the fridge, and retrieved a beer.

"Grab me another, too. Thanks," Aaron said. Megan brought both beers over to the counter. He pulled a glass from the cupboard and passed it to her. "Now, tell me what's going on. What'd Marvin get himself into this time? Is he okay?"

Megan didn't respond until she'd poured her beer and taken the first long pull of it. "Marvin's going to be okay—once the bullet wound in his side heals. He says a sniper shot him. I looked around up the hill behind his place. I found a spot where a shooter could have hidden and taken a shot or three. There are no shell casings, but gum wrappers, a candy wrapper, and a water bottle point to a shooter spending some time there watching the cabin. He was smart enough to take his shell casings but not smart enough to hide his presence."

"Who the hell would want to shoot that old man? He's harmless, just a veteran who wants no part of other people," Aaron commented.

"That's what I have to figure out. As far as we know, Marvin has no enemies. Maybe it's a case of preventing him from seeing something. Premeditated, you know? Someone planned a crime and knew the only person in the area would be an old man who might see them unless they convinced him to stay inside." Megan took another swig and pulled her notes from her pocket. "What kind of crimes take place out in the high desert—away from civilization? Drug deals, human trafficking?"

"*Sonofabitch!*" Aaron jumped off his stool and quickly paced around the breakfast bar. "I know what could be going on out in the desert. Roger has been missing a few cows, and so have some other spreads. Rustlers would need to bring in a rig to haul out the cows. That washed-out BLM trail the old man lives off of would work. Lots of room to turn it on the desert floor, load up the cows, and get out of there with no one the wiser."

"Are beef prices running high enough to make rustling worthwhile again?"

"If you have buyers, rustling is way easier than running your own spread. All you need are a couple of horses and a rig to haul out the cows."

"Well, shoot. Rustlers. Why didn't I think of that? They would know about Marvin in that old line shack if they were locals. They would have seen him in his old truck if they had done any reconnoitering. I'm glad they thought to scare him instead of killing him, but they came close to doing both." Megan downed the remainder of her beer, suddenly feeling less stressed. Finding rustlers might not be that easy, but finding a person with a killing vendetta against an old man would be more complex and likely more dangerous.

"I'll talk with the hands at the R-bar-M. I know it's none of our crew, but they might know if anyone in town is spending out of their pay grade," Aaron offered.

"You do that; I appreciate it. I'll hit A Bad Idea tomorrow afternoon when it opens and question Donny. He'll have noticed if anyone is over-spending too." Megan's mood lightened now that she had a plan of action. "I'll go back out to Marvin's cabin in the morning and see if I can backtrack the shooter. He was careless about what he left behind. Maybe he wasn't careful in hiding his tracks either. I might be able to tell if a larger rig pulled off that road to the line shack, too."

"Well, now that you've worked things through, are you ready to eat? Bethany sent over a lasagna, homemade lasagna. All I need to do is microwave it for a couple of minutes." Aaron walked over to the stove, where a ceramic casserole dish sat.

"Yes, yes, and yes! You should have told me it was Bethany's lasagna. I'll get us a salad while it heats." With a surge of renewed energy, Megan jumped up and dashed for the fridge while Aaron served up two plates of food. He heated each dish for two minutes before he brought the plates back to the breakfast bar. Megan grinned at the garlic bread. "Bethany sent bread too?"

"She wanted you to have a good meal. You know she always makes two or three of these things when she cooks one. Best dish to send around or to freeze for another day." He carefully set the dishes side by side before sitting beside Megan.

A companionable mood settled as they ate the delicious meal. Only the sounds of scraping cutlery and groans of pleasure broke the silence. Finally, a whine brought Megan's attention to Sparkle, who was sitting at her side, eyeballing every forkful of food Megan ate. Megan couldn't help but tease the dog. With her last crust of garlic bread, she scraped it through the sauce very slowly, trying not to laugh at the dog's expression.

"I don't know, Sparkle. This food is far too good for a dog." Her hand moved in slow motion, bringing that last bite to her lips.

Sparkle whimpered and drooled, watching the food ever so intently.

"What do you think, Aaron? Has Sparkle been good enough to deserve this last bite?" Megan waved the treat from left to right, watching the dog turning her head to follow the morsel. Laughter won out, and Megan offered the bite to Sparkle, who gently took it from her fingers.

"One of these days, she'll snap the treat and your fingers," Aaron warned, laughing with her.

"I try not to tease her too much, but sometimes I can't help it." Megan stood, taking her dishes over to the sink. "Let's leave the dishes in the sink. I'll wash them in the morning with my coffee cup," she told Aaron.

"Oh, no, you don't. We'll wash the dirty dishes together. I enjoy sharing the simple chores with you." Aaron pinned Megan against the sink with a smile. "Besides, it gives me more chances to molest you," Aaron said as his fingers began to tickle her sides.

Laughter, healing and relaxing, bubbled out of Megan. "Stop." Megan giggled as she pushed at Aaron's hands. "You *know* we'll never get the dishes clean if you keep tickling me.

We'll be lucky if I don't drop anything." Megan's voice rose to a squeal in her laughter.

"I didn't say we would *finish* washing the dishes or that we would get them clean. I just said we would wash them together." He pulled Megan into his arms and kissed her, effectively silencing her giggles.

When Aaron's hands moved from tickly to fondling, Megan ran her arms up to circle his neck, pulling him closer. The exchange heated, and the dishes were forgotten as the couple headed upstairs to Megan's room. Sparkle heaved a deep sigh and curled up on her bed in the living room, knowing better than to follow them up the stairs.

*****

"Wake up, sleepy-head. You're going to be late for work, and Roger will tell Bethany, who will then harass me about keeping you overnight," Megan called up the stairs to Aaron. It was her second time trying to wake him without going upstairs. If it didn't work this time either, she would have to risk going back into the bedroom where he slept. If he pulled her back into bed with him—neither one would get to work before another hour had passed. Megan smiled when she heard the bathroom door close. As much fun as it would be to spend time rolling between the sheets this morning, she had a lot to do, and Aaron needed to get over to the R-bar-M. She poured his coffee when he entered the kitchen, grabbed her around the waist, and nuzzled her neck.

"Good morning, gorgeous. How did you sleep?"

"When we finally *went* to sleep, I slept like the dead. I know you did too, or else you would have heard me get up and let Sparkle out this morning. I had to call you twice. Did you have a rough day yesterday? I never asked you last night. I was kind of caught up with my job. I'm sorry." Megan tilted her head back to kiss him.

"I was out searching for those lost cows with Roger. We followed them down to one of the gullies, and then the trail faded away in the rocks. It was a long day in the saddle and nothing to show for the effort. If what you and I think is right, I understand why we found nothing. Wonder how the rustlers managed to herd those cows and not leave any shod horse prints. We saw some mustang tracks, but nothing with shoes was out there."

"Hmmm...maybe, they're riding unshod horses to avoid being tracked? Horses wouldn't stay sound long, but this kind of rider would simply find another horse. I'll check with Doc Rayburn to see if he's worked on any lame horses lately. Not that they would call a vet." Megan shrugged, disgusted at the thought of horse owners who would ignore a lameness if it didn't suit their schedule or plans.

"Another thought. Maybe the rustlers have cattle dogs that do the work, and the riders just push the herd," Aaron voiced another possibility.

"Where did you lose the tracks? Any specific gully?"

"It's just a rocky seasonal creekbed that empties into the Blue Ditch. We didn't go all the way to the Ditch because it would have put us out past dark. Roger and I could take the quads out and follow the gulley to see if the cows were herded out of it before reaching the Blue Ditch."

"Not yet. Let me talk to the other ranchers and see if they followed errant cattle in that direction. Marvin's line shack isn't far from the Ditch. I can see where the thieves would want him secured if they were moving cattle. I'll call you later if I need you and Roger to follow those tracks. You better get going. Kiss me goodbye." Megan turned her face up for his quick peck as he grabbed his coat and headed for the door.

"Are we still on for Thursday? There's a new movie in town." Aaron paused at the door for Megan's answer.

"Yes. I'll be ready for some distraction. See you then, if not before." She waved at his back and watched him drive away. Megan looked at her watch and squealed. "Oh, *crap!* Here I am chasing him off to work, and now *I'll* be late." Muttering under her breath, she pushed Sparkle outside, snatched her jacket and hat, locked her door, and sprinted for her SUV.

Once on the road, she used her hands-free voice-controlled phone to call her office. "Shirley. Hi. Listen, I'm going to run a couple of things down this morning. I'll be in the office by noon. I can respond to calls, so go ahead and put emergencies through and take notes on other calls. Okay?"

"Sure, boss. Nothing much going on here, anyway. Even Henry hasn't called. *This* is the way I like to see things. The only call was from the JCX. He's lost some cattle and wants to talk to you. I'll tell him you'll call this afternoon if he calls back. That's the third rancher this week who's mentioned missing cows. Is something up?" Shirley asked

"Yeah. I think we've had some rustlers in the area. Do me a favor and check the counties around here to see if there's been more action than the normal stray cow or two. I just wonder if the thieves are traveling through or if they are local," Megan wondered as she turned onto the rough BLM road that led to Marvin's cabin. "Got to go. I'm about to lose reception anyway. See you later." Static sounded at the same time as she signed off, so Megan was unsure if Shirley had heard her last statement. In this case, it wasn't an issue.

The rutted dirt road took all her attention. She slowed to a crawl, watching where she was driving and looking for vehicle tracks going off the road on either side. She found more than she anticipated about a mile short of Marvin's cabin. She stopped to examine the tracks going off the road on either side. The marks to the left looked like a lone vehicle, likely a pickup or even a large ATV. Possibly the shooter since Marvin's cabin was so close. She'd follow that trail later. The tracks to the right were what stirred her investigative instincts.

More than one vehicle had left and returned off this dirt road on the right side. One of the vehicles had been a truck and trailer. The narrow dirt track had forced the truck driver to go off on the left side to turn right without putting the trailer over a massive boulder. As it was, the boulder showed scars where at least one tire had scraped it. The driver was experienced, but turning a truck with a gooseneck trailer in a tight spot was *not* easy.

Gooseneck trailers would always cut a curve sharper than the towing truck— Megan knew that from personal experience. She examined the tracks on the right and saw where the truck had stopped, corrected, and tried to miss the boulder. She looked at the boulder. The gooseneck would have the tires on one side with significant scrapes on the rim and possibly even the wheel-well. She took photos of these tracks, the boulder, and the tracks on the other side of the road.

Megan stood there, deciding which set of tracks to follow first. She knew where the shooter must have stopped, so she followed the stock truck trail. Her SUV was designed for the back roads in the wilds of the high desert. High clearance allowed her to stay on the track, pushing over sage and smaller boulders like her quarry. A wide clearing opened on the left, and the bigger rig turned into it. Megan stopped, shutting off the SUV.

Ahead of where she stopped, she saw the ground had been trampled by livestock—lots of livestock. Leaving that for later inspection, she walked into the clearing, noting that at least one vehicle had been towing a smaller trailer. She photographed where that trailer had let out at least two unshod horses. Dog prints were dancing around the hoof prints. Another riddle resolved. Thieves on unshod horses using cattle dogs for herding stolen livestock. Damn, these boys were slick, covering all the bases.

Well, maybe not *that* slick if the marksman they used didn't know to police his spot, removing all traces and evidence. Also, the suspects somehow didn't think there would be an investigation of the shooting. Instead of the one closest to the line shack, they could have used one or two other BLM access points. Megan grinned. If they were this careless, she should be able to find them. Quickly, she photographed the ground and the tracks. The tracks didn't show much, no specific tire prints or voids to help determine what truck and trailer, but the photos would help her show that more than one vehicle was involved.

She visualized the clearing with both rigs sitting there in her mind's eye. She discovered round spots every eight feet spreading out from the larger rig. Corral panels next to the ramp? They would act as a chute to narrow the cattle down into a line to load. These guys weren't amateurs. They'd done this before, either as thieves or as ranch hands moving a herd to another pasture. She would almost bet as both.

Megan back-tracked the cattle on foot, finding where the group was driven up out of the arroyo to the loading zone. The arroyo was dry rocks, with no water yet this spring. Rocks would hide the tracks, and the gully likely ran for miles past several spreads. Yeah, this would make stealing from more than one ranch simple. Cut a fence, have the dogs herd stock down to the dry creekbed, and then to the next spread. Pretty smooth.

A sound to her left brought Megan's hand up to her pistol as she whirled to see what was there. A soft mooing solved the question, and she relaxed, though she still kept her hand on her weapon. A large sage partially protected by a huge boulder hid the cow. A bleating moo sounded next, and Megan knew there was a calf too. Megan moved cautiously around to where she could see both cow and calf. The calf was new, possibly even born last night or today. It wasn't still wet, but it was very wobbly when it stood up. Momma cow must have dropped behind the boulder to calve and was missed when the cattle dogs rounded up the other animals for loading. Megan noted the brand on the cow. She backed away, leaving the pair, and walked back to her SUV. She speed-dialed the needed number. It was picked up on the second ring.

"Hey, babe. I was just going to call you. I talked to the guys, and none have seen anyone throwing money around." Aaron didn't give Megan a chance to speak first.

"That's okay. I've got a gift for Roger. I found one of his missing cows. She's here with a calf. You'll need water, food, and a trailer to haul her out of here. You might be able to drive her home, but the calf is less than two days old." Megan explained the situation.

"Great news! Not all five, but a cow and calf are always welcome back into the herd. Where are you? I'll get there as soon as I can."

Megan explained her location and the location of the cow. It would take Aaron at least a half-hour to get there, maybe as long as an hour. She glanced at her watch and decided to be there when the rig arrived. It was only an hour. She could follow the tracks on the left of the BLM road while she waited. She remembered her emergency stash that she kept in the back of the SUV, a shrink-wrapped flake of hay and a gallon jug with a metal dish. She lugged the items back to the arroyo, within sight of the cow but not close enough for the animal to get protective of her young. She sliced open the shrink-wrap, making a mental note to replace both, spread the hay, and poured the water into the dish.

While she worked, the cow mooed, clearly needing the food but unwilling to get closer to Megan. "It's alright, momma cow. I'm going to leave you to eat. I don't want to hurt you or your baby." She kept her voice soft and coaxing as she backed away from the food. Cautiously, the cow moved toward the pile, and the water shimmered in the sun. Megan left her to eat, returning to her SUV with the shrink-wrap and empty jug in her hands. Aaron would return the water pan later.

Happy to have found at least one of the missing cows, Megan drove back to the rutted BLM road, crossed it, and slowly followed the tracks she was sure led to where the sniper had hidden to shoot at Marvin's shack. Ahead, she saw a line of boulders that must have stopped the vehicle she was tracking, so she stopped driving and began trailing on foot. Sure enough, the tracks ended where the rifleman had parked and later turned around. She found bootprints that exited and then reentered the vehicle. She followed the prints to the rocks. The trail ended there, but she clambered over and down until she was at the spot she had found yesterday, the one the shooter used to fire on Marvin.

In the distance, she heard vehicles and figured it was R-bar-M hands there to collect the cow and calf. She took a few daylight photos of the sniper's nest before climbing over the rocks to get back to her SUV. She photographed the spot where the gunman's vehicle had sat. She was careful to get photos of each tire imprint in the dirt. She measured the axel length and the turning radius to see if she could understand what type of vehicle the sniper used.

Megan was tucking her notepad back into her hip pocket when she heard a truck coming toward her. No mistaking that particular rumbling rattle. A smile creased her face when it topped a rise, and Aaron waved.

"Hi, babe! The boys got the cow and calf. Surprisingly, she's not in bad shape. Here's your water pan." He hopped out of his big dually truck and jogged over to her. When he reached her, his arm circled her waist, and he pulled her close for a light kiss.

"Did you want to bring back this pan so that you could snatch a mid-morning kiss?" Megan laughed after kissing him back and taking the pan from him.

"Anytime I get a chance for a midmorning kiss, I'll grab it." Aaron leaned in for a second, deeper kiss.

"Hmmm—we better knock this off, or we could head down to Marvin's cabin," Megan suggested. Then a shudder ran through her at the memory of the old man's dwelling. "On second thought. Let's bookmark this for later. I wouldn't want my dog living in that old line shack. I wonder if the Boy's and Girl's Club would like to clean it for him? You know, as a community service project," Megan wondered aloud, a project taking shape in her mind.

"That or the Methodist Women's League might take it on. Does it need repair or simply cleaning and new linens?"

"As far as I could tell, new glass in the window, linens, cleaning, and maybe stocking the freezer with things he could cook on the woodburning stove. I didn't see any evidence of the shack needing a new roof, but the chimney likely needs cleaning." Megan and Aaron walked over to her vehicle as they discussed the project. She put the water pan into the back, next to the empty jug, before turning and kissing him lightly. "I've got to go. Will you take over talking to either group? It would be wonderful to clean the place before he comes back out here."

"I'll put Bethany on the case. She's getting bored staying at home—when she's not chasing Charlie." With obvious reluctance, Aaron let Megan go. He stood there until her SUV disappeared, waving as she topped the last rise.

Chapter Eleven

Megan drove straight to the Co-op. Norman possibly knew or would have some guesses about who could be moving stock in an extended trailer using cattle dogs. The Co-op had the best prices on feed for all animal species in the area. From dogs to llamas, if it needed to be fed, the Co-op sold the feed it required. The Co-op also was the place to hear all the local gossip and ranching news.

The parking spots in front of the store were taken, and three rigs were waiting to load up at the back dock. Megan chuckled as she drove around the block to park in front of Stephanie's Closet. Nothing like this time of day in a small town. Morning chores were done, and now the ranchers and cowboys were running errands before afternoon and evening feeding times.

She waved to Stephanie before she crossed the street to enter the Co-op. It was like a scene from a movie—all talking stopped when she stepped into the store. All heads turned, and eyes followed her as she walked up to the counter.

"Good morning, Norman, fellows. What's the word on the range? Norman, have you been tracking how many ranchers are missing cattle or think they could be missing a few steers or cows?" Megan waved to the hands and ranchers before giving Norman her full attention. He would know what was happening if it involved livestock.

"Well, there's three ranches on the west side of town that are missing cows, and the 4JC is missing a yearling bull.

It almost sounds like someone is trying to set up a spread. Ain't heard of any steers missing, just cows, cow and calf pairs, and a bull. All branded, and the bull is micro-chipped. Of course, that only helps if they try to run it through a legitimate auction." Norman shrugged and turned to ring up the sale in front of him.

"Anyone here missing any livestock or even any cattle dogs?" Megan watched the shoppers each shake their heads at her question.

"What's going on here, sheriff? I heard twenty-some-odd cows were missing between three ranches. Have you found any sign of them?" A gruff voice spoke up from the back of the store.

"I found where some stock was loaded into a gooseneck trailer by at least two thieves using cattle dogs. They missed one cow that had found a hiding place to calve. I would guess that it had to be close to sundown, and they didn't have time to search for her. They might have made two runs, but hard to tell in that hardpacked ground."

"Sheriff, I didn't think the price of beef was high enough right now to make rustling a worthwhile enterprise," the older cowboy mused as he paid for his purchase.

"I didn't either—unless someone needs livestock. Cows are close to calving time if they don't have calves already. If Norman heard correctly and they took a young bull too, these animals might never make it to market." Megan made a mental note to talk to the local vet about notifying her if he got called out to tend calving cows. Most cows had no problems, but a young heifer could experience difficulty with birthing a large calf. If Dr. Rayburn watched brands, he could tell her if the cow's brand wasn't her owner's ranch brand. Ranchers did buy and sell stock among themselves from time to time, but those sales were well documented in both spreads' logs.

Megan realized that Norman didn't have time right now to talk, and with this audience, it wasn't likely that he would speak freely. Her pocket vibrated. She pulled out her cell and read the message. *How soon will you be in the office? Something's come up that needs you here.* It was strange to get a text from Shirley. *C U in 5.* Megan sent back. She waved at Norman, giving him a hand-to-ear signal for "call me" before turning for the door. She trotted to her vehicle and soon parked it in her spot at the office. One thing about a small town square is you could just about get anywhere around it within five minutes, driving or walking.

"Hi, Shirley. What's going on?" Megan greeted her receptionist without breaking her stride toward her office.

"I put Ted Hawthorne in your office. He's a mess. He even brought his mother with him; they demanded to see you." Shirley called after Megan's retreating back.

Megan slowed as she neared the closed door to her office. She paused to listen to the conversation within.

"You better hope the sheriff doesn't arrest you. We don't have bail money, and the house is already mortgaged. Whatever made you think shooting at a line shack was okay? Couldn't you tell someone lived there? *What were you thinking?"*

"But Ma, you know how much we need money, and iffn' I could earn a hundred bucks just for sitting in the rocks and firing a couple of rounds toward the cabin—I didn't see no harm." A sob sounded from the man. Ted was in his early twenties. He had enlisted in the army a year ago and washed out of boot camp due to his slow intelligence. Ted ranked only just self-sustaining and barely made it out of high school. He worked some for all the shops in town, sweeping sidewalks and helping off-load shipments. All jobs that required either no supervision or close supervision. Megan figured it was time to find out what exactly they were talking about. She walked into her office and sat down.

Ted Hawthorne was tall and gangly, with wrists hanging out of the sleeves of his flannel shirt; his sandy hair brushed the collar on one side of his head and looked like a five-o'clock shadow on the other side. Bangs hung down across his forehead, almost hiding his eyes but were unable to disguise the tears on his cheeks. He flipped his hair back with a toss of his head, and his eyes desperately made contact with Megan's.

"Good afternoon, Deborah, Ted. Shirley told me you needed to speak with me. How may I help you?" Megan figured she would let him explain what happened without her hurling questions at him. "Do you mind if I record this? It helps me keep things straight when I make reports."

Megan didn't hit the record button until Deborah nodded.

"Sheriff. You gotta' believe me. I never meant to hit anything when I shot at the cabin. I was told just to shoot to keep Marvin in there. I thought he was on the other side of the room when I fired at that chair. Honest. I didn't know he'd moved into it. Is he gonna' be okay?"

"Let's start at the beginning. Why were you shooting at Marvin's cabin? I'm required by law to tell you that anything you say can be used against you, and I suggest you have an attorney present."

"We can't afford no lawyer, sheriff. Ted and I barely make enough to cover living day-to-day." Deborah sat, wringing her hands. The worry expressed in her body language far exceeded that in her voice.

"Let me see if I can get a public defender or one of our locals who can advise you pro bono." Megan wanted to hear what was going on, but more importantly, she wanted what was best for Ted. Poor decisions made by a mildly handicapped man shouldn't ruin his life. This kind of thing could cost him more than just his freedom.

"If it won't cost us anything, I'd like to have someone here who knows the law. Someone who can stand up for my boy in court if it comes to that." Deborah nodded, deciding to get outside help for her child.

Megan reached over and turned off the voice recorder. "Good move. Let me see who we can get. You can wait in here until they arrive."

Megan walked out the door of her office and into the solid chest of Deputy Joseph Kaleo. "Morning Joe, did you need to see me?"

"Uh, yeah, well, I..." Joseph stuttered, seemingly upset at being caught listening at Megan's door.

"It's okay. I understand, but now you're going to stand right here to keep the Hawthorne's safe while I talk to Shirley." Megan waited as Joe realized she meant to keep the Hawthornes from leaving, not to keep others from entering her office. The light dawned in his eyes, and Joseph gave her a grave nod of understanding.

"Sure thing. I'll make sure no one comes out or goes into your office until you return."

Megan made her way to Shirley's desk in the front reception area. Shirley was on the phone, nodding and smiling when Megan got there. She held up her finger at Megan.

"That's right, Kathy. How soon can you get here? Great. I'll tell the sheriff, and we'll see you in ten minutes." Shirley hung up the phone. She gave Megan a huge smile. "That was Kathy Cornwall. You know, the new pastor's wife? She's a retired attorney, and she's volunteered to help Ted with this problem. She's on her way over to advise him during questioning."

"I won't ask how you knew Ted would need an attorney, but how did you know about Kathy Cornwall? They've only been in town for two weeks."

"Sheriff, you know nothing is secret in a small town. When her husband took the job as pastor, she sent her credentials to the Montrose courthouse. They sent us word, knowing it was information we could use. Besides, when the Cornwalls took the Mitchell's house instead of the rectory, the rental paperwork showed her occupation, and Betty called me."

Megan shook her head. Small town grapevines could put intelligence agencies to shame any day of the week. She stopped at the pop machine, unlocked it, and pulled out three sodas—one diet, one full of caffeine, and one sugary lemon-lime. Joe moved to the side, opening her office door when he saw her coming, balancing the cans.

"Okay, here's what's happening. We're moving down the hall to the conference room." Megan nodded for Joe to open the door. "We're taking this to the conference room. Kathy Cornwall is on her way to help you. She's a retired lawyer."

Ted and his mother rose to follow Megan down the hall.

"Bring my tape recorder, would you, Joe?" Megan asked.

In the conference room, she put the lemon-lime at the chair closer to her own and the diet at the seat just beyond it. Taking the end seat, she set her cola down before opening it. "Ted, have you met our new pastor at the Methodist church?"

"You mean, Pastor Glen? He's cool. He plays the guitar and coaches soccer after the service. He's teaching me to be a goalie." Ted's eyes took on the glow of hero worship.

"His wife, Kathy, has offered to help you. Drink your soda slowly; we may be here for a while. Deborah, would you come with me a minute?" Megan left Ted with his drink. Holding her soda, she took Deborah back to her office.

"Sheriff, are we supposed to pay Kathy?" Money seemed to be a significant concern to Deborah.

"No, she's agreed to work without pay. I'm not sure, but she may want you to plead that Ted wasn't of sound mind when he decided to shoot at the cabin. I know you're Ted's mother and his legal guardian. Is there anyone else you've assigned to handle his affairs in case something happens to you?" Megan hadn't wanted to talk in front of Ted. Somehow, even though he didn't always understand what others were talking about, it just seemed wrong to discuss him as though he wasn't in the room.

"I had Pastor Robert as a designated guardian in my will. Now that he's moved to Denver, I haven't approached Pastor Glen yet, but I will as soon as I know them better."

"Maybe, you should have Kathy draw up those papers too. She might even be a better choice as a guardian since she's an attorney." Megan heard voices and looked beyond the windows of her office to see a woman greeting Shirley. "Looks like she's here. I just wanted to know who to contact if you're not available." Megan and Deborah moved back to the hallway.

"Sheriff, this is Kathy Cornwall, the new pastor's wife. She told me she hadn't met you yet," Shirley introduced Megan to Kathy. Together, they all filed back into the conference room where Ted sat playing games on his phone and drinking a soda without a care in the world.

Megan knew this lack of attention to what had so distressed him five minutes ago was a symptom of his mental capacity. However, it still felt wrong for him to be so carefree in this situation. She didn't need to make introductions because Kathy knew the Hawthornes from church.

"Sheriff, I need about five minutes with my clients to settle the details. Do you mind?" Kathy sat down in Megan's seat, touching Ted's hand to focus his attention on her.

Megan and Shirley left the room quietly. "Shirley, get Henry for me. I need to ask him a few questions about what he's seen lately. If Norman calls, put him through unless I'm in the conference room," Megan instructed as she led Shirley back down the hall.

"You got it. I'll hold any other calls and take messages until this conference is over. Right?"

"Thanks." Megan turned into her office, noticing that Joe was standing next to the conference room door. She nodded her approval before closing her door. She had just sat down when her phone rang. That was quick. She picked it up, expecting it to be Henry or Norman.

"Sheriff Holloway here."

"I'm surprised it rang through. Shirley usually catches calls to your number." A familiar voice said.

"She's calling Henry for me. Norman, I'm glad you called. Can you spare a few minutes?"

"Sure, Megan. How can I help?" Norman's voice sounded serene and unworried.

Megan wished she could feel that way. This week was getting more and more complicated.

"Ted Hathaway works for you a lot, doesn't he?"

"Yeah, I've got him doing things that don't require mental expertise. I don't think he reads above third grade, and his problem-solving is about the same level. I still don't know how that boy got to the Army recruiter and managed to enlist. That recruiter needed to be shot for accepting him." Norman ranted against the man who allowed a moderately handicapped young man into the Army.

"I know, right? I wrote a letter of complaint to the Army. Don't know if it did any good, but I had to do something. I need to know if you've seen him talking to strangers, maybe with a dog?" Megan felt the question was leading, but in this case, she needed data more than needing Norman to come forward with information.

"You know, we've had several new customers in the past couple of weeks. One is the guy who came off his horse on Saturday, and the other two men I've never seen before or since."

"Did you see Ted with either?"

"Yeah, when the two guys got out of their truck, a dog jumped out and ran over to Ted. Animals can always tell who needs them the most. Ted put down his broom and fell to his knees to pet the pup, and one of the men grabbed its collar, yanking it away from the boy. Ted looked like he wanted to cry. The men got the dog into the truck and came into the store to buy cattle feed and dog food. Ted reached his arm in the window to pet the dog while the guys were in the store but grabbed his arm out before they saw him."

"Have the men been back? What kind of truck, or at least what color was it?"

"I think it was a Ram, the color could have been silver, or maybe there was a tint to the silver. Kind of sand-ish. I haven't seen 'em since. They didn't start a tab like most ranchers run for monthly payments. Come to think of it, the truck had Utah plates, so maybe they were passing through," Norman mused.

"Keep your eyes open, and if you see them again, call me. Oops, my other line is blinking. Shirley must have reached Henry. I'll keep in touch and don't expect Ted today if he's scheduled. I've got him here with me." Megan dropped the call before Norman had a chance to react.

"Sheriff Holloway here."

"What do you need, Sheriff? What's Ted doing in there with his mother?" Henry's sounded the most concerned Megan could remember hearing.

"Hi, Henry. Ted's here because he might have seen something. But that's not why I called you. What have you seen of a Ram dually pickup with Utah plates? Might have been around on Friday or Saturday morning?" Megan hated giving Henry so much information, but she needed to know if the old man had seen that particular truck in town. Henry was an encyclopedia of vehicles, and if any new or different cars or trucks came through town, he'd notice.

"Utah plates? Hmmm. I don't remember a dually, but I saw a big Ram 2500 pulling an empty stock trailer up on the highway. I was headed to Montrose, and this guy just about shut me down. I noticed the truck had Utah plates, but I didn't get the number. Really irritated me, and I was gonna' follow him to give him a piece of my mind. He turned north onto some sort of ranch or BLM road not that far out of town, and I thought better of picking a fight out in the middle of nowhere."

"Good move. What day did this happen?"

"It was Saturday. I had the day off. Lilabell and I had spent the day together, and I was heading to Montrose to get her something special. I'd say it wasn't too long before sundown. I kind of wondered what they were doing, but I know people sometimes sleep in their trucks off the highway when they don't have funds for a hotel, so I wasn't too worried."

"Thanks, Henry. Keep your eyes open for Utah vehicles. Let me know if you see more. It might have something to do with the missing cattle, so don't go playing the hero. Call it in if you see them, *don't follow them.* Am I clear on that?"

"You bet. Rustlers tend to have guns. The only person I want to be around who handles a gun is Lilabell. She's a crack shot and not afraid to use her weapon."

"So, what did you get Lilabell?" Megan felt Henry wanted her to ask. The man was horrible at keeping anything secret.

"I wanted to get her a ring from Chris, but she's not ready for that, so I bought her and Ida Mae both a day at the Guest Spa in Gunnison. Maybe by the time Chris gets some more rings made, Lilabell will be ready to accept one from me." Henry's voice was soft and whispery as he dreamed of the day to come.

"You two are getting that serious? I thought it was more of a 'first you date Lilabell, and then you date Ida Mae' kind of thing. When did you switch back to Lilabell, anyway?" Megan scratched her head. If this kept up with those three, she would need a playbook to keep track.

"Oh, Ida Mae was just helping me make Lilabell jealous so she would get over being mad at me. It worked too. Two dates with Ida Mae and Lilabell was a peach ready for picking. We've never been closer, except when her husband was alive, of course." Henry amended his statement.

A knock sounded on Megan's door, and Joe stepped into her office.

"Let me know when congratulations are in order and if you see any Utah vehicles. I gotta go." She broke the connection.

"Ted, his mother, and Kathy are ready to answer questions now. Do you still want me at the door?" Joe looked hopeful.

"Yes, if for no other reason than to keep anyone but you from overhearing the conversation." Megan strode down the hall and into the conference room. Joe took his assigned place.

Chapter Twelve

In the conference room, Kathy had moved to Ted's left, leaving the end seat for Megan. Deborah moved to the chair across from Ted to Megan's right.

"Theodore Hathaway, you are here of your own accord to tell us about something you did. You understand that if your actions warrant a court proceeding that anything you say here can and will be used against you in such court action?" Megan pointed the recorder at Ted to better pick up his responses. Ted nodded his head in answer to her question. "Ted, please answer yes or no for the recording of this interview."

"Yes, Sheriff. My ma and Ms. Cornwall explained everything to me. I'm ready to tell you what happened." Ted's mother covered his clenched hands with hers to give him comfort. Kathy Cornwall smiled her encouragement to the man-child.

Megan read Ted the remainder of his Miranda rights to legalize the proceedings. "Ted, why don't you tell us what happened." Megan tried not to confuse Ted with what she knew of the actions.

"I was sweeping in front of the Co-op on Saturday morning, and these two guys were discussing which would have to sit all afternoon watching a cabin. From what I heard, they were trying to win a bet against the cabin owner. See, he's got an outhouse, and one of the guys bet ole Marvin they could keep him from usin' the outhouse for a whole day. If Mavin could get to the outhouse, Marvin would win the bet. I heard them bitchin'—oops, sorry, Momma. I mean, complaining how boring it was gonna be to keep Marvin hole up in his house all day and night so they could win this bet. One of them tol' the other it was a stupid bet, and what did he bet five hundred for?" Ted paused, frowning at his soda. "Thinking about it now, it seemed like a strange bet, but I wasn't there when the bet was placed. One fella commented that it would be great to find someone who wanted to earn a hundred bucks. I broke in and told them that I could use a hundred bucks. What did they want me to do for it?"

Megan bit her tongue. She wanted details about the two men but understood that Ted had to tell the story completely before she could get him back to the men who hired him on a fool's errand. "What happened next?"

"Well, I was done at the Co-op, so I followed them out to the ridge above Marvin's line shack. It was barely noon, and the cabin was quiet. The dark-haired man helped me get down to the rocks above the hut, where I could shoot through the open window. He gave me fifty bucks, two sodas, a candy bar, and a rifle. Said I was to sit there and make sure Marvin didn't make it to the outhouse. Said if'n I shot a round or two through the window once Marvin was up and moving around, he'd be too scared to come outside. For any reason. The guy laughed, and it was an evil sound. Gave me goosebumps."

Ted ran his hands up and down his arms, shook his shoulders, and took a swig from his soda. "I guess I knew then that there was no bet. But we need the money, and I couldn't see any reason not to shoot into the line shack. It's not like I was hired to shoot ole Marvin—just to keep him inside. I figured I could do it until dark and collect the rest of the money. Dark-haired guy left, and I stayed there in the rocks for hours. Marvin must have been hungover or something. He didn't move and didn't move. I began to wonder if'n Marvin was home. I got up to piss, and when I came back, Marvin was at his front door. He must have gone to the outhouse while I was trying to find a safe place to take a leak. Damn it all! Sorry, Momma. I was so angry that I didn't do what those guys hired me to do. I fired over his head at the door. Meaning to scare him into the cabin. It worked. He high-tailed it inside and slammed the door. I could see through the window and watched him for another hour or so. I needed to go pee again, but I was gonna' to make sure he didn't leave the cabin this time. I took careful aim and shot through the window into the highback chair. I almost peed my pants when Marvin screamed and jumped up out of the chair! *I thought he was at the stove! I never meant to hurt him. I like Marvin. He gives me chewing gum!"*

Ted broke down into tears, shuddering and sobbing, his heart seemingly breaking at the thought that he'd hurt the old man. His mother stood and put her arms around her son, rocking him against the chair where he sat, trying to ease his suffering. "Hush, baby. You did something very wrong, but you didn't mean to harm anyone. We know that. Hush, now. Blow your nose, and tell the rest of the story." She patted his hand as she must have since his earliest childhood. Slowly the sobbing came under control. Kathy Cornwall passed Ted tissues to wipe his tears and blow his nose. Childlike, the man did as directed by his mother.

"I didn't know what to do. Marvin was up and out of the chair, his rifle pointed out the window. I knew he was gonna be okay cause if he'd been shot bad, he wouldn't be able to stand. Right?" Ted looked around the room, hoping for confirmation of his reasoning. "I stayed where I was all night long. On Sunday morning, he opened the door, and I shot at the door again. I was happy he was moving around; I had to finish what I'd been hired to do. I had to keep him there until noon on Sunday. At noon, I headed for home. Those guys had told me they would leave the other fifty under a rock where the track I was on met the BLM dirt road. It wasn't there. I looked under every boulder within fifteen feet of the turn. Nothing. They lied to me. *I shot Marvin, and they LIED to me!*" Ted broke down into sobs again.

Megan stood. Making eye contact with his mother, they stepped away from her son a few feet. "Can you get him to calm down enough to answer some questions? I need to know more information about those men who hired him, and I need the rifle he used."

"Give me a few minutes. I'll get him to settle down. Is Marvin going to be okay? Knowing that would help a lot in getting him to stop crying."

"Marvin is going to be fine in a few days. The wound was clean, and he drank enough booze to keep any bacteria at bay," Megan assured the woman. She walked out, colliding with Joe, who was still standing at the door.

"You heard? I need you to keep this quiet. I don't want a word of this to get out to anyone. If it does, it's your job. Am I making myself clear?" Megan trusted Joe but also knew the speed of gossip in this town.

"No problem. But why? Some scumbags hired a boy, or rather a man, of slow wit to do their dirty work and then stiffed him on the payment. Ted isn't competent enough to make decisions, and these guys figured that out real quick. They abused his trust. What difference does it make if the town finds out? Everyone loves Ted." Joe seemed honestly confused.

"Because everyone loves Ted, we don't want it to be common knowledge that he was tricked. Some would hold it against him, and that's not in his best interest," Megan explained.

"Oh. I guess you're right. I think even Marvin will forgive him, but some of the newer residents might not understand how the people of Riverview stick up for each other." Joe's expression looked pained at the thought of people who might not stand behind Riverview's handicapped population. "What are you going to do now?"

"I'm grabbing my soda from my office and going back in there to see what I can find out about those rustlers."

Five minutes later, Megan knocked and opened the conference room door. Ted's mother held him, but she patted his back and stepped back to her chair at Megan's entrance. Ted straightened in his seat and lifted his sad eyes to Megan's face while his advocate drew out a clean sheet of paper.

"Ted, I need you to answer some questions. I want you to remember every detail you can, okay? The only wrong answer you can give me is if you lie to me, and we know you don't believe in lying." Turning the recorder on again, Megan took her seat.

"Ted, can you describe each of these guys who hired you? Anything special that you noticed?"

"Well, one was taller than me, and one was just a little shorter. The dark-haired man was older and taller, but he weren't old, only older than the shorter guy. Called the short one 'Shorty' a couple of times. I could tell the short guy didn't like the name. He didn't say a word, but if looks could do damage, dark-haired guy would have been bleeding." Ted nodded sagely.

"What did the short guy look like? Could you see eye color on either of them?" Megan would pull the video from the Co-op surveillance, but it was black and white.

"Shorty's hair was a red-blondish color. He wore a ball cap and sunglasses, so I couldn't see his eyes. The older guy had dark hair that hung outside his cowboy hat, and he had sunglasses too. When Shorty paid me the fifty, he had a really slick leather wallet chained to his belt. I could use something like that. I lose my wallet at least once a month.."

"What was special about the wallet besides it being attached?"

"It had one of those Indian things carved into it. You know, the round hoop with feathers and cross ties? Someone told me the name of it once; I think it starts with a d." Ted's brow puckered as he tried to recall what he'd been told.

"A dreamcatcher?" Kathy offered.

"Yeah. There was a wolf in the middle, and then the lines out to the edges with feathers carved as hanging from the hoop. It was cool."

"Good job. Now, what else can you remember? Did they have a truck or a car?"

"They drove one of those six-wheeled pickups. The kind that rattles and rumbles when it starts up, and it had a back seat. The cattle dogs could hardly hop into the back. It was so high off the ground."

"How many dogs were there? What color were they?" Megan asked, knowing the man would likely remember more about the animals than his employers.

Ted's face brightened, and his brow cleared. "There were three of them. Two were in the truck, and one sat next to Shorty. He wouldn't let me pet any of them. Said they was working dogs and not pets." A scowl marred Ted's childish face. "I managed to pat the one by Shorty when he turned to open the truck." A sly smile stole across Ted's visage. "Of the two in the truck, one was black with a white stripe down his face and across his chest. He had longer hair with folded ears. The other was a rusty brown with black eyebrows and ears standing up. Shorty's dog was a mottled color. Kinda spotted like one of those Indian ponies. It had the strangest blue eyes."

"Good job. Now, what do you remember about the truck?"

"It had six tires, you know, like the ranch trucks that haul those long trailers."

"Do you remember the color of the truck? Did it look new? How about signs or stickers?" Megan asked.

"It had one of those window stickers…you know, the boy taking a leak with a mean look on his face?"

"Good. What else?"

"I think it was a diesel—cause it rumbled and rattled when the tall guy started it. It sounded loud to me, so it could have been souped up," Ted offered.

"What color was it?"

"It looked kind of brownish. It was hard to tell cause it was dirty and had a lot of scratches and a dent on the front. Like maybe they'd hit a deer or something. My grandpa's truck had a dent like that after he hit a deer one time."

"So it looked kind of old and beat up?"

"It was beat up, all right. But it didn't look all that old. Maybe five years or so, I don't know." Ted's brow creased in concentration.

"That's okay; don't worry about it. The dented fender and color will give us something to watch for," Megan reassured the man.

"You know, I did see somthin' strange on Saturday. While I wus sittin' up in the rocks, I saw a guy come out of the gully that goes down to the Gunnison. He limped. I wanted to call to get him help, but I knew I couldn't. I wus about to go help him when he climbed over onto a road. You know, one of those that go back to ranches out in the open country? Anyway, I could barely see him, even with the binoculars I pulled from my truck, but he pulled the brush away from something, and it was a car. He drove off, so I didn't worry about him anymore. That was just before Marvin started moving in his shack," Ted explained.

"Ted, you sat up there a long time. Did you see anything strange other than the limping man?" Megan figured he didn't have much more to tell about the rustlers, but he might be a witness to the destruction of Billy's truck.

"Ya' know? I did see some stuff happening. I couldn't tell who, but someone drove a single headlight truck up the BLM road that goes around the state land and toward the Blue Ditch. That was late on Saturday night. The sound of the truck woke me up, and I almost fell off the rocks cause I forgot where I was sleeping." Ted's eyes grew wide as he remembered the fright.

"Could you hear anything? Like party noises or such?" Megan didn't want to lead him, but she wanted to know who was in the truck dumped in the Blue Ditch.

"Nope. I heard a grinding, scraping, thump coming from the Ditch, but nothing else. For a while, there was a light over there. I figured it was the headlight before the battery died."

"Thanks; Billy's loaner truck was found in the Blue Ditch on Sunday. No one knows who dumped it there. But, from what you tell me, it wasn't drunks having a party." Megan stood and put her hand on Ted's shoulder. "I need to check a few things and speak with Kathy and your mother. You sit here with your soda. Would you like Officer Joe to come in and keep you company?"

"Naw, I'll be okay. Momma says I need to think about what I did and figure out why it was wrong besides the fact that Marvin got hurt."

"Okay, we'll be back soon. Joe's outside the door if you need anything." She released the youth's shoulder and headed for the door, followed by Kathy and Deborah.

"Wait, Sheriff. I just thought of something. On Sunday morning, I got up at sunrise to go take a leak. You know, I saw that limping man again. He came up from the Blue Ditch. He began following the rocks around the open land, kind of like he didn't want to leave any tracks. I went back to watching Marvin's cabin and didn't pay any attention to him. When I went to leave, he was a good half-mile from the Ditch. He sat on a rock like he was tired." Ted's face reflected surprise and happiness that he remembered another detail.

"Thanks, Ted. We'll be right back." Megan led Kathy and Deborah back to her office.

"Sheriff, did Ted help you enough? Is there any way you can save him from going to jail?" Deborah collapsed into the chair facing Megan's desk.

"I'll need to verify with the District Attorney, but with the details Ted provided, the charges could be reduced to misdemeanors. It's more important that we catch the cattle rustlers. The term 'State's Witness' comes to mind. Also, he's a material witness, possibly, in another case." Megan sat at her desk, making eye contact, first with Kathy and then with Deborah. "I think, for now, we can release him into your custody, Deborah. Just don't let him leave town. He needs to stay home for a few days, out of sight of the rustlers, if they come back to tie up loose ends."

Deborah burst into tears. "Thank you so much, Sheriff Megan. I can guarantee you that Ted will be restricted to his room for the next week—or until you tell me I can release him. It will be just like locking him up, only with better food." She jumped up and began wringing Megan's hand.

"Kathy, you can help by writing up a report with Deborah detailing Ted's mental status. We want the judge to realize that he can understand right from wrong but is more easily fooled than a person without his handicap. Have the statement available for me tomorrow, and I'll take it to the D.A."

The phone on Megan's desk began to ring. Knowing Shirley wouldn't put through any call, Megan waved the two women from her office and picked up the phone from her desk.

"Sheriff Megan Holloway here. How may I help you?"

"Sheriff, this is Norman. I finally caught up and remembered you had some questions. Go ahead and pick my brain. I'm in my office, and my nephew is manning the counter so I can talk."

"Hi, Norman. You were really swamped earlier. Glad you called. I know you heard me say I'm looking for the thieves who have been rustling cattle, but I'm not sure you caught what I said about them using dogs and mustangs or unshod horses." Megan pulled her notepad closer and picked up her favorite pen. "Have you seen anyone new to the area with cattle dogs, a long gooseneck trailer, and possibly buying horse and cattle feed?"

"What makes you think they are new to the area, Megan?" Norman asked.

"I hope they are new. I don't want to arrest my friends and neighbors for these crimes. They hired Ted to distract Marvin so they could collect the rustled cows without being seen. I know there are at least two men in the ring, could be more, including a ranch where the cows can be kept and a butcher who wouldn't notice a brand on any cows he butchered."

"I saw the two guys talking to Ted on Saturday morning. You're right; they had dogs. Haven't sold them any cattle feed, just dog food." There was a rustling of papers as Norman searched his desk. "They paid cash. I just found the receipt we use for cash sales. They're not a common thing in Riverview. No name, just a truck description for the person loading from the dock."

"Has anyone new been buying cattle feed recently?" Megan hoped there would be a couple of buyers. Some cattle ranches were beginning to run short of hay and would supplement with feed at this time of year.

"Only the usual list of buyers. No, wait. That new guy building off the corner of the 3C's bought both cattle feed and some calf manna and milk replacer. Said he was going to a spring auction and needed fodder when the animals were delivered. He also bought some horse feed for when he gets a horse. I wonder after that wreck if he's going to be getting a horse?" Norman mused.

"Hmmm...interesting. Roger sent one of his hands over to the ranch when Nick turned up missing, and they found no livestock to feed. I wonder when he's expecting the delivery. Keep your eyes open and if that Utah truck comes into town, call me. Don't approach them; sell them whatever they need, but contact me as soon as possible. Get a plate number if you can do it without being obvious." Megan instructed.

"Sure thing, Sheriff. Did you see the flyer for the Cattle Dog competition? Those Utah cowboys might be going to it. Good size purse, and they've got three dogs." Norman offered.

"Give me the details. Maybe I'll find the time to attend."

"I'll scan it and send you a copy of it. Much easier than trying to remember all the details." Norman offered.

"Thanks. I'll look forward to getting the file. I trust you to keep all of this to yourself; no need to let the thieves know what we're doing to catch them." Megan warned.

"Not a problem. That's why I called you from my office—privacy. You let me know if there's anything I can do for you, and you tell Ted his job is here waiting for him."

"Thanks, Norman." Megan broke the connection. She headed out of her office, stopping by Shirley's desk. "You've got things under control here, right?"

"Sure. Where're you going?"

"I need to go see Doc Rayburn about some livestock. Norman is going to send a file over. I'd appreciate it if you would print the file and put it on my desk." Megan set her Stetson firmly on her head, picked the SUV keys from the wall hook, and set off to find the veterinarian.

Chapter Thirteen

Megan enjoyed the drive to Dr. Rayburn's clinic. She never ceased marveling at the scenery surrounding Riverview, no matter which direction she traveled. The day had turned beautiful, with the sky showing the color blue that only elevation and lack of pollution can give it. From her youth in Texas and her military travels, Megan knew most of the world would never see the color of sky she was graced to admire here in Riverview. By the time she pulled into the clinic parking lot, the day's stress had melted away, and she could feel her grin returning. Yep, there was nowhere else she would ever want to live—unless Aaron needed to move. She would leave Colorado for Aaron, but little else would draw her away from this land of majestic vistas and amazing people.

Seeing only three vehicles in the clinic parking lot, Megan felt relief that she wouldn't be interrupting much of Dr. Rayburn's day. One was pulling a stock trailer, but the other two were sedans belonging to the owners of smaller animals. Maybe Doc would have time to talk to her for a few minutes. It was easier coming by than trying to get him to the phone. Also, he might remember more if she were standing there than he would while sitting at his desk. There were too many distractions for him at his desk.

She heard hogs squealing in the long barn to her right, so she headed in that direction. Someone was out there, and it likely was the vet with the owner. Rounding the edge of the barn, she saw a huge sow in the first stall, stretched out and obviously in labor. Dr. Paul Rayburn squatted at the south end of the sow, helping the delivery of each piglet by applying a tugging pressure when needed. At the sow's head knelt a teenager Megan couldn't quite place. He looked about sixteen; the sow might be his Future Farmers of America, FFA, project. He watched every move Doc made while he stroked the sow, trying to keep her calm. The sow shrieked loudly with the emergence of each piglet.

"I warned you not to let her get so obese, Michael. Fat sows don't have enough muscle to push piglets out past that fatty layer." Paul Rayburn tried to educate the young farmer while assisting the sow.

"But, you know how much she likes those yams. It was either feeding the culls to her or the horses, and Pa wouldn't let the horses have 'em. Says it can founder 'em."

"Your Pa is right. Yams are high in sugar and can founder any animal given too many of them. You can feed yams as a supplement or a treat in moderation. You just can't give them as a steady diet to any creature." Doc looked up and saw Megan.

"Hi, Sheriff. What brings you out this direction?"

Megan worried about questioning Dr. Rayburn in front of Michael. Still, in a small town, Michael most likely knew everything going on. There were no secrets in a ranching community when it came to livestock.

"Paul, do you have any additional customers? Anyone with cattle or cattle dogs? I know about Nick's new spread, and Norman told me he's been buying calf manna; has he brought any livestock into the clinic?"

"I sold him some milk replacer and colostrum for newborn calves. He expects to have some babies over on his place, and I don't think he's got any cows. He did mention some sort of online sale of orphan calves. I've never heard of anything like that in this neck of the woods." Doc eyed the distressed sow and reached down to feel for the next piglet. "How many live ones does this make?" he asked Michael as he eased a pink and black squirming piglet free of the sow.

"That's number ten, alive. The first two were stillborn, one at my place and one in the trailer. Millie couldn't push them out quick enough to keep 'em alive, or else, they were not viable from the get-go."

"I'll check them over later to see if I can tell. If Millie's going to lose piglets every litter, she's only fit for bacon," the vet advised the teen.

"Yeah, I'd hate to start my breeding program all over again. Pa says the same thing, and I won't be advancing my FFA project by breeding inferior livestock." Michael looked dejected. "Well, if'n those piglets would never have made it, and I gotta start again, at least we'll have pork for a good year or more. I might be able to trade one of the meat piglets for another breeding sow." His face mirrored his thoughts from gloomy to hopeful in one sentence.

"Sheriff, you know, I did answer an emergency call on Sunday. I met a livestock hauler up in the rest area. He had a cow that needed help calving. We pulled the calf, and I told him to let the heifer rest for at least a couple of hours before starting out again. I don't know if he did. He paid in cash, but I got his plates because I don't like working on the side of the road."

"How many animals were on the truck? Was it an eighteen-wheeler?" Megan asked.

"No, it was one of those red steel stock trailers, double axel. Pretty rusted and also pretty full. They managed to get the one cow out before I got there—I don't know how they expected to get her back inside and not have her calf trampled. They haven't called back, so I guess they made it out of the area."

Paul leaned over the sow again, reaching his hand into her, feeling for any remaining piglets. "Feels like that was the last one. Not a bad size litter for her; only problem was she couldn't push them out because you let her get too fat." He stood up, rubbed the small of his back, and stepped out of the farrowing pen.

Megan waited while he spoke to the young farmer about proper care of the sow and her piglets. "Let her rest at least an hour and put the piglets separate from her to haul her home. She might step or roll on them if you don't."

"Sheriff, if'n that stock trailer the doc saw on Sunday is of interest, I saw one over at Nick's new place. It was behind the barn Sunday evening when I drove past on my way to see Julie." Michael spoke up as the group stepped away from the sow and back out into the daylight.

"When did you sell the milk replacer to Nick?" Megan asked the veterinarian.

"That was last week, but it's a powder, and you mix it when you need it. Do you think Nick bought that calf from those haulers?"

"Considering he is in the market for orphan calves, it would be convenient for them to drop the calf off, pocket the money, and drive away. I'm not sure how they would know about him, but it seems possible."

"Sheriff, you can locate anythin' using a smartphone." Michael reminded them.

"Paul, did you notice the brand on the cow? Haulers often haul for more than one spread at a time. Did they say where they were taking the livestock?" Megan inquired.

"I didn't get to see any of the other livestock in the trailer. The cow in labor was penned in a portable corral. I thought it kind of odd for them to have panels mounted to the side of the trailer, but I got busy fast and had little time to worry about the issue." Paul stopped to dispose of his long glove in the trash before continuing. "I believe the brand on the cow was 3C's. I didn't think much about it because Angela had mentioned she wanted to cull her livestock the last time I was out there. The old man had let the cattle breed and eat without ever culling, so the herd had some real losers in it."

"Keep your eyes open and call me if you find any cows at a different ranch than their brand indicates. There's been some rustling, and it seems to be all pregnant cows that are being taken. Sort of a 'steal one and get two' kind of deal." Megan shook Dr. Rayburn's hand and nodded at Michael. "You keep your eyes open too. We can beat these thieves if we all watch brands."

Megan left the pair and drove back toward her office. She collected a BLT and sweet ice tea from Betty's Diner, escaping before Betty had a chance to corner her for rumors about the current crime spree. Megan liked getting information from Betty; she didn't like being the source of local gossip. On her way out, she told the few diners and Betty, "Ya'll keep your eyes open for an extended length red stock trailer possibly hitched to a Ram with Utah plates. Call me if you see it, don't mess with them; I just want to know where it's seen last." She made it back to her SUV before the first text came in.

"On Monday, I saw one over by that new ranch on the corner of the 3C's ranch."

"I saw one of those things turning in on a BLM road Saturday afternoon."

"I saw it. This morning. It turned in on a Forestry road that runs through the land leased to the R-bar-B Pack Station."

Megan chuckled. There were only about four people in Betty's. It looked like each had seen the rig at different times. The third text grabbed her attention. She responded, "How long ago?"

"Bout an hour or so. Want me to show you where?"

"No, I know the road you mean. Thanks."

Megan called her deputy, Joe Kaleo. "Joe, I need backup right now. Bring along anyone who's there with a weapon."

"Whoa. What's going on? Do I need to call in the Highway Patrol?"

"No need for HP. Just get yourself moving. I think we can catch the rustlers with a load of freshly stolen cows. The suspect vehicle and trailer were seen going up the Forestry road that runs behind the R-bar-B Pack Station. We can block their escape route and apprehend them with a full trailer if they're doing what I think. Roger is running some cows on the land they leased from the Forestry department."

"You thinking it's the road Roger used to rescue Bethany when she came off Coup?"

"That's the only road that goes into the forest behind the R-bar-B. Only road in and only one road back out. It deadends about ten miles from the highway, right next to grazing land leased to the R-bar-M Ranch. Step on it. I'll meet you there. NO sirens." Megan didn't want the rig to dump whatever they were hauling before she and Joe cornered it. As she put her rig in reverse, she speed-dialed Aaron.

"Hi Babe, how's your day going?" Aaron sounded happy and relaxed. He wouldn't be for long.

"I need some rifle back up. Just to be safe. Joe and I are going to make a stop on the rig we think is rustling cattle. Can you take about three or four of the guys up the Forestry road where Bethany and I came out that time? You know, the one that runs up to that open glade? Go quietly. Just take places overlooking the road about half a mile from where it joins the highway. I don't want to give them hope to make it past us. That would be an excellent place for our roadblock. I don't want any shooting unless they open fire first."

"On our way. You won't see us unless you need us." Aaron cut the connection.

Megan smiled. The R-bar-M hands were former military, several snipers, so she knew she could count on their skills. Most had been deputized over the past couple of years, so she wouldn't need to do it again. She turned west on Highway 50, enjoying the view for the short distance to the Forest Road on the left, a short distance past where the trail from the R-bar-M Ranch crossed the highway to the R-bar-B Pack Station and Campground. The dust still hung in the air from Aaron and his crew. Joe pulled his Jeep past her SUV before she pulled up at the Y, turning her SUV to block the road. He did the same with his Jeep, angling it up the road to prevent the rustlers from reaching the highway. Megan doubted even a determined rustler would be able to push two vehicles out of the way to escape.

She spotted some movement in the rocks to the left side of the road and turned to inspect them. Aaron stood and waved before resuming his position. On the other side of the dirt road, in the trees, a man stepped out and waved to Megan. He then became part of the forest once more. Good. All set. Now to wait.

"Sheriff, what makes you think the rustlers are up this road?" Joe asked as he walked over from his vehicle.

"The suspect's rig was seen turning onto this road about an hour and a half or so ago. I think they should still be up there. Loading cows isn't a five-minute job when you need to set up a catch pen or chute before driving them into the trailer." Megan took a bite of her cool BLT. Not bad, but still cold. "If they don't come down in a couple of hours, I'll drive up and find them. I don't think we'll need to wait that long. Get into your Kevlar and take the safety off your weapons."

She turned away from her deputy and spotted Officer Perkins, Joe's latest trainee. He looked nervous, so Megan motioned him over.

"Hi, how do you like your new job? Is Deputy Kaleo treating you okay?"

"Uh, yes, Ma'am. Deputy Joe is teaching me all my duties and treating me just fine." He kicked a pebble with his toe, giving it all his attention.

"We're waiting for a probable suspect in the cattle rustling case to come down from the high meadow where they possibly picked up more stolen cows. You'll need to put on the extra Kevlar vest in Joe's Jeep. Make sure you have your weapon loaded and the safety off. I hope we won't need to use guns, but having them ready is our best protection. Do you have any questions?" Megan explained.

"I was wondering what ya'll were doin' blocking this road. Did you see that guy up in the rocks? Is he one of 'em?" Timothy Perkins motioned with his hand low and shielded by his body toward the rocks overlooking their position.

"He's one of our secret helpers. I don't expect these men to start shooting, but we've got the drop on them if they do." Megan took a swig of her soda and the final bite of her delayed lunch. In the distance, the sound of possibly more than one vehicle could be heard, getting louder by the second. "Sounds like it's showtime. Get your vest on *now*! Hide behind your vehicle, and no shooting unless they shoot first." Megan pointed to the Jeep while opening the door of her Durango to use it as cover. She grabbed her Kevlar vest from the back seat and slipped into it, quickly fastening the assorted locking straps to keep it in place. The nose of the first truck edged around the curve as she checked her pistol, holding it in her left hand so she could work the bull horn with her right.

A beat-up Chevy truck pulling a two-horse trailer in the same condition cleared the bend. Behind it was the Ram pickup, its stock trailer was still hidden. Both vehicles slid to a stop on the loose gravel road. All movement ceased as the rustlers took in the image of the roadblock ahead of them. Megan knew there was no way the rigs could back up, but the people in them could run. She really hoped they wouldn't be so stupid, but if they had brains—they wouldn't be out rustling cattle. She grabbed her bull horn and flipped it up loud.

"This is the Sheriff of Riverview. Turn off your vehicles, throw out your weapons, and put your hands out the windows. Don't move once your hands are visible. We have you blocked, and the woods around you secured, so trying to run will only get you shot. *Do not try to exit your trucks!* Wait for us to approach you." Megan lowered the bull horn and waited to see what they decided to do.

Movement in the trailing truck drew her attention. A pistol fell from the passenger side window, followed by a rifle dropping from the driver's window. What looked like a machete flew from the passenger just before he extended his hands. The driver did the same but only had a buck knife.

Those in the lead vehicle took longer to decide. Megan could see the passenger with what looked to be a cell phone to his ear. She hoped he was calling an attorney. He moved his hand from his ear and then reached to pull a pistol from under his shoulder with two fingers. The gun went flying out the open window, followed by a knife. The driver pitched out a rifle, a knife, and a pistol before placing both wrists on the edge of the window with his hands hanging down the truck's side.

A whistle sounded from the trees where Aaron was hiding. Megan looked up to see him motioning to the trailer towed by the rear truck. "Someone is making a run for it from the gooseneck!" Aaron yelled, pointing to the rocky left of the road.

"*Sonofabitch!* Why is there always one person who thinks they can escape?" Megan muttered.

Megan spotted Aaron's dirtbike leaning against a tree. She holstered her pistol, grabbed the dirtbike, and took off through the woods along the road without hesitation. The bike bucked and kicked under her as it climbed up the hill beside the road. At the top, she could see a man on foot scrambling up an embankment away from her. Pulling her pistol, she fired one round at the rock face next to him in warning.

"*Freeze!* The next round will find your body!"

There was only a slight pause between the round hitting the rock and the man raising his hands in submission.

"On your face, hands above your body. You move, and I *will* take you out. I don't enjoy chasing idiots," Megan called.

She watched until the thief complied with her order. Over her shoulder, she saw Aaron coming down to help Officer Perkins cuff the others while Joe kept them covered. She dismounted the dirtbike, sliding down the embankment to the ledge where the thief was spread-eagled. "You're going to have fun sliding back down this hill with your hands behind your back. I told you not to run."

Cuffing one hand, she pulled it behind him and reached for the other. The crook made a feeble attempt to pull away and earned a knee to his groin as Megan landed on top of him. "Ah, ah, ahahh… That wasn't a smart move either. Maybe you'll learn that I mean what I tell you."

The man groaned under her, trying to catch his breath while she secured his hands. That done, she pulled him to his feet and pushed him ahead of her to the edge of the ledge. "Sit."

He stood looking down, not saying a word and not moving to follow her order. "I'm not above helping you to fall down this hill. I'm giving you a chance by letting you sit and slide down it. You climbed the damn thing. Now. *Sit!*" Megan helped him balance as he managed to sit awkwardly on the ledge. "Better. If I were you, I'd put my hands up as high on my back as I could reach and use my legs to keep me from sliding too fast. But, you can choose to slide down this hill any way you wish—so long as you get your ass to the bottom."

Megan had seen Aaron cuffing the driver of the Ram. He moved toward the back where the door to the gooseneck stood open and closed it before looking up at the pair on the ledge above the road.

"Do you need any help?" Aaron asked.

"Just stand ready to help this guy get to his feet. He's cuffed and ready to go. I'll ride your dirtbike back to where I found it. Are you okay working all three in this rig?"

"Yeah, they're all cuffed. I'll shove them in the truck cab and pull closer. Then I'll transfer them to Joe's Jeep. I can have my boys drive the rigs to the R-bar-B Pack Station. They've got corrals and room for these cattle while we sort out the ownership."

"Good idea. I'll be down in just a few minutes. In the meantime—*catch!*" Megan pushed the thief in the small of his back, accelerating his movement off the ledge and down the embankment.

Megan watched the thief scoot before turning back to Aaron's bike. She was back at her SUV a moment later, ready to receive the suspects. "Joe, you should be able to fit four in the Jeep. I'll take the runner. Aaron, thanks for your help. I've got to secure the vehicles at the R-bar-B Pack Station before running this idiot to town, so I'll follow you."

Joe and Officer Perkins had their passengers secured and drove toward Riverview five minutes later. Aaron left his bike in the trees to protect it from theft. Not much chance of it being stolen out here, but no sense leaving the dirtbike in plain sight. He hopped into the lead truck, directing his ranch hand into the truck with the gooseneck trailer. Both trailers were full of livestock, and there were dogs in the tack room of the bumper-pull trailer. Megan led the way to the R-bar-B, pulling aside to allow the two rigs to pass once she arrived at the pack station.

Megan lowered her windows by half and parked in a shady spot for the sake of her prisoner. She had no qualms about leaving him sit—but she wouldn't leave a dog in a closed-up vehicle.

"I expect you to be here when I get back. No place you can go, and I don't think you can get the door open since the locks back there are disabled. Might as well just sit here and think about this mess you're into." The man only glared at her. He hadn't said a word yet, and Megan didn't mind his silence. The quiet ones often talked the most once they started to rant. Locking the SUV, she walked to where Aaron had parked the bumper-pull and the goose-neck rigs.

"We need to get some photos of the rigs, the cows coming off the trailer, and the trucks' interiors. Can you herd the cattle to that pen over there?" Megan asked, pulling out the camera she'd taken from her Durango.

"Let me know when you're ready. I think the cow dogs will work for me." Cow dog cues tended to be almost universal among the ranchers. At any given moment, a cowboy could need a dog to respond, even if it weren't his, so the commands were commonly the same.

Megan nodded and walked around the rigs snapping photos. She paid special attention to the dinged wheel well, most likely damaged by the boulder up by Marvin's shack. Once the outside was photographed, she opened the tack room door to release the dogs, snapped shots, and stepped into the snug space. She photographed the equipment and paraphernalia needed for cattle rustling. She found and tagged a cash box. After sealing it with crime scene tape, she labeled it and put it on the front seat of her vehicle.

"You can't take that." The first sentence uttered by her prisoner gave Megan the idea that the box was exactly what she needed to check out.

"Evidence. If the cows on your trailer are stolen property, even the fleas on those dogs would be evidence. If the cows are yours, all of this will be returned." Megan slammed the door and relocked the vehicle.

She photographed all the livestock in the gooseneck, even the newborn calf up in the neck of the rig. She pulled the calf out carefully. Ignoring the squalling, she held it between her knees next to the pen's gate. "Okay, bring out the cows as slowly as you can."

Aaron stood by the sliding door and let the cows out one at a time until one cow managed to push out with another. He signaled the dogs to move both cows into the pen, each cow passing Megan to reach the relative safety of the corral. When the wilder cow pushed past Aaron's control, he shut the door behind her. This gave the dogs and Megan a chance to contain the extra cow. The loose heifer charged toward the calf and stopped, eyeballing Megan with distrust.

"Whoa, girl. It's okay. Here's your calf." Megan pushed the baby to the cow, who nudged it into the pen. Just inside the gate, the cow began licking the calf while the calf happily attached itself to her udder. Megan took a photo of the calf and cow pair, making sure the brand of the cow was visible.

"We know whose calf that is. I'm ready for you to start again. How many more? Can you see?"

Aaron moved around the side of the trailer. He released the middle gate of the rig, allowing the cows in the front access to the sliding door. "There were six in the back section. I think there might be eight in the front. These are some very pregnant cows. Hope there are no injuries from being loaded in their condition."

Carefully, he slid the exit door open again, allowing one cow out at a time so Megan could photograph each leaving the trailer. Every photograph would show the cow, her brand, and the trailer to the D.A. This should be a ton of evidence to convict the rustlers. Fifteen minutes later, the job was done, and the cows milled around the pipe-paneled enclosure. Of the fourteen adult animals, there were three different brands on them. The calf, of course, had no brand, but his mother was a 3C's cow. R-bar-M brand was on two cows, 3C's brand on another five, and the remainder had come from the Rocking-S. This rig had been around.

"Looks like these guys pulled cows from all the local spreads. Wonder where they were taking them," Aaron mused.

"I don't know, but I think it's weird that there were no running irons or knives in the rigs. I would expect thieves to want to try and change brands the first thing with stolen beef."

"Joe picked up those carving tools these guys carried as knives. Maybe some of those will have traces of beef blood. I think I'd prefer to use a hot iron to change a brand, but some people are vicious and prefer knives. A cut mark has to be pretty old not to look like a knife wound." Aron said. "Another thing. There are only pregnant cows, no steers in this rig."

"They must have a buyer who doesn't care about the brand on the stock; only the meat he's pulling off," Megan commented. Meat had no brand, and many people didn't care where or how a steak was butchered, only how it tasted and how much it cost.

"Thanks for your help today. I think tonight I just want a quiet evening alone. Do you mind?" Megan asked.

"Of course not. Some 'me time' is good for you. I'll see you Thursday, if not before. Call me if you need anything. Always happy to help. I'll get one of the boys to run John and me back to our bikes. You've got more than enough to handle." Aaron put his arm around Megan and kissed her forehead. "Drive safe."

Aaron and John left in one of the R-bar-M ranch trucks while Megan finished sealing and marking the evidence from the rustlers' trucks. She showed each horse coming out of the smaller trailer, even lifting each hoof to demonstrate the horses had no shoes. All could be essential parts to connect these horses and rigs with the theft up by Marvin's cabin. The horses were given runs up at the barn.

In the gooseneck of the larger trailer, where she'd found the newborn calf, Megan found another rifle and a tightly bound bundle wrapped in cowhide. After more photos, she marked both as evidence and pulled them into her Durango. She found a ledger under a cookstove in the tack room of the horse trailer. Megan noted how well it was hidden, photographed the scene, and put the register with the other items on the passenger front seat of her SUV. Her prisoner said nothing, only sat glaring at her from the secure back seat every time she opened the vehicle.

The cattle dogs lay quietly next to the gooseneck trailer, watching her every move. They presented a different problem. She decided to take them into protective custody until other arrangements could be made. These dogs would suffer horribly if they were put into pens. No, Sparkle would have three friends at her ranch for a while. She opened the rear of her SUV and called the dogs. They mounted the vehicle as though this was the most common event of the day. Megan rolled her eyes at the thought of more mouths to feed but smiled as she shut and locked the door.

She drove to her ranch and dropped the dogs off after introducing the three neutered (thank goodness) males to her spayed female Great Pyrenees. Sparkle made no fuss about having the boys in her yard, and the boys, in turn, sniffed noses and then went about marking the yard as their own.

Megan smiled when Sparkle showed teeth to the male who came up to take a spot on the porch. He didn't argue, only went back to join the others lying in the grass. Okay, so a boundary had been set, and the boys wouldn't be coming into the house. There was shelter under the porch for them. They would be fine.

"You take care of your guests, Sparkle. I'll be home in a while." Megan checked the outdoor water bucket, filled it, and took off for town.

Chapter Fourteen

Back at her office, Megan found mild chaos. With her prisoner ahead of her, she watched a moment while Deputy Joe attempted to show Officer Perkins how to book new prisoners. Meanwhile, those prisoners wailed and demanded a lawyer incessantly. She shook her head and let out a piercing whistle that arrested all conversations and wailing. Megan stared around the office in silence until she was sure each man was watching her.

"Let's take the noise down a notch. Each one of you will get your one call to whomever you wish. Give the name and number to Shirley when she asks. No more screeching or shouting. It won't win you any points or favors in this office. *Am I perfectly clear?*" Megan glared at each prisoner in turn until the man nodded. She hadn't raised her voice over a carrying note needed to reach the back of the room, but every person there seemed to understand she wouldn't accept any nonsense.

"Shirley, walk from man to man and take down the name and number they wish to reach. Confiscate all electronics making sure each is marked with the name of its owner." Megan smiled at Amanda, standing at Shirley's shoulder with a notebook. "Busy first day. It's not always like this. Keep a decent distance between you and the prisoners. I don't want any of them getting ideas of snagging a hostage. You never can tell what a desperate man might think of in a situation like this."

Joe was cuffing the hands of prisoners in front so they could sign the paperwork, but Megan noticed he only did one person at a time. She nodded to her prisoner, pointing him to the only empty chair in the room.

"Sit there. Officer Perkins, this man has shown he likes to run. Could you find that bicycle cable in the evidence room and use it to attach him to the railing behind that chair? I wouldn't want him to try another escape. Thanks" Megan nodded to the officer as he went to the evidence locker. When he came back with the cable and ran it through the cuffs of her prisoner and around the rail, Megan nodded again. She watched as the room seemed less chaotic. Shirley and Amanda moved from prisoner to prisoner while Joe worked industriously on paperwork. Joe motioned Tim Perkins over to his desk and began showing the new recruit how to fill out the forms needed for booking prisoners.

Megan returned to her Durango, pulling out the cash box, ledger, rifle, and bundle wrapped in cowhide. These items she carried to her office, where she would mark them as evidence and put them in her safe. The rifle could go into the gun safe, but the smaller items would be more secure in her large safe.

A huge sigh escaped her when she plopped down in her desk chair. Her head seemed to spin with today's events, not to mention the past week. Too much. She enjoyed Riverview because of its quiet and peaceful nature. The past few days had been far too busy for her liking. She glanced at the pile on her desk and groaned. Nothing would get done if she didn't get started. She pulled on a pair of rubber gloves to protect any prints on this evidence. Turning on her voice recorder, she reached for the cashbox.

"Cashbox found in the cab of the Chevy truck pulling the two-horse trailer." She broke the evidence seals she'd put on it. She nudged the latch and opened the box. "Box contains twenty-two one-hundred-dollar bills, eleven fifty-dollar bills, seven twenty-dollar bills. No ten's, five's, or one's." Megan stacked each denomination to the left of the box. She picked up the box, noting a rattle when it moved. Carefully, she pulled out the divider tray, tilting the box left and right, looking for what was rattling under the tray. The box slid out of her hands, landing on her desk with a bang. One of the loose items, catching the light, glimmered up at her.

"Holy shit!" slipped past her filters as she touched and then picked up first one, then a second stone. Diamonds. Was someone paying for rustled cows with diamonds? Were these stolen gems? This could be big! Megan pulled out a little evidence baggie and slid the diamonds inside with shaking hands. She zipped the baggie closed before holding it up to the light, admiring the glimmer of the stones through the clear plastic.

Megan hadn't seen loose diamonds since Sparkle had been used to smuggle stones last year. A smile crossed her face. Chris still had his machine that mapped diamonds; she needed to get these to him to map and verify. They could be fakes. "Two loose gems located in the bottom of the cashbox, possibly diamonds. Christopher Long will map and verify each stone."

With that statement, she turned off her recorder. She doubted these were fake. Someone had paid for stolen cows with diamonds. Hmmm—untraceable payment? It didn't make much sense to her, but the person using the stones must have had a valid reason. Maybe, the buyer figured it was an untrackable way to pass off stolen goods. Or it could simply be the buyer had no cash.

Megan put the bills into evidence bags and those bags into the box, which she resealed before locking it into the office safe. The rifle she marked and locked into her gun safe, the ledger, and the cowhide bundle she secured into her bottom desk drawer after marking each as possible evidence. When everything was done in her office, she opened the door to a much quieter reception area. One of the suspects was on the telephone located on Shirley's desk; Shirley and Mandy were standing next to Joe's desk, deep in conversation with the deputy. Officer Perkins stood an arm's length from the man on the phone, and the other suspects were nowhere in sight. Megan figured they must be locked up in the three cells behind the evidence locker. Not very comfortable, but they would hold until the dust settled and the charges were filed.

"Joe, did you contact the ranches about the cattle? Have any of those spreads sold any cows recently?"

"Talked to the foremen of each. This time of year, they wouldn't have sold any cows. Not even any cow and calf pairs. We need to pull the numbers off those ear tags to verify data on each cow. R-bar-M Ranch is hauling its portable squeeze chute over to the R-bar-B Pack Station. They offered to run the cows through and call with the data. Better them than me. Cows spook me," Joe admitted. His Hawaiian origins didn't include time spent outside the cities and ports.

"I thought Hawaii had cattle on one of the islands," Tim Perkins commented.

"Not the island I came from. Just because there are live cows around doesn't mean I ever wanted to work around them. I like steak, but not one charging at me."

Tim Perkins chuckled before cuffing the man who had just hung up the phone. "Boss, these dudes are getting restless. They want to know the charges."

"Well, if none of the ranches sold those cows, I figure the charge will be cattle rustling. Joe. Don't forget to call the brand inspector to verify those cows before we release them to their owners. We need all the documentation we can get." Megan reminded her deputy.

"Yeah, Roger had already called him. He should be there to help sort the cows by brand tomorrow," Deputy Kaleo responded.

"Good. Another solid piece of evidence. I hope these guys don't have any family waiting for them to come home. It could be a while." Megan nodded at the prisoner being escorted back to his cell. "I'm heading home. I'll stop over to see Chris with this evidence. I'm taking the official list of items stolen from his Gunnison shop. I'll see you in the morning," Megan explained as she headed for the door.

Megan's hopes soared as she crossed the square, heading for Chris's Custom Jewelry. Of course, these stones might have belonged to a person who didn't have money to buy the cows and bartered them. Still, somehow, Megan felt on the verge of an exciting discovery. Anyone with the money to have two diamonds the size of these most likely wouldn't be trading them for cows. As she got closer to the shop, she noticed the lights were out. Chris's Custom Jewelry was closed for the day. Looking at her watch, she was stunned to see it was just after six.

Well, that explained the twilight that she hadn't noticed. Her stomach growled at her sudden realization that she'd had very little to eat hours ago. Changing her direction, she wandered over to Betty's for dinner.

"Hey, Sheriff. You're just in time for the last of tonight's special. Chicken strips and fries with a side of coleslaw," Betty called as Megan entered to sit at the counter.

"Hmmm, I was hoping for meatloaf with mashed potatoes and gravy."

"You know that's tomorrow. Today is only Tuesday."

"Seriously? It's only Tuesday? Could have fooled me. Chicken strip dinner is fine. Can I have tater tots instead of fries? Oh, my usual sweet tea, too," Megan ordered.

Forty-five minutes later, she was pulling into her driveway, feeling guilty the animals had not been fed at their regular times. She could have called Aaron to come over to feed, but she wanted some quiet time tonight and didn't want to owe him the favor.

The cattle dogs greeted her as though they belonged and had been waiting patiently for her return. Sparkle growled at them, letting them know to back off from *her* human.

"It's okay, girl. They're just the working dogs. You're the house princess." Megan rubbed their heads and scratched ears as she made her way onto the porch. Sparkle didn't let the male dogs even look into the house. She chased them from the porch before they approached the door.

Megan wasn't sure what the working dogs had been fed in the past, so she decided to give them only kibble for tonight. She'd ask the rustlers tomorrow what they fed their dogs. Once the dogs were all eating, she went out to the barn to feed the horses and get some soul relief from them. The horses always managed to ease whatever stress she was experiencing. She had even come out at night when the nightmares were awful. Grooming Radar released the horrible memories and the pain of her wounds.

She groomed both horses while they ate their grain, talking to them as she worked.

"So it seems the rustlers used dogs and portable pens to run cows into the trailer. But where did they hang out while finding buyers? I should check the truck stop and see if anyone remembers the rigs. Chris had both his stores robbed. I wonder if he has an enemy? Either that or the haul at the first store was good enough to make it worth the drive to rob the second. Hmmm. Maybe it's more a case of the thief having experience robbing jewelry stores. Maybe has connections for fencing stolen gems. What do you think, boy?" Megan paused with the brush an inch from Lucky's gleaming black-and-white coat. He looked up from his grain, snuffling her shoulder for a possible treat.

"No opinion. What good are you?" She rubbed his withers before leaving his stall to work on Radar.

"Hello, boy. The robber in both heists had a limp. Is it a new injury or a chronic condition? Could be either. But we better find him before he heals if we want to use that as a connection between the two crimes." Megan's mind ran through all the locals she could think of. She knew three who might be limping. Marvin Stowers had a limp from his days serving his country. One of the cowboys at the 3C's hobbled from his rodeo days. He'd blown out his knee in the steer wrestling. Those two would fall into the chronic condition category. Nicholas Davis was currently injured from his fall. He had a pretty airtight alibi for Saturday. However, Monday in Gunnison was possible. IF he'd not been at home on

Monday." Megan picked up the mane brush and combed through Radar's thick mane.

"Too bad he's got such an alibi for Saturday. I would prefer the crimes to be done by outsiders. I'd hate to think one of the locals could bash Chris over the head. Nick is still an unknown in this area. Wonder where he came from?" As she finished Radar's mane, Megan made a mental note to check Nick's history. She also wanted to investigate unsolved small jewelry store robberies. See if these two followed a known MO. She gave each horse a treat before turning off the lights and making her way back to her cabin. The cattle dogs took a few pets and a dog biscuit each before she entered the house and locked up for the night. With her brain still mulling over all the events of the past four days, Megan managed to fall into a deep untroubled sleep.

Chapter Fifteen

The bell over the jewelry shop door jangled at Megan's entrance. She reached the counter before Chris came out from the back holding a construction hammer.

"Good morning, Sheriff. What brings you here so early. I'm not really open for another hour." Chris set down the hammer to shake her hand.

"I tried to come by last night but missed you. I've got a couple of stones I need you to map and document." Megan pulled the sealed evidence baggie from her zippered jacket pocket.

"Anything to report on either of the robberies? I've heard a little from the detective in Gunnison, and he hasn't got much to go on." Chris's face looked much better today, less bruised, with a more healthy skin color. He took the baggie from her. "Let me get my gloves. I wouldn't want my fingerprints to smudge what might be on these."

"I haven't gotten very far on your robbery. We know it was a man with a limp driving Billy's stolen loaner truck—but no one got a decent look at his face. I need you to check the web to see if these stones have been reported as stolen." The gems sparkled under the bright store lights within the bag. "I found them in the cash box of some rustlers, and it'll be interesting to find out if someone paid for stolen cattle with stolen gems."

"No problem. I can scan the gems while you're here if you have a few minutes. After the robbery, I don't know how secure this store is. I'd rather give them back to you."

Chris walked the stones to the stone mapping machine next to his workbench out of sight of the front door.

Megan followed. She'd been through this before. After diamonds had been discovered inside Sparkle, Chris had shown her how his machine worked. He pulled on rubber gloves before dumping both gems onto a black velvet cloth.

"Sheriff, did you notice the smudge on this one stone? The bigger one? Looks like blood. I'll scan it, but the smear could affect the identification." Chris laid the larger stone in the tray and slid it into the machine. He turned back to Megan. "Seems like we've done this before."

"Yeah. Was it only a year ago?"

"Just a little over a year. Remember it was fall because you convinced those city crooks that rattlesnakes were migrating." Chris chuckled, remembering the story Megan handed to the crooks to get them to make a play to retrieve their lost smuggled stones. His machine dinged, and Chris removed the larger diamond. He replaced it with the smaller gem and slid the tray into the device again. Chris looked at the readout on the mapped stone. *"Shit, Sheriff,"* Chris swore and looked at Megan.

"What? Was the readout completely unusable?" Megan inquired.

"No, I can use it. The results are clear enough that I can identify the stone. It was in a pendant in my shop at Gunnison." Chris carefully slid the stone into the baggie and passed it to Megan. "I'll get you the mapping results from the day I made the pendant. The Gunnison shop will have to check their records to see if it was sold, but I only sent it up there a week ago."

"You're saying this is one of your gems?" Megan was surprised but not shocked. If they hadn't nabbed the rustlers as they came out of the forest, these stones would have been out of the county, maybe even the state, by dinner time.

If the diamond was stolen from the store in Gunnison, someone between here and there used it to buy stolen cows from a rustler. Unless the rustlers were also jewel thieves. Megan waited to hear if the other stone was stolen from Gunnison or possibly from this store. She had no doubts now that it would trace back to one shop or the other.

Chris went to his filing cabinet and pulled out a file. He opened it and retrieved a sheet of paper which he brought over to Megan. The sheet showed the mapped identity of the stone and a photo of this particular stone in a beautiful filigree setting. "The setting is 18k. I would expect they melted it down for the gold. *Bastards.*"

Behind him, the machine dinged again. Chris pulled out the results, leaving the gem still in the scanner. *"Sonofabitch!"* He stomped over to his file cabinet again, retrieving another file and removing another sheet of paper. "Sheriff. Damnit, all to hell. This stone came from that belt buckle stolen from my window here. If that bastard melted down all the work I put into carving that buckle, you better catch up to him before I do. I spent two weeks making it."

Megan rubbed Chris's shoulder, trying to comfort him. She could understand his new sense of loss. Finding stones from pieces he had spent time making created a fresh wound. The thought of the destruction of his labor and artistry had to hurt.

Behind them, in the shop, the bell over the door jingled, signaling the arrival of a customer. Chris left Megan standing at the machine, comparing the printout of the two gems just mapped to the records of jewels Christopher had for sale in his shops. One record was an exact match, and the other started the same but soon changed with a note on the mapping that the stone was muddied. She was deep in thought about the proof in her hands when Chris appeared behind her.

"Sheriff, I think, I'm not positive, but I think that the customer out front has a pair of earrings stolen from the Gunnison Gallery," Chris whispered.

"I've got the official list for you if you'd like to compare it." Megan reached into her jacket pocket and passed the folded paper to the jeweler.

Chris scanned it, nodded once, and then again.

"Bingo!" For the first time since she arrived, Megan saw him smile. A malicious smile. "Sheriff, the earrings the customer wants me to match with a pendant are listed as stolen from Gunnison. The matching pendant is the same pendant I made around the larger gem I just mapped for you. The earrings and pendant set were sent to the Gunnison store about a week ago."

"I think we need to find out where your customer got the earrings." Megan nodded and followed Chris back out to the front counter.

Krystal looked up from her phone. Her face fell at the sight of Megan, but she didn't look worried. "Hello, Sheriff. I didn't expect to see you here. You and Chris have something going on?"

"No. One man in my life is enough for me." Megan politely smiled despite biting her tongue and clenching her fists to avoid slapping her former employee.

"Krystal, I can make you a matching pendant. I'll need you to leave at least one of the earrings with me. I need to see what I did when I made the earring. Filigree work can be complicated."

"Those are pretty, Krystal. You're lucky to have them since so much of Chris's work was stolen this past week. Did you buy them, or were they a gift?" Megan attempted to keep her voice casual, trying not to alert the woman that the jewelry was stolen.

"My boyfriend gave them to me as an anniversary gift. We've been dating three months, and I'm moving onto his ranch the first of next month." Krystal didn't realize the earrings were stolen and bragged about her good fortune.

"I didn't realize you had a significant other. What ranch does he work for?" Megan asked.

"He doesn't *work* for any ranch. He *owns* a ranch. How else would he be able to afford these earrings and a getaway to Gunnison?" Krystal snipped.

"Lucky you. My fiancé is only a foreman," Megan complimented her.

"I need the name of the ranch if you'll be moving there so soon. I need to know where to find you," Chris began filling out an order form, waiting for Krystal to give them the name of the spread and hopefully her boyfriend.

"I don't know if Nick has named his ranch yet. He's been building it since he bought the land from the 3C's. I'll be moving in with Nicholas Davis. First, driveway past the gate of the 3C's." Krystal looked very pleased with both herself and the man who would be keeping her.

Megan nodded while Chris continued writing down details. Megan moved around the counter and stepped behind Krystal. Pulling out her handcuffs, she reached for

Krystal's right hand. "Krystal Marie Parker, you are under arrest for possession of stolen property." Megan snagged Krystal's left wrist and brought it around her back to cuff it to the right. "You have the right to remain silent...." Megan began reciting her prisoner's Miranda rights as she guided the shocked woman toward the door.

"I'll call your office and have someone open the door for you," Chris yelled after the pair. He speed-dialed, watching Krystal start sobbing as she was frog-marched across the square to the city offices.

"Hi, this is Chris Long. Your sheriff is coming in with her hands full. Someone needs to open the door."

"What? Oh, gotcha' I can see her coming now. This is way too rich—Krystal in handcuffs. I am sooo tempted to get a photo," Shirley chuckled and cut the connection. Hopping out from behind her desk, she ran to open the door before Megan steered Krystal up the steps.

"If you can not afford an attorney, one will be provided to you. Please feel free to ask for assistance." Megan finished reciting the final stipulation as they entered the door. "Officer Perkins! Here's a person to book. Confiscate her phone, and she gets her call when I get back. Am I clear? Charge is: 'Receiving Stolen Property.' When you get her booked, show her to the interview room. Our holding cells are full from yesterday." Megan nudged Krystal toward Officer Perkins and continued to her office.

Megan knew she needed to find Nicholas. She doubted that Krystal would tell her much of anything now that she'd been arrested. Krystal might even recant what she had said to the jeweler in Megan's presence. This situation needed to get wrapped up and fast.

"Joe! My office. Now!" Megan's voice stopped Deputy Joeseph Kaleo in his tracks.

Joe had been walking toward his trainee. Perkins looked lost, staring helplessly at the bawling woman in his custody. Joe shrugged at the man and turned toward the Sheriff's office. "Yes, boss?"

Megan led him into her office and closed the door. "You and I are going out to that new spread off the 3C's." She walked to the weapons locker, unlocked it, pulled down the chain, and took out her favorite rifle. She knew her gun was loaded and her belt complete, but she took an extra box of shells. Her vest was still on the seat in her Durango from yesterday. With any luck, this could be done without firing a shot, but she didn't know exactly how many they would find at the ranch. Maybe just one. "Pick your weapon and grab extra shells. Where's your vest? You can load up as I drive."

Quickly, Joe did as directed, then trotted his big frame after his boss. "I'll grab my vest from my Jeep. What's going on?"

"I'll explain in the Durango. How many sets of cuffs do you have?" Megan queried.

"I've got the three sets we used on those guys we arrested and a handful of zip ties," Joe detailed his inventory of personal restraints.

"Good. I've only got my stock of zip ties since Krystal is wearing my handcuffs. Let's hope we find only one man to capture and restrain." Megan slipped on her vest before she mounted into her Durango, impatiently waiting for the big man to don his vest and climb up beside her.

"Krystal has a pair of stolen diamond earrings. She named Nicholas Davis as the person who gave them to her. Nicholas has a limp from his wreck at the Saddle-up fundraiser. He has no provable alibi during the first robbery in Riverview. He spent the day of the Gunnison robbery in Gunnison with Krystal. It might be difficult to prove the Riverview case, but we got him if we can find him with stolen gems." Megan turned on her lights, leaving the siren off. Her Durango threw gravel on their way out of Riverview. Joe grabbed the hand strap above the passenger seat, muttering a prayer as the SUV turned sharply onto the highway. The scant traffic wisely pulled out of their way. The Durango gained speed on the straight stretches and hugged the curves around the hills.

"I should have known. I saw Nick's pinky ring without its gold nugget, and I found a gold nugget on the floor of Chris's store. That and the trail had been undermined. I should have gone into that more. I knew there was something fishy about that wreck. Damn. I hate it when I miss the easy stuff."

"Uh, slow down, boss. If he's coming to town, we'll see him. If not, we're going to catch him at his ranch. On Saturday, he didn't have any ranch hands. I haven't heard of anyone finding work out in this direction. Just take it easy, or else we aren't going to arrest anyone from a hospital or the morgue." Joe's Hawaiian complexion had lightened to a pasty-looking beige.

Megan looked at him and let up on the gas. "You're right. I just don't want him to get away or hide the gems. Shoot! Call the judge and get her to text me a warrant for search, seizure, and arrest at the property owned by Nicholas Davis. Tell her we expect to find stolen property by the word of Krystal Parker." Megan knew the judge would do it, but she still needed to see it before entering Nick's property. She pulled into the 3C's drive and turned off her lights. They could wait here, where any traffic going to or from Nick's would have to pass by them.

Joe relaxed his braced position to text the local magistrate. "Done."

"Does it show she read it? If not, call her." Megan didn't have the patience to wait and wonder if a text had gotten through.

"Shows received." Deputy Kaleo kept his eyes on his cell phone, waiting for the word to come through, showing the judge had signed a warrant.

"You know, if he is there and sees us driving up in my Durango, he might try hiding the diamonds or escaping. You know the layout from driving him home on Sunday. Is there any way to approach the house and barn without being in plain sight for five minutes?"

"Naw. What few trees were growing, Nick took down. His cabin is on a rise, giving him a fine view almost to the highway. A person could come up from the 3C's land along the creek and not be in sight of the cabin." Joseph described the lay of the land and the lack of cover from the highway.

"Hmmm…That's an idea. Let's go talk to the hands of the 3C's." Megan started her Durango, her mind whirling with plans as she drove to the ranch yard. Two of the cowboys she'd interviewed a couple of days ago were in sight, walking toward the barn. "Joe, you take the Durango. Once I'm set, and you've got the warrant, drive slowly up Nick's driveway. I'll go through the barn to the house's back door while you knock on the front door. Any questions?" Megan asked as she pulled the SUV to a stop next to George and Daniel, the foreman.

"I think it'll work if you have time enough to sneak up on him before he can destroy evidence," Joe replied.

"You text me when the warrant is valid, and I'll text you when I'm set. That's when you drive up the driveway." Megan opened the door of her Durango.

"Hi, guys! I need some help," she called.

"What do you need, Sheriff?" George asked.

"I need one of you to give me a lift over behind the new spread. You know, Nick Davis's place." Megan pointed in the general direction she wanted to go. "If you have a quad, that would work best because I need to slide off it without you stopping."

"I can do that, but it'd be a smoother ride using side-by-side," George suggested.

"If you were heading out to check fenceline, which would you take? Which would Nick expect to hear along that border?" Megan asked.

"Most often, the quad unless we're going to repair something," George offered.

"That's why we take the quad now. After I slide off the back, I need you to continue along the fence line for a mile before returning to the ranch yard. I'll catch a ride back to town with Deputy Kaleo." Megan explained as she and George moved over to the four-wheeler.

About ten minutes later, the two riders on the quad saw the fence line running between the 3C's and the land Nicholas Davis was developing. George slowed to a fast walking pace and turned up the fence.

"I'll point out the best spot to hop off. It's a short way beyond the hill." He yelled over his shoulder. He gave the machine more gas to pull it up the steep hill. At the top, he let off the pressure, and they coasted to the bottom. "Just up here is a dry creekbed. If you follow it, you'll get within about ten yards of Nick's barn."

"Thanks. Don't let off the gas. I'll slip off the back." Megan slid to the back of the quad, took a deep breath, and let go of George's jacket. A final push against the seat, and she stumbled to her feet behind the moving machine. She felt abandoned as she watched the quad work its way up the next hill, the sound fading as it went.

Megan followed the creekbed to the left, the direction George had pointed. From ahead, a distance away, she could hear the twang of an old country song. Strange, Nick hadn't impressed her as a country music lover. However, he was a rancher, small though his spread might be. She paused to listen and realized the mooing in the background didn't sound like a radio. Had Nick gotten his first shipment of cattle? The timing was spot on for them to be stolen. Megan's hopes of simultaneously closing two cases began to grow with each step closer to Nick Davis's barn. She couldn't help but smile.

When the lowing and the music swelled, Megan climbed the side of the creekbed to peer over the top. Bingo. The barn was about twenty yards away, and a small pen with a shelter held four very young-looking calves. As much as she wanted to move forward to inspect them, Megan sat down to text her deputy. If the warrant had yet to be handed down, she would be sitting here until it was legal to approach her suspect. Anything found before that wouldn't be admissible as evidence. All their efforts would be for nothing.

Got it yet? I'm set. Megan texted.

Just came thru. You ready for me? Joe responded.

Give me 5 and drive here. I'll be at the back door. Megan grinned. This would work. Even if Nick didn't have the diamonds, she would bet her next paycheck that those calves were from stolen cows. He might have fenced the remaining stones and settings in the three days since the first robbery. They still had Krystal's earrings to show he was connected with the Gunnison crime.

Megan unsnapped her holster, drew her pistol, and flipped off the safety before she began moving toward the barn in a low crouch. At the breezeway entrance to the barn, she stopped to listen. The calves were bawling, but the music came from outside the barn. Interesting. She wondered if Nick had hired a hand or two since Saturday. The calves were new since Sunday when Joe brought Nick home. Megan listened for any sounds of movement inside the barn. Only the noise of at least one horse munching hay. Overall, there was a stillness to the barn and its inhabitants. Other than the incessant bawling of the calves—there was no one in the barn.

Megan stood against the wall, moving cautiously through the barn to the other side, closer to the house. She paused to survey the area and decide on the safest path to the back porch. No matter how she worked it, she would be in plain sight should Nick or anyone else look toward the barn.

Movement caught her eye as a figure walked through the house, crossing in front of first one and then a second window. Obviously a male, he walked toward the front of the house. Megan made a quick decision and a dash across the open space between the barn and the back porch until she could no longer see the window. Quietly, she moved onto the porch, stepping softly on each step until she managed to put her back against the wall next to the door. Her heart was pounding so loud in her ears that a train could have approached without her hearing it. She barely heard an approaching vehicle over the person's footsteps in the house.

The footsteps froze. Megan overheard blinds being drawn; she couldn't tell if up or down. Then the sound of a man running toward her location. Megan couldn't wait. Nick was either trying to get away or moving to destroy evidence. With her pistol at the ready, she pounded on the door.

"Sheriff Megan Holloway here. Nicholas Davis, we have a search warrant. Open up!" Megan yelled over the sound of her knocking. "Riverview Sheriff's Office! We have a warrant! Come out with your hands up, *NOW!*"

Megan stepped back against the wall, waiting to hear what her suspect would do next. She heard the toilet flushing—stupid son of a bitch. City folk just never realize that a septic system can be pumped. Everything belongs to the person who owns the property and flushed the john. It wasn't like a city where what you flushed flowed into the sewers of the population. It might not be a fun job, but they had him now. It would take a couple of days for Tim Perkins to clean out the septic tank. Lucky him.

"Nicholas Davis! There's no place for you to go. Come on out with your hands up. We don't want to hurt you over some stolen jewels or rustled calves. Quit stalling and come out!" Megan called again.

"What the fuck are you talking about?" Nick's voice came from close to the back door. "I'm coming out, and I'm not armed."

The door handle began to move, and Megan pointed her pistol where she expected chest height on her suspect. The door swung open slowly.

"Show me your hands! I want to see both hands, *now!*"

"Don't get your panties in a twist. My hands are visible and empty. No need for any shooting. I've done nothing wrong." Nick waved his hands out the door and followed them out.

"Is there anyone else in the house? Anyone else on the ranch?" Megan motioned Nick to turn around. "Put your hands on the wall above your head, spread your legs, and don't budge. Answer my questions."

"Only me here. I don't have any cowboys hired yet."

Megan stepped back to be out of reach should her suspect try any fast moves. She heard someone coming through the house and watched the door in case the person approaching wasn't her deputy. The back door opened, and Joe filled the doorway before he stepped out onto the porch.

"Cuff him," Megan ordered. "Read him his rights. I'll call the brand inspector to check out those calves."

"Do you have someone to care for your livestock? I'm likely confiscating the calves, but I saw a horse in the barn. Do you need it to be boarded? I don't think you or Krystal will be coming home for a few days."

"What're you holding *her* for?"

"Receiving stolen goods. Which Krystal stated she received as a gift from you. Joe, Take him around and seat him in the back of the Jeep. You search the house for anything from the jewel robberies. I'll deal with the brand inspector."

"Someone needs to feed Buck. That pasture doesn't have enough grass yet this season." Nick said as Joe finished securing his hands.

"I'll see that it gets done unless you want him boarded. I think the R-bar-B could take him in. If the Sheriff's department does it, it's five dollars a day for one of us to stop by and throw him food. Stall cleaning will add ten dollars a day to the fee. R-bar-B has paddocks at about half that, " Deputy Joe told the man as they began to walk around the house. "You have the right to remain silent...." Joe's voice faded when they rounded the corner.

Chapter Sixteen

Megan pulled out her phone as she walked back toward the barn. This time, there was no need for speed or bending over. They had Nick in handcuffs. Checking through her contacts, she found the brand inspector's number. By the time she reached the barn's door, she had him on the phone.

"John Sewell, here. What do you need, Sheriff?"

"If you are available, I need your assistance. We've got some calves here at that little, new ranch next to the 3C's. They have ear tags, but I think the tags are faked, and they're rustled as no cows are around. You helped Roger with those cows we confiscated yesterday, didn't you? These calves could belong to those cows," Megan explained.

"Is that spread at the end of the new road cut in on the east corner of the 3C's?"

"That's the one. How long before you can get here?" Megan asked.

"I'm heading out the door. Should be there in about twenty minutes if the highway's not blocked by construction. You know they're working between Gunnison and Riverview," John Sewell replied.

"Okay, get here as soon as you can. I expect I'll have some antsy ranchers on my hands by the time you get here. If we don't find the cows, these calves might be all they get back for their losses," Megan said.

"You know, if the ranchers start fighting over them, we'll need to blood type and look for genetic markers to compare with each spread. I think you should get the vet out to pull blood and check them over."

In the background of the call, Megan heard a car door slam and an engine start.

"Will do. You drive safe and get off the phone. I don't want you to get a ticket for distracted driving. Especially if I'm the cause." Megan cut the connection and dialed the vet. She scowled when the call went to voicemail.

"Paul, this is Megan. I'm at that new spread next to the 3C's. I need you to check over some young calves and pull blood on them. Call me as soon as you get this. Thanks," she cut that connection too. Now, she was stuck here until both the brand inspector and the veterinarian arrived. She walked up to the house, wondering if Joe had had any luck in his search.

Inside the house, Joe was meticulously going through cabinets in the kitchen. Megan nodded at him.

"I'm not sure we will find much concrete evidence until we clean out the septic tank. I heard him flush before he came to the door. He must have been desperate to dispose of gems and gold in that manner, but I guess he thought his freedom was more important than money."

"This is the last set of drawers here in the kitchen. I checked everything in the fridge, even in the freezer, but nothing looked odd. Opened and dug through the leftovers and butter. No gems in there, and a couple of those containers were rank." Joe shuddered, obviously revolted by the memory.

"You go ahead and take the prisoner to town. Book him on suspicion of possession of stolen goods. Send Officer Perkins out here. He will need an empty septic pumper, hip boots, and a face mask. Don't explain why in front of the prisoner. If he doesn't realize that the stuff he flushed will be in our hands shortly, let's not tell him." Megan chuckled and patted Joe on the back.

"Good job, by the way. Those rustlers should be begging to talk to get a better deal by the time I get back. Nicholas will be aching to know if we found his hidden stash of gems. You can lock him in the courtroom. Cuff him to the railing. I don't want him comparing stories with any of the others."

"You going to send any suspects to the county lock up? They've got space to separate our prisoners," Joe commented. Riverview just wasn't set up for this kind of a crime wave.

"Not yet. I'll have to send the group out tonight with the two additional suspects. Still, I want everyone close at hand for statements and interviews. Things take so much longer once they get to the county jail because we need to travel to Gunnison." Megan looked around the kitchen, noting all the open cupboards.

"I'll be back to the office as soon as the brand inspector and vet do their thing with the calves. Tim is a country boy, isn't he?" Megan could not bring his interview or application to mind for some reason.

"Yep. Pretty good hand, too. His daddy is foreman at a ranch up by Montrose," Joe reassured her.

"Good, we'll put him on livestock management while everything gets settled. Did Nick say what he wants to be done with his horse?"

"He's kind of shocky, not making a lot of sense. Seems to think he'll be home for dinner. I'd say we have to care for the animal here until he puts in writing what he wants." Joe advised. He'd been deputy when Megan took over as sheriff and understood the unique needs of rural living.

"Yeah. That sounds about right. Once you have Nick booked, start a list of things we need to cover during the interview. Put that at the top." Megan walked Joe to the door, noting the other rooms looked unsearched.

"You started with the kitchen, didn't you?" she inquired.

"Yep. The rest of the house is all yours." Joe chuckled as he went down the steps toward his Jeep, clearly knowing Megan would be searching the house for evidence for a few hours. "See you back at the office."

Megan waved them off, turning to survey the house in front of her. It couldn't be larger than fifteen hundred square feet. She felt that Nick flushed something he didn't want to be found in his possession. Most likely gems from the two jewelry stores, but he might have other data that would be good evidence. Could he have a schedule or a diagram of each store? She shook her head and turned into the first room, pulling on her latex gloves as she entered.

The living room had minimal furniture. A couch, a recliner, a couple of end tables with drawers, and a bookcase that housed the television in its center. Megan started with the end table closest to the door. She opened the drawer, pulled it out, and checked the underside for secret hiding spots. Using her penlight from her keychain, she examined the hole where the drawer rested. Nope, nothing there. Next, she shook out the paperback and shuffled through the papers under it, but nothing looked interesting, so she moved on to the sofa.

None of the cushions were removable, so Megan was forced to wedge her hand between each crevice, feeling for hidden items. She found coins, a wadded-up napkin, a pen, and a paper clip. These items she stacked on the end table. She glanced around the room, feeling that this was a waste of time. But then, until the vet and brand inspector arrived, she had nothing but time to waste.

Megan moved quickly around the room, checking each item in or on a piece of furniture. At the fireplace, she shone her penlight behind the decorative art above the mantle. Bingo. The light picked up an edge of paper inserted or taped to the back of the piece. Even at five-foot-seven, she could hardly reach the bottom of the large print, much less lift it down from the wall. Crap. She looked around the room. She needed something to stand on. The end tables were glass-topped; they wouldn't work. Beyond the living room stood a dining room table and four chairs. It took Megan less than a minute to drag the closest chair over to the fireplace.

Megan was standing on the chair, stretched out above the mantle, when a knock sounded at the front door. She froze.

"Who is it?" Megan lowered her voice. Her heart was racing; she was utterly vulnerable in this position.

"Dr. Paul Rayburn. You called, needing a vet?" His familiar voice slowed the racing of her heart. Megan knew she would have been in serious trouble if the person at the door had been an associate of one of the suspects.

"Come in, Paul. I need your help."

The door opened, and Paul Rayburn ambled his over six-foot frame into the living room. Seeing Megan's position, he hurried over to put one hand on the art and one hand on the back of the wobbling chair.

"Get down from there before you kill yourself. What are you trying to do?"

"I need this picture off the wall and laid out on the table, face down." Megan used Paul's shoulder to stabilize her position on the chair.

"Why didn't you just wait. Where's Joe or Officer Perkins?" Paul looked around for the missing officers.

"Tim Perkins will be here in a little while. I fulfilled the search warrant while waiting for you and the brand inspector. How was I to know that print was heavy?" Megan stepped down from the chair and moved it, allowing Paul access to the piece in question. She watched the tall man easily reach up and lift the framed print off the wall.

"Damn. This thing weighs a lot more than I would expect. The frame must be made with the heaviest wood out there." Paul carried the art to the dining table, turned it over, and laid it face down. "What the heck?"

"I could tell there was something not exactly right when I looked behind with my flashlight. I just couldn't see what," Megan said as they stood looking at the back of the picture.

The expected gallery paper had been augmented by a layer of what looked to be poster board taped at the print's center. Megan stepped forward and examined the pocket created by this method. She pulled her phone from her pocket, using the camera feature to get a photograph. She shot photos of the pouch, its visible contents, and as much of the frame as possible. She handed the phone to the vet.

"It's going to use up battery, but put the camera over to video so we can show the items being removed," Megan instructed. She waited while Paul set the camera to video before she pulled out a notebook, several papers folded together. In the bottom of the pouch, she pulled out a cloth-wrapped packet. Megan set all the items on the table next to the print. First, she unwrapped the package. If the camera was going to run out of battery, she wanted this part on video. After she cut the tape, the cloth fell open, revealing a handful of stones, mostly what looked to be diamonds. Paul audibly caught his breath.

"This is *déjà vu*. Only this time; you're finding the stones," he muttered quietly.

"Yeah. At least my patient is only art," Megan replied, remembering the day she stood at Paul's shoulder as he removed a bag of diamonds from a dog's abdomen. He'd saved the dog she named Sparkle that day. Unfolding the papers revealed diagrams, maps, and notes about Chris's stores and a couple of chain stores in Montrose and Gunnison.

"Looks like this guy was thorough about investigating his victims. I recognize the diagram of the mall. There are three different jewelers there," Paul said.

"It looks like he's marked the cameras in the mall, the parking lot, and the closest intersections. We got lucky that he didn't disable the camera close to the Gunnison Gallery. It belonged to another store, so I guess he missed it." Megan studied the map of the street where the gallery was located.

"I guess now we know where he got the funds to build this place. Wonder why he chose to settle in Riverview?" she mused.

"Why not? Low crime, beautiful scenery, peaceful community—Riverview is a magnificent place to sink roots." Paul looked at the other item on the table and then at the cell phone, "Battery is shot."

"That's okay. I've got what I need. The book is maybe a journal or some such. Admissable, but not critical to conviction." Megan took back her camera.

The sound of approaching vehicles snapped her head toward the front window. A large truck with a septic pumping tank pulled to a stop behind the vet's treatment truck. Officer Perkin's cruiser pulled in behind it. Both Tim and the truck driver came toward the house. Megan waited until they reached the front door before yelling for them to enter.

"Hey, boss. I brought what you told me. Did something drop down the sink?" Tim Perkins asked.

"Well, with what we just found, I don't know what our suspect flushed. He flushed something down the toilet when I knocked. It's up to you to find out what," Megan directed Officer Perkins to find what Nick felt the need to flush.

"Has any water been run or toilets flushed since the one flush in question?" This question came from the truck driver.

"I'm Milton Parker of Parker's Pumping Service. There's a chance if the toilet is far enough from where the pipe exits the house that the flushed item could still be in the pipes."

"Well, it's up to you and Officer Perkins to figure that out. Nothing has been flushed since we entered the house. One way or the other, you're going to have to clean out the system from front to back and save anything that doesn't look like it belongs in the septic," Megan instructed the pair.

Megan pulled a plastic bag from one of her pockets, put the items found on the back of the art inside it, and sealed the bag with evidence tape. She wondered if Nick had any other stashes of stolen goods or evidence around the house. She wanted to look, but with the vet here and the brand inspector just pulled up, she needed to show them the calves.

"Tim, once you get Mr. Parker started on cleaning out the septic, you need to finish going through the house looking for evidence. The kitchen and living room are done. Be sure to look under things like drawers and beds. This guy is pretty paranoid; he hides his treasures well." Megan waited for Tim to nod his understanding before following Paul Rayburn to meet the brand inspector.

Behind the brand inspector's truck were three more pickups arriving. They pulled around the vehicles at the house, driving up to the barn's main door.

"Uh, oh, Sheriff. Looks like the ranchers have heard you've found calves. We better put some speed on if we want to keep them from claiming stock and taking them home," John Sewell, the brand inspector, said as he began trotting toward the barn.

"I swear. Nothing is ever secret in a small town. Those boys better *not* try to take my evidence." Megan passed the men when she began running to take charge of the chaos in the barn.

Six men in jeans, boots, and western hats stood by the pen holding the four calves. Each seemed to be pointing and arguing with the others. Voices were rising, and Megan feared physical contact would follow any second. Putting her fingers to her mouth, she gave her piercing whistle, guaranteed to stop just about everything. It did. The men froze before turning as one entity to watch her approach.

"Gentlemen. Don't even start. If you feel one of these calves is from one of your cows, you will need to provide

DNA proof to the Brand Inspection Office," Megan explained calmly.

"But Sheriff, what'll happen to them until the tests get back? They could die without proper care," the foreman of the 3C's asked.

Megan turned to Paul, "Do you have space for them? A pen and shelter?"

"My girls are raising swine for their 4H projects this year. My pens are taken. How about we mark them and give them over to one of the ranches to raise? George, you've got three boys in school. Do any of them want some extra money for taking on these calves?" Paul asked.

"My oldest is working with me, but my youngest, Bobby, just started middle school. He could use the experience. If'n he does good, I'll see he gets the money. If'n he slacks off, I'll see the job gets done and keep the money. How much?"

Megan looked at the ranchers. "How much are these calves worth? The owner of each calf will end up paying for its upkeep. Unless we can get the cost charged against the suspects." She waited while the men talked and looked at the calves.

"I need to expand my herd. If these calves are taken care of properly, I'll buy them. I can pay two dollars a head per day—up to three months," Roger Meadows offered. "I'll get you the DNA for my bull, and maybe I won't have to buy one of them."

"Roger, I think we should auction these calves off to the FFA kids. I know my bull sired that bald-faced blackie. The kids need animals to raise. We can buy them at the fair," George suggested.

"Okay, by me. Let's get our DNA profiles to the vet so the calves can be sold off before they're grown." Roger slapped George on the back.

The men stopped the vet on his way through the barn. Each gave a description of the calf they felt belonged to them and promised to send the Brand Inspection office the DNA profiles of their bulls. George stayed behind.

"Sheriff, I'll be back with my trailer. D'ya need my boy to take that horse too?" he asked.

"No, Tim will take care of the horse. He just can't be out here four times a day to feed these calves."

"I'll send Sam back with the trailer. He got his license and needs practice."

With that, he left the barn. Minutes later, all three trucks were on their way to the highway and back to work. Excitement like this was only good for an hour or so break in the daily ranching routine.

"Looks like you got that cleared up. Now, let's start marking and taking samples from these little fellows." Paul and John stepped into the pen and snagged the first of the four calves. The bawling increased as the calf struggled to get free.

While the men were fighting the calf, Megan looked around. There had to be milk replacer for these youngsters. Spotting the bag of powder over by the hydrant, Megan snared a bucket and moved to make some lunch for the babies. It was almost impossible to overfeed them at this age, and if they weren't fed often enough, they would suffer.

Megan chuckled at the creative cussing coming from the calf pen. Some of those words she'd never thought to use in those phrases. Strangely very few were four-letter known swear words. It seemed first, Paul would exclaim in pain and follow it with a very descriptive set of terms, and then John would do the same, using his version. Megan had to wonder if there was some sort of contest going on.

"You guys are good. I didn't know 'cute-little-heifer' could be used as an insult." Megan said when she set the bucket down outside the stall. "Said in that tone, it sure wasn't a compliment."

"Well, Megan, we never know who will be around when we need the power of words—so we've come up with phrases and terms to fill the need that won't offend delicate sensibilities," Paul explained.

"Yeah, anymore, saying what you want to say can get you fired if you say it in front of the wrong person," John agreed.

"Would you mind pouring this into that trough when you get done? Watch which eat and which don't. George needs to know. I'm going to take the evidence I've found back to town. John, when you're done, check with Roger about recording the data on those cows we pulled from the rustlers' trailer. Paul, you might want to check them too. A couple look ready to drop calves anytime."

Megan left the men working and walked back to the house. She found Officer Perkins gently pulling things out of a closet, checking all pockets and boots as he worked. He was so intent on his activities that he didn't hear Megan enter the room.

"Tim," she said.

Megan jumped back when Timothy squealed and grabbed his weapon.

"*Stand down, Officer* !" Megan commanded, taking another step out of the room.

"Shit! Sheriff, I could have shot you!"

"I think you're not ready to work alone yet. Grabbing your weapon is seldom the right move in a small town."

"I'm sorry. I was just so engrossed with this guy's stuff."

"Not good enough. If we're staking out a house and expecting a villain to arrive, then maybe, just maybe, drawing your weapon would be appropriate. Think about what could have happened. Right now, I'm taking your cruiser back to town. You hitch a ride with the septic pumper. You'll need to keep the chain of evidence anyway."

"Yes, Ma'am. We managed to wash a packet out of the pipes by flushing again. Maybe that's what Nick thought you'd find when you called him out." Tim reached for the front thigh pocket on his uniform pants and removed a baggie marked as evidence. He passed it over to Megan.

"Thanks. Good work. More charges against this suspect. I'll see you back in town once you've gone through the septic tank contents." Megan waved, walked to the dining room to collect the other evidence, and left the house. She pondered the problem of Officer Timothy Perkins on the way back to Riverview, wondering if he would ever mature.

Chapter Seventeen

With her arms full of confiscated evidence, Megan had a hard time opening the back door to the station. At least she managed to key in the security code before any alarms started sounding. Once she entered, she let the door close behind her and headed to her office. The new evidence went on a specific shelf she had cleared in her bookcase for pending investigations. She didn't want this evidence to be confused with what she'd been examining earlier. Heaven forbid if she got the two sets mixed. Even though each piece was labeled, sorting through a combined mess could jeopardize the legal chain of evidence.

Megan gazed at the piles of tagged evidence. There was too much happening, with one crime after another. This was Riverview, not New York City. Even minor crimes were infrequent around here. Maybe domestic disputes and a few drunk and disorderly cowboys, but not jewel heists, cattle rustling, grand theft auto, and assault with deadly weapons.

Well, by all appearances, the rustlers had been caught. The jewel thief was possibly cooling his heels in the courtroom, and Ted had confessed to taking shots at Marvin. She needed to tie the attack on Marvin to the cattle rustlers. Ted might not be the best witness, but he could identify the men who hired him. That would give her another charge against them besides rustling. Megan wasn't sure any testimony given by a mentally challenged witness would be enough. Still, it might scare them into confessing or bargaining for lesser charges.

She needed to connect Nick with the stolen truck. He had to have used it in his scheme of being a missing rider while he robbed Chris's Custom Jewelry. She already had him for the Gunnison heist. Krystal would sell him out to save herself. Once the confiscated gems were mapped and if the stones were in the system as belonging to Chris, Megan knew she had him by evidence too.

She wondered which of the rustlers she should question first. Was one more likely than another to want to deal their way out of the main charge? Regardless, she needed to get statements from each. She wondered if they had found attorneys yet. She wasn't going to volunteer the preacher's wife to them. Gunnison had a larger pool of public defenders. *Crap.* She might as well send the rustlers and Krystal on to the county jail. She wanted to keep Nick here. She could keep Nick for twenty-four hours before filing all the charges against him. Decision made, Megan walked out of her office. Turning right, she walked to the holding cell area. Five heads turned to watch her when she entered the accessway.

"Gentlemen. I'm sending you and another prisoner to the county jail in Gunnison. There, you'll be able to find public defenders or paid attorneys to handle your defense. You are being held on cattle rustling accusations and one count of receiving stolen merchandise. I suggest you begin thinking of what you can tell us that might get your charge reduced. Colorado doesn't take kindly to rustlers. You should be deciding how you want to plead and respond to the charges. I'll be in Gunnison to question you by this time tomorrow. Have a nice trip." Megan turned and walked out to the open squad room.

"There you are, Joe. Call the Preacher Cornwall of the Methodist church. See if he'll rent the church van to the Sheriff's department. You'll need to set it up for transporting criminals. No one is to sit in the front. You can anchor them like baby carriers. Just use handcuffs and zip ties to secure them. You'll be taking six to Gunnison. Krystal and the rustlers. I don't want you talking to any of them other than telling them where they are going. I've already told them the charges they're facing. They don't need to know any details. Let them stew for a while."

"Okay, Sheriff. What're you planning on doing with Nicholas Davis?" Joe pulled out his cell phone and paused before calling the preacher.

"I'm keeping him here until the contents of the septic system have been logged so I can tell if there are more allegations against him. So far, he'll be charged with possession of drugs, possession of stolen gems, and possession of stolen cattle. If I can put him at either location, he's going down for robbery and assault at the jewelry stores—both of them." Megan watched Joe as she spoke.

"You think he actually robbed Chris? He was lost in the desert when that job happened." Joe scratched his head in confusion.

"Perfect alibi. I only need to connect Nick with the store and possibly Billy's truck. I think I can. I think he overstepped his intelligence this time." Megan listened to Joe talking to the preacher and smiled when he broke the connection.

"Preacher says so long as we have the van back in one piece by tonight for him to pick up the Bible study group, he'll let us use it," Joe reported with a grin.

"Good. I'll go talk to Krystal for a few minutes." She left the squad room, walking to the conference room where Krystal had been put. She couldn't help but wonder if Krystal knew anything about the local robbery. Megan doubted Nick was idiot enough to provide Krystal with information to put him in jail. Still, stranger things had happened lately, and he *did* give her those stolen earrings.

"Hi, Krystal. I can escort you to the ladies' room if you need to go to the bathroom before your trip to Gunnison," Megan offered as a conversation starter.

"What trip to Gunnison? I can't go to Gunnison. I've got my son to pick up," Krystal's voice rose an octave with each sentence.

"I thought you called your sister to take care of your son. I'll give you an extra call if you didn't. Your son will need to spend a few days with her, maybe longer, unless you prefer me to call Children's Services." Megan unlocked the handcuff securing Krystal to her chair as she spoke.

"I asked my sister to pick up Jason and watch him this afternoon. No one said anything about me not going home today." Tears began to trickle from her eyes, and her face crumpled when the realization hit her that she was in real trouble this time.

"You've worked around here for over a year. You know the drill. We arrest suspects and send them to Gunnison to be jailed until they can be arraigned by the judge and a court date set." Megan helped Krystal to her feet, urging her to move toward the door.

"Yeah, but..."

"But, nothing. You were in possession of stolen property. Those earrings were taken from the Gunnison Jewelry Gallery owned by Christopher Long. That makes you an accomplice." Megan stopped in front of the door to the ladies' room. "I'll wait out here for you. I don't think you want to try climbing out that window."

Megan nudged Krystal in the back and watched as the dazed and dejected woman entered the bathroom. She hoped Krystal would overthink the situation and come out begging to make a deal. For that, Megan would call Kathy Cornwall back to help word the statement to nail Nicholas Davis to the wall. Megan didn't have long to wait.

Krystal stormed out of the bathroom, her tears were gone, and fury lit her eyes with an unholy glow.

"Would a statement from me be enough to stay here in Riverview and be released on my own word?" she demanded.

"I don't know. You would need an attorney, wouldn't you?"

"Hell, no. My life is pretty well shot if that rat-bastard has involved me in a jewel heist. I'll do whatever I have to if I can get charges dropped. I had no idea those earrings were stolen." Krystal allowed Megan to put the handcuffs on again, but her fists were tightly balled, revealing her anger.

"I'll put you back in the conference room and give you a notebook to write your statement. While you do that, I'll see if I can round up someone to advise you. I don't want any recanting later, and if you have someone giving you advice, that is less likely to happen."

Megan didn't mention that another witness to the statement would protect both of them when this came to trial. Her attorney couldn't break client confidentiality, but the attorney could verify that no coercion was used against Krystal.

Megan marched Krystal into the conference room, sat her at the desk, and handcuffed her non-writing hand to the chair again. Looking around the room, she found the writing paper and pens. She put a pen in Krystal's hand.

"I know that's not very comfortable, but I'll send Shirley in to help you." With that, Megan walked out of the room, humming to herself. Maybe, just maybe, Krystal would know enough. She could always hope.

"Shirley, call Kathy Cornwall. Ask her if she could help Krystal write out a statement. I want it all legal and binding. She can have Krystal donate to the church as payment if she wants. When you get done with that, help Krystal. Writing on a looseleaf notebook one-handed isn't easy."

"You left her handcuffed? Can I take a picture? I'll not share it, but I can use it for a good chuckle to lighten my days," Shirley pleaded.

"No. Call Kathy." Megan strode to her office.

Megan examined the rifle taken from the rustler's trailer while sitting at her desk. It was tagged, as were the cash box, the ledger, and the cowhide wrapped bundle. Since she had inspected and packaged the contents of the cash box, she took it and the rifle over to the evidence safe, putting them in one corner of the tall section.

"Good thing this safe is almost big enough for a body. I've never had so much to put in there at one time," Megan muttered, looking at the varied objects already in the safe. One item caught her eye—the baggie with the gold nugget from Chris's Custom Jewelry floor. A chill washed over her giving her goosebumps. "I *know* where this stone is from," she mumbled, picking it up to examine it again.

Her memory flashed back to the day Nick was found out on the plateau. He had a ring with rough edges, and he moaned about losing the gold nugget from its center. Megan remembered seeing the photo of his hand, wearing the ring with a gold stone in its center, as the lock screen on his smartphone.

Sonofabitch! She had him. Nick lost the gold nugget from his jade ring during Chris's Custom Jewelry robbery on Saturday. That put him in the store. If the gems found at his ranch matched the stolen merchandise, she had him for the assault, theft, *and* possession of stolen merchandise. A burden lifted from Megan's shoulders. Now, she needed to connect the stone to the ring solidly. The stone had glue residue. Maybe the ring did too. If the glue and the stone matched the photo, she had Nick by the short and curlies. A heady sensation of certainty brought a smile to her face. She reached for her phone and called Officer Perkins.

"Officer Perkins here. What's happening, Sheriff?"

"Are you still going through the ranch house?" Megan inquired.

"Yes, Ma'am. I'm almost done. I haven't found anything of note. Nothing that looks out-of-place or hidden." Tim sounded disappointed.

"Go back to the bedroom. Look in his jewelry collection for a ring with a green stone in the middle. I need you to find it. It has some glue stuck in the center, and the sides have gold nuggets on the band," Megan described the ring she remembered. "Bag it carefully. Try not to knock any of the glue off. Call me if you don't find it." Megan broke the connection, taking the baggie with the nugget back to her desk. A memory crossed her mind, something that happened the day she gave Nicholas a lift back to the R-Bar-B. She carefully put the nugget into her desk drawer, locked it, and headed out to find Joe.

"Joe. Did Nicholas have any jewelry in his personal effects when you booked him? You know, a watch, tie tac, rings?"

"Of course. I've put Nick's stuff in a personal effects envelope and sealed it while he watched. Why?" Joe looked up from the report he was writing.

"Do you remember a ring? Kind of a large pinky ring? It would have gold nuggets on the band." Megan didn't want to describe the ring in more detail.

"You know, he did have two fancy rings. One was in his pocket, the other he wore on his left little finger," Joe recalled.

"Call Officer Perkins, tell him he doesn't need to dig around as I asked. He can call it a day and return with whatever evidence he's found. Tell him to bring Nicholas' computer," Megan ordered. She trotted to the section used for the prisoners' personal belongings. On top of the packages belonging to the rustles and Krystal was a fat envelope marked " Nicholas Davis" and today's date. The envelope was sealed with evidence tape, and Nick had initialed next to Joe as office procedure required. Hearing voices and footsteps, she turned to find Kathy Cornwall and Joe walking toward the conference room. Grabbing the envelope, she caught up with them.

"Wait a minute, Kathy. I need you and Joe to witness something. Come with me." Megan led the pair to the courtroom, where Nicholas Davis sat on a chair next to the railing with one hand attached to the wooden rail. Megan halted the trio.

" Nicholas Davis. This is Kathy Cornwall. Kathy can act as your legal advisor to observe and testify about what we are about to do. Do you accept her in this capacity?" Megan had turned on her recorder before she asked the question.

"I don't know her. Counselor, what do you suggest? Will you represent me, at least for right now? Should I agree?" Nick looked Kathy over, seeing a softly rounded, mature woman with gray in her hair and history reflected in her face and eyes.

"Sheriff. Let me have a few minutes with this man to confer. I can't give advice, even pro-bono advice, without first knowing the situation. What are the charges?" Kathy had taken a step toward the prisoner but turned to regard Megan and Joe.

"So far, we are working on two counts of possession of stolen property, one count of possession of drugs, and possibly assault and robbery. Only the possession charges are definite so far. We're investigating the other charges to turn over to the D.A." Megan and Joe left Kathy to confer with her possible client.

"Is she licensed in Colorado?" Joe asked.

"I don't know. No money is changing hands, and Kathy is only advising Nick, not representing him in court," Megan explained.

The door to the courtroom opened. Kathy motioned Megan and Joe to return. Megan switched the recorder back on as they entered the room.

" Nicholas Davis has accepted me as his legal advisor. He will need a practicing attorney before his arraignment in Gunnison. Still, I can represent his interests here in Riverview," Kathy announced.

"Joe, uncuff Nicholas from the rail. We need to move to the table," Megan pointed to the closest attorney's table in the courtroom. Kathy followed the motion and moved to one of the chairs, seated herself, and waited for Nick to take the chair next to her.

"What's going on, Sheriff?" Nick demanded.

" Nicholas Davis, do you recognize this personal effects envelope? Did you initial the evidence tape sealing it?" Megan waited while Nick inspected the envelope.

"Yeah, I initialed the tape next to the deputy's initials," Nick finally verified.

"Is the envelope still sealed as it was when you initialed it?" Megan continued.

"Looks like it. What's this about anyway?" Nick seemed to be losing patience. Kathy reached over and patted his balled fist where it lay on the table.

"I need to open this envelope to retrieve an object that I believe is covered by our evidence search warrant served on you today. With or without your permission, I am cutting this tape in front of you and these witnesses," Megan stated, pulling out her pocket knife to cut the seal. Keeping her hands visible over the table, she sliced through the tape, opened the envelope, and carefully dumped its contents on the table.

"Do you recognize all the items on the table as those you watched being put into the envelope?" Megan questioned Nick.

"Yeah, that's my stuff. When do I get it back? I feel naked without my watch," Nicholas groused.

Megan had not moved her hands away from the top of the table while he looked at his belongings. Once he agreed that the pieces belonged to him, Megan put on gloves and carefully pulled a gold and green ring from the pile. She held it in one hand, turning it around to Kathy and Nick and then back to herself to note the glue and scrapes on the green stone.

" Nicholas Davis. Do you own this ring with a jade center and nugetted band?" Megan asked.

"Yeah, I've had that ring for years. It's pretty useless now that the main gold nugget is lost from the center of the jade. Why?" Nick was beginning to frown.

"You have a photo of it as a screen saver on your cell phone, don't you?" Megan wanted him to admit the photo she'd seen was of this particular piece of jewelry. She picked his phone out of the pile.

"How did you know?" Nick snarled.

"Remember, I found your cell phone where you came off your horse down by the Gunnison River. I saw the photo when I checked to see if the phone was locked. I was hoping to find a relative to contact." Megan explained.

"Oh. I forgot. Yeah, there's a photo of it on my lock screen. Like I said, it's my favorite ring, and I've had it for years."

"Joe, Nick will need another personal effects bag. Sealed and secured as this was. The Sheriff's department will be keeping this ring and cell phone as evidence in the robbery of Chris's Custom Jewelry in Riverview, Colorado." Megan cautiously dropped the ring into a small evidence baggie. She sealed the bag. She placed Nick's cell phone into a larger evidence baggie, locking and taping it.

Megan turned to Kathy.

"Would you mind staying with Nick while his belongings are secured again? Once that is finished, Joe will escort you to the conference room, where another person is waiting for your assistance. You're almost as busy as I am this week." Megan waited for Kathy to nod before leaving the room with her treasures. She couldn't restrain herself from giving a fist pump of celebration in the hallway. *"Yes!"* she laughed, "We've gotcha! All I need to do is match the glue and the photograph."

"Excuse me, Sheriff?" A man walking toward Megan addressed her.

"Yes, how may I help you?" Megan asked.

"Here's the keys to the church van. It's full of gas, and I hope you intend to fill it before giving it back." Steady brown eyes regarded Megan as he passed her the keys.

Megan realized this was Pastor Cornwall. She'd missed church for a couple of weeks, so she'd yet to meet him.

"Thank you, sir. I've met your lovely wife. I'm Megan Holloway. Sorry I haven't been to church lately. It seems that recently the town has been keeping me busy seven days a week. It's been one thing after another. I hope to make it to church on Sunday." Megan reached out to shake hands with the new pastor. He had a warm, dry, firm grip that belied the age on his face and the gray in his hair.

"Michael Cornwall at your service. We don't need a contract or anything for this loan of the Church bus, do we?"

"I don't if you don't, but maybe we should write something to protect the church if anything happened to the vehicle on the road," Megan suggested.

"Will it take long? I'll need a ride back to the church, and then I'm on my way to visit some parishioners who are housebound."

"I'll get Shirley to type up something. It won't take a minute or two."

The courtroom door opened, and Joe led out Kathy. Both stopped next to the entrance to the conference room. Kathy smiled at her husband.

"I didn't know you were coming by, dear. You could have brought me," Kathy said.

"I'm surprised you're here. Is Ted in trouble again?" Michael asked.

"Not this time. I'm helping suspects and witnessing things for the Sheriff. What are you doing here?"

"Sheriff's office is borrowing the church van. I brought it over. Can you drive me home, or we can make calls together." Michael suggested, "How much longer will you be needed?"

Husband and wife turned to Megan.

"Kathy is helping Krystal with her statement, and while she does that, Shirley can put together something for this use of the van. I hope both can be done in about five to ten minutes. Krystal has been working on her statement for the past twenty minutes," Megan explained. "I don't see any reason why you won't be able to leave here together without much delay." Husband and wife nodded in agreement.

Joe opened the door to the conference room, allowing Kathy to precede him. Shirley looked up from where she held the corner of the writing paper steady for Krystal to work. Shirley jumped up, nodded to Joe and Kathy, and came out the door before it had a chance to close.

Once in the hall, Shirley looked from Megan to Pastor Michael in question.

"Shirley, I need you to write something up for our department to use the church van. A liability release for the church that shows the van will be our responsibility until we return it." Megan expected and hoped Joe would be back before the pastor needed the van. He *should* be. But things can and do seem to happen lately around this town.

"Yes, Ma'am." Shirley turned to the pastor. "Come over to my desk." She led him away.

With everyone set off to different tasks, Megan walked to her office, humming under her breath. Today was turning out to be a good day. At her desk, she unlocked the drawer, took the baggie with the nugget out, and marked the two baggies as evidence taken from Nicholas Davis connecting him to the jewelry robbery in Riverview. She slid all three individual bags into a larger one and set that bag into the evidence section of her safe.

She sat down to write her reports to send with the rustlers to Gunnison. She would also include accounts to the District Attorney for all local crimes. Thinking of Michelle Brewer, the D.A., she knew the woman would be calling her as soon as she finished reading the robbery and rustling accounts. It sounded more like a work of fiction than a week in the life of a small town in Colorado.

Chapter Eighteen

Megan's earlier elation returned. She felt almost giddy with the proof and knowledge. Now, she could combine the crimes. Megan decided to work on the evidence against the cattle rustlers before starting on the complications of the crimes committed by her star villain—uh—suspect. Having made that decision, she pulled the cowhide wrapped bundle from the items she had confiscated from the stock trailer. She turned on the video camera covering her desk and work areas.

"This item was collected from the stock trailer belonging to the men suspected of cattle rustling. Suspected rustled cattle filled the trailer when deputies and I stopped the vehicle," Megan gave it a case number before she continued. "Pending Case 1803CT on May 20th." Megan carefully broke open the string used to tie up the bundle.

"As shown in other visual evidence, this package was stashed under the ledger that I will record next." Megan unrolled the contents, revealing six rubber-banded bundles of cash. They all looked to be hundred-dollar bills. "Rustling must be pretty lucrative," she muttered.

In front of the camera, Megan counted each banded pack. "Twelve thousand dollars," she stated for the record. Marking the total on her evidence sheet, Megan stuck a slip of paper in with the money. She rewrapped the collection using the same cowhide and string. This time, she added evidence tape over the string knot to keep the chain of evidence. Megan had taped and marked the cash box earlier, so she commented for the video, "Cash box was found to hold loose diamonds that Chris's Custom Jewelry has authenticated. The data on one stone matches a gem he set into a piece of jewelry stolen from his shop in Gunnison."

With that explained, she reached for the ledger. Opening the book, her eyes rounded in surprise. It wasn't the sales log she expected but rather a journal of animals stolen and to whom they were sold. "This book was confiscated along with the cash box, the wrapped bundles of cash, and a rifle from the stock trailer," Megan told the video camera.

"The cattle thieves didn't worry about revealing their clients' names," Megan said. She held the book up to reveal pages of hand-printed dates, descriptions, and names of their buyers. "The only thing missing are the names of the ranches originally owning the cows."

Megan read further. "This ledger also details the birth of calves. Eight cows have calved from the beginning of this rustling spree, and the calves have been sold to three clients. One of the clients who purchased four calves is Nicholas Davis, our suspected jewel thief." She had wondered why these rustlers were taking pregnant cows. Now, she understood. There was a market for orphaned calves.

All the buyer needed to do was tag the calf as being born to one of their cows, and no one would be the wiser. Cows sometimes had twins, and no one would suspect an extra calf (or three) on the ranch. If questioned, the buyer only needed to explain the cow died in calving. Unless there was DNA evidence from breeders who lost cows, the calves would simply blend into the buyers' herd. Certainly, an illegal way to expand your stock, but kind of a slick scheme.

The rustlers stole pregnant cows, held them until they calved, sold the calves, and then sold the cows to illegal meat processors. Legitimate packing plants required documentation of ownership. Double money for the same risk. Megan wondered if the rustlers would turn over the processors if given the proper incentive. She jotted down that idea for the D.A.'s office to handle.

Megan couldn't help but wonder where they stayed while waiting for the calving. The pipe panels they carried would create a decent-sized pen, but they would need parking, and it had to be back in the wildlands to avoid detection. "Crap," she muttered as she stood and headed for the holding cells.

"I need to talk to one of you. Just one. Any volunteers?" Megan watched the men look each other over as no one moved. "Okay, no volunteers. I'll take our escape artist. Joe, uncuff him so he can come with me." The man had been cuffed to the bars of the cell to keep him from causing more havoc.

Joe and Megan led the man to her office. All the other offices were either occupied or far too public for the discussion Megan wanted to have with this man. Megan pointed to the chair across from her desk. "Cuff him to the chair," she directed Joe.

"Now, as you are aware, you've got at least one more charge against you because you attempted to escape. How would you like to mitigate that charge? I need to know where you've been hiding with the stock you rustled. You don't have to be exact. Just give us a road location, and we'll do the rest. It might save you when it comes sentencing day," Megan suggested.

"What makes you think those cattle are rustled? We bought them. All of them. We were legally hauling them when you stopped us for no reason," the man declared in a hurt voice.

"If that's how it happened, why did you try to escape? We declared who we were, and you had no call to leave the convoy. Yet you did or at least tried to. Where were you going? *Sonofabitch*. Joe, escort the prisoner back to his cell. We don't need his help," Megan commanded. "Meet me back here when you're done."

Minutes later, Joe returned to Megan's office. "Yeah, Boss? What was that about?"

"I'm an idiot. We stopped those yahoos on a road that goes into the Forestry land. No ranches back there, just an old abandoned cabin or two. Roger has some stock up there, but these rustlers would have to search for days to find those cows in the forest." She paced around her desk, furious that she hadn't figured this out earlier.

"Those boys were heading out with a load. A load of cows they probably stole over the past month. The place they've been using has to be one of the cabins up that road. Come daylight, Officer Perkins and I are heading up there to determine which cabin was used and make sure no one else is holding cows waiting to calf."

"I could go with you. Tim Perkins is kind of green for that kind of job, isn't he?" Joe questioned.

"Green he might be, but he knows how to ride, and we need to slide up there without the roar of vehicles. I don't expect any other rustlers to be up in the woods. I think they were on their way out with the final load. Things around here had begun to be too warm for them," Megan assured him. "Besides, you know Aaron won't let me go up there with just Perkins as my backup. I expect he'll either be with us or just behind us to make sure nothing happens."

"I'm just about out of here with the prisoners. Was Nick or Krystal joining us?" Joe asked.

"We've got a sealed and notarized statement from Krystal. She can drive herself to Gunnison for arraignment. There might not be any charges against her as state's witness, much to Shirley's dismay. On the other hand, Nick needs to spend the night here while we collect evidence against him," Megan said. She nodded toward the door as Shirley came in with a document for the sheriff to sign. "Have a safe trip. You'll get overtime for this. No need to rush." She waved Joe out the door.

Megan looked at the sheet and signed it. Now, the van was legally rented by her department and covered by insurance. "Shirley, I need Krystal's statement typed and signed by all of us. Once that's done and entered into evidence, you can go home. Thanks for staying so late."

"No problem, it's been a busy day for all of us. I don't remember a day so productive in getting the bad guys off the street in all the years I've been here. Well worth the extra time to have them under lock and key," Shirley stated. "I'll have the statement ready for your signature in just a few minutes."

Ten minutes later, Megan watched Krystal sign her statement. Shirley signed as a witness, and Kathy signed as a witness. Megan signed as the officer in charge before she attached the handwritten document to the printed one.

"Did your husband leave without you?" Megan asked Kathy. If the woman needed a ride, Megan could see she got where she needed to go.

"He had to take one of our invalids his dinner. He'll be back any minute to collect me," Kathy replied.

"Shirley can give you a lift if you need it. Can't you, Shirley?"

"Yep. I'm on my way out. Where do you need to go?" Shirley asked.

"I'm fine here. In fact, I see my husband pulling up. Bye!" Kathy called over her shoulder as she trotted out the door.

"Have a good night, Shirley." Megan waved her off before turning back to the conference room where Krystal still sat.

"Now that we have your statement, I'll turn you loose. I need you to sign this statement that you will appear before the judge on Tuesday morning at nine for arraignment in Gunnison." Megan watched the woman sign. "If you don't appear, a warrant will be issued for your arrest, and you will be charged. Do I make myself perfectly clear?"

"Yes, Ma'am. I understand. If I don't want to be thrown in jail, I'm to be in Gunnison Tuesday morning at nine," Krystal parroted Megan's statement.

"Don't make me regret this. You won't like it if I do."

Krystal nodded and hurried out the door.

Megan looked at Mandy, who had taken over for Shirley. "If you have any questions or the place burns down, call the mayor. I'm out of here as soon as I move Nick to his cell." She didn't notice the grin on Amanda's face as she entered the courtroom. Nick was in a cell five minutes later, and Megan was heading home, too tired to stop and grab a hamburger.

Her cell rang on her way, the unique tones she'd given Aaron. She pulled over, disheartened that she had forgotten they had a date tonight. Crap. She was so exhausted, but she didn't want to miss seeing him.

"Hi, honey. I forgot about our movie date," Megan began with an apology.

"I know what's gone down today. I cooked you a steak and left. It's on the counter, just waiting for you. Might even be warm, or you can nuke it," Aaron said.

"God, how I love you. Here I am feeling guilty about canceling, and you're so sweet that you understand why I need to skip this date. *And you made me dinner.*" Megan felt her throat clog with unshed tears.

"I love you too. I want you healthy and happy above all things. We've got our entire lives for date nights. When things slow a bit, you can come over and make me dinner to pay me back for tonight. Now, eat what you can of the stead and get a good night's sleep. Oh, I fed the horses. You need to feed Sparkle and yourself. Sleep tight, sweetheart." The connection broke.

Megan sat in her patrol car, letting the tears of love flow for a few minutes before blowing her nose, wiping her eyes, and driving home. All she could think was how lucky she was to have Aaron in her life.

Chapter Nineteen

"Huh? What the...?" Megan rolled over, trying to clear the fog of deep sleep to realize what noise woke her. Opening her sleep gritted eyes, she managed to read the numbers on her bedside clock. "Six-thirty-eight?"

The noise sounded again. This time she recognized the commotion. Someone was pounding on her door while Sparkle and the rustlers' cattle dogs barked like hellhounds. Barking dogs didn't seem to slow this intruder down. Megan's slowly waking brain tried to figure out who would be visiting at this time in the morning.

"All right. *All right!* I'm coming, I'm coming. Sparkle! *Hush!*" Megan yelled at her dog but didn't know how to call off the visiting canines. Sparkle quieted, but they continued to serenade the person pounding on her door. "At least they aren't attacking," she muttered as she pulled on her sweats and housecoat.

"Hold your horses! I'm coming," she called down the stairs between the dogs barking and the fist-pounding. The dogs continued to bark, but the knocking stopped. Megan checked the peephole before she opened the door.

"Perkins, this had better be serious. I haven't even had coffee yet."

"I'm sorry, Sheriff. Joe told me you expected me out here to go into the Forestry land to look for more crooks. He said I should bring a saddle. I don't have one anymore. I gave up riding when I left steer wrestling." Tim explained as he stood in the doorway holding his hat.

"I'll bring a saddled horse for you to ride. That still doesn't explain what you're doing on my doorstep at o-dark-thirty. Come on in, and I'll make coffee." Megan motioned the man in and walked to the kitchen. The coffee pot was on a timer, ready to brew, so all she did was flip the switch.

"Cups are above the pot. I'm going to get dressed. Apparently, my day is starting early." Megan left her deputy standing next to the gurgling coffee maker, looking mildly confused.

Megan felt proud when she made it back to the kitchen in just fifteen minutes. She even managed to take a quick shower. Her new handheld spray unit kept her hair dry. In the kitchen, she saw Tim had poured himself coffee and was reading last week's paper that she'd left sitting on the counter. Megan grabbed her gunbelt from her locked gun display cabinet and secured it around her waist. She slid her pistol home after checking the wheel to confirm it was loaded. She'd grab her Kevlar out of her SUV on the way to the barn.

"Now, where were we. As I understand it, Deputy Kaleo sent you over here. Did he tell you to come over immediately? Didn't it ever occur to you that I might not be ready to hit the trail at this time of the morning?" Megan struggled to keep her temper. She thought Joe understood how much she hated being called before her work hours.

"He told me I would be riding with you this morning. I didn't have anything else on my schedule, so I came on over. I'm sorry if I woke you, Ma'am." Perkin's face was as red as the mug he'd chosen for his coffee. He studied his mug of coffee rather than look up at his boss.

Exasperated, Megan heaved a huge sigh and poured her coffee. This wasn't why she was sheriff. Training raw recruits should be done in some city, not out here in the country. When Timothy Perkins applied, he gave an impression of maturity and common sense. He'd spent four years in the Army. That should have matured him; it had undoubtedly aged her. Well, her college time had matured her before her enlistment. Still, she knew tons of soldiers who had started out fresh from high school and developed into responsible adults under the discipline of the military. Perkins looked and often acted like an inexperienced teenager. Lord, was she *ever* that young?

"Well, you're here now. We might as well get started. I'll call the R-bar-M to let them know we'll be on their leased Forestry land. I don't expect anyone out there shooting, but if they know we're riding through, we should be safe."

Megan snagged three granola bars and her travel mug of coffee. Sparkle barked at the door to be let in, and Megan remembered she hadn't fed any of the dogs. "Crap." She speed-dialed Aaron before she grabbed two cans of dog food from the pantry. Aaron's phone went to voice mail, not unexpected at this time of day.

"Hi, Babe. Just wanted you to know that Officer Perkins and I will be riding up in the Forestry land today. We're going to see if one of the two abandoned spreads up there has been used to store the stolen cattle. I don't expect so, but riding up to them will give us an advantage. No engines, no way for any rustlers to expect us. I don't want you or the hands to go up there searching. Leave that to us. It could be dangerous if any rustlers were left behind, with or without more cows. I'll see you for dinner tonight, right? I'm cooking." Megan cut the connection, stuffed her mouth with one granola bar, and filled three bowls with dog food. She opened the door for Sparkle.

"Tim, grab that bowl and feed Sparkle. I'll take this food out to the cattle dogs. I need to throw the horses their breakfast and hitch the trailer. I'll be back in a few minutes," Megan said over her shoulder and took the food out to the dogs.

Ten minutes later, she was back in the kitchen, wearing her Kevlar vest, stuffing snacks, fruit, and water into her saddlebags.

"Sheriff, I feel kind of useless sitting here with the dog. What can I do to help?"

Megan pitched him the truck keys. "Hitch the trailer. Get your Kevlar vest on before you do. I'll get the horses saddled while they work on their hay." She put the mini-first-aid kit in the saddlebag and, as a safety precaution, attached her SpotGen locator to one of the grommets on the leather saddlebag. Surprisingly, even in the mountains, it worked well to give your location if triggered. She heard Perkins start the truck as she brought the two bowls of water out to the dogs. "Good boys. Here you go. You stay and be good dogs." Sparkle could have the house and her fenced backyard.

Both horses looked over their stall doors as Megan entered the barn again. "Guess what, boys? Both of you get to work today."

She saddled each one with little fuss while they were eating hay. "Sure is sweet having horses that behave this well," she muttered to Radar, her number one mount, as she stroked his soft neck.

Since she was unsure of Perkin's ability to ride, he would ride Radar. She hoped the man would be a decent rider. He'd been raised in Texas, the same as she had, but that didn't mean he was born in the saddle like she was.

"Sorry, boy. You know the drill. Take care of him and follow Lucky and me."

Megan hooked the lead rope to Radar's halter and led him from the stall. Tim Perkins had pulled the trailer up to the barn and opened the metal door. He stood next to the far door, ready to close it as needed. Megan threw the rope over Radar's neck before sending him into the slant-load rig. She stepped to the sliding divider, glad it had slam latches. In the barn, Lucky called, thinking he was being left behind.

"I'm coming, I'm coming," Megan called to the spotted gelding as she re-entered the barn. Grabbing his lead rope from the wall hook, she snapped it on the gelding's halter. She opened the stall door and stood back as he marched out of his confinement toward the trailer where his herd mate waited. As Lucky passed, Megan threw the lead rope over his neck and followed him to the trailer.

"Once he loads, close your door," she said to Tim. He nodded and began to close the trailer door once Lucky had hopped in.

"That's pretty slick. Do they always load this easy?"

"Yeah. When I only take one, the other screams and chases around the pasture as the truck pulls out. I've had people tell me as soon as the rig is out of sight, the horse in the pasture returns to eating. So I don't worry much."

"Herd instinct. I had a gelding once who lost his herd mate. I had to buy another horse to keep him company. He grieved for a week until I did. Wouldn't hardly eat and called over and over for his buddy. They do tend to bond more than most people understand. I think most of it is a case of 'I need a herd mate or the wolf will eat me,' but it's also a social thing. They need company," Perkins said as he handed the truck keys to Megan before walking to the passenger door.

Megan walked around the rig, checking the hitch, the electrical connection, the tack door latch, and the stall door latches. She would do the same if she had hooked up the rig, but she was twice as careful when someone else did the chore.

"How much riding have you done?" Megan needed to know. Some of the trails they could be taking were challenging at best. A green rider might have problems staying on even the best trail horse.

"Shoot, Sheriff. My brothers and I used horses instead of bicycles until Pa moved us to the city for high school. We were cowhands before we could read. I can still ride. I only gave up my horse when I quit steer wrestling because he was too good to become a pasture pet. You don't have to worry about me. Wherever we're going—if the horse can make it, I can stay on," Tim assured her.

"Okay, I'll take your word for it. Radar is the best trail horse I've ever had. We've run fifty-mile competitions, and he's finished in the top ten and best condition. He's not in that shape right now, coming out of winter. But you won't run out of horse with him under you. Just stay out of his mouth. Trust him. He knows more about what he's doing than you do. If you start jerking his mouth, he'll start dogging it until it drives you crazy. Keep a light touch on the reins," Megan warned. Radar was a character and knew to the degree precisely what he could get away with on just about any ride. He wouldn't do anything dangerous, but he would drop back and drag his feet until his rider loosened the reins.

She barely finished her lecture when they arrived at where she wanted to park. Another rig was parked ahead of them with two lead ropes hanging from the trailer. Riders were on the mountain. Megan looked closer and recognized the R-bar-M truck and trailer. Aaron. *"Damn it,"* Megan muttered as she walked around to unload her horses.

"Who's rig is that, Sheriff? Were you expecting more riders?" Tim asked.

"No. I specifically told the rancher *not* to come over on this side of the highway today. I had to let them know we were going up the mountain. It's their leased land. I really hope those boys don't get into trouble. If any rustlers are still up there, they've got to be nervous because the crew didn't come back."

Megan let Lucky out, grabbing his lead rope and passing it to the deputy. Radar whinnied and stomped inside the trailer, eager to follow his buddy out. "Just hold on. Get your butt off the divider, and I'll open it," Megan told the horse as she slapped his hindquarters to push him off the divider gate. Radar stepped forward and tried to turn his head to see. *"AAACCCKKK!!"* Megan growled in her nastiest tone. Radar straightened and held still while she opened his divider.

Once freed from his trailer section, Radar waited for Megan to lead him out of the trailer like the gentleman he was trained to be. His voice rumbled in her ear as he called softly to his buddy held by Officer Perkins on the side of the dirt road. Megan handed Tim Radar's lead rope so she could get the bridles from the tack compartment. She also snagged her rifle from the cab of her truck. She prayed she wouldn't need it. The horses were tacked up, saddlebags secured behind the cantle, and ready to hit the trail a few minutes later. Megan donned her helmet and ignored the snigger from Perkins. "I was taught that those who have a brain use helmets; those who have nothing to protect, ride without. There's an extra in the tack trunk if you want it."

Megan pulled her mounting block from the truck's bed, stationing it behind the trailer so she would remember to put it back in the truck later.

"Kind of fancy, ain't it, Sheriff?" Perkins pointed at the red two-step mounting block.

"Nope. Easier on the horse than pulling myself up by the mane or the saddle. Try it. Radar will appreciate your effort," she explained, mounting Lucky. Lucky stood next to the block while Megan checked the scabbard and saddlebags. "See. No-fuss, no muss. Just easier on the horse."

Megan stepped Lucky away and nodded to the mounting block, smiling when the officer grumbled and led Radar over to it. Some guys equated mounting blocks with crutches and wheelchairs, something only used when you couldn't mount without it. Tim looked to be one of those people.

"Radar likes to lead, but I'll do the honors on the way out. You can lead when we come back."

"No problem. You know where you want to go. I'm just here to support your play," Officer Perkins replied, tapping his pistol where it rested on his thigh.

Megan walked Lucky at a brisk pace up the dirt road. The first spread was about five miles distant, and she knew where to cut into the woods to approach it from the blind side of the cabin. She had discovered the place when she and Bethany were marking a new trail. That was the day they had found the mummified corpse when Bethany landed on it as her horse fell. Megan hoped this ride into the woods would be less eventful than that one.

After a quarter-mile, she put Lucky into his gait. Radar moved into his Fox Trot and then a lope to keep pace with his herd mate.

"Daaaymmm. I've never ridden a horse this smooth. What kind of horse is this?" Tim asked as he and Radar caught up to Megan and Lucky.

"He's a Missouri Fox Trotter. Lucky is a Spotted Saddle Horse with a suspicion of Tennessee Walking Horse. He's not papered, so we don't know exactly. Lucky can out-gait Radar, but Radar is better on rough ground. They sure are a hoot to move out on smooth trail." Megan laughed over her shoulder as she sent Lucky up the embankment into the woods at the exact spot where the old trail started.

This trail had been used during the days of settling this area, and the wild game kept it worn enough for riders to use it if they could find it. Megan remembered how she and Bethany had found their way out of the woods after Bethany's fall. This trail would take them to the split, where the cabin trail turned to the right. Lucky slowed his gait to a ground-covering stride while Radar maintained his slower fox-trot. The two horses got to the junction quickly. Both knew where they were. They'd traveled this trail before. Megan eased Lucky to a stop and let Radar come up beside her.

"Where do we go from here? Looks like neither trail is used very much," Officer Perkins observed.

"If we go to the left, we'll end up at the pack station. To the right, about another mile or so is the first place I want to check. I hope the riders ahead of us don't go crashing in without any caution. A cornered rustler is a desperate criminal." Megan had a bad feeling about Aaron and whoever he roped into the jaunt getting into a battle with a possible rustler. She hoped she was wrong, but this first cabin was in the best condition with an easily fenced pasture. It would work for holding cows without many improvements.

"Let's keep moving. I want to catch up with the others if we can." Megan clucked, and Lucky began his fastest walk short of gaiting. This section of trail wasn't rocky, and being sheltered kept the ground softer than the exposed northern face of the mountains. She looked over her shoulder to see that Radar kept pace a few yards behind her. The trail wound around and down to cross a creek. She was glad the weather had been dry.

They were climbing up to the top of the ridge that overlooked the small open valley where the cabin sat when the sound of gunfire echoed around them.

"Sonofabitch!" Megan cussed. She kicked Lucky into a gallop up the hillside as she unhooked the scabbard, pulling out her rifle. She slid her horse to a stop before they cleared the woods. The cabin was about four hundred yards away.

"Stay in the cover of the woods and ride to my right around the cabin. There's a dirt track. We need to stop anyone from escaping. Can you do that? Anyone on horseback is a friend. I'd prefer you not to shoot my fiancé," Megan directed.

She scanned the scene below her, searching for movement. Two horses moved from behind the cabin into the field, loose horses. Never a good sign. Lucky called to them. Megan cringed, hoping it wasn't loud enough to draw attention. The horses didn't look up from their search for spring grass. She turned back into the woods, tying Lucky up to a tree where the other horses were out of sight. He settled to munching on the sprouting leaves of the brush around him.

That done, she moved in a crouch from the trees to the closest boulder. She scooted from one boulder to another farther down the hill, ducking behind each. Megan plotted a course to within about fifty yards of the building. Once she got that close, there was no brush, trees, or boulders to hide her movements. She worried that there had been only silence since those two shots were fired. There was no movement that she could see. She might be able to make it to the lean-to stall to see what was happening inside the cabin. But first, she needed to be around the side with no windows. She about jumped out of her skin with a warm breath ruffled her hair. She whipped around, startling one of the grazing horses that had come to investigate her into stepping back, but he didn't leave.

Megan looked at the cabin and the distance she needed to cover. Flat open ground, only spring grass growing. She felt the plan fall into place as she looked from the curious horse to the cabin. It might work.

Megan grabbed the horse's trailing rein. Using it, she turned the horse toward the cabin, putting herself on the far side. She asked the gelding to wander toward the building. The seconds ticked by like minutes, each step they took felt exposed. Time could be critical if anyone had been shot. "Come on, boy. Just mosey over there. There's good sheltered grass growing. Honest," she whispered. She worked to keep her body at the gelding's shoulder so that her legs might not be evident to anyone glancing from the cabin.

The other horse followed along after his herd mate and the human. Megan smiled. That would be natural.

Horses were worse than teenage girls...one never went anywhere without the other. When her moving concealment halted by the edge of the lean-to, ducked his head, and began to graze, Megan slipped into the stall, hugging the wall. She paused and listened. Voices.

"You can't tell me you two were just trail riding. Not with rifles in your scabbards. Trail riders carry canteens and lunch. All you've got is one bottle of water between you. I'll ask you one more time. What. Are. You. Doing. Here?"

"This is bear country. Everyone carries a rifle if they're smart. We rode up from the pack station. Somehow we got off the track and ended up here. I told you, we're lost. We didn't mean to trespass. How do we get back to the R-bar-B? Has either of you two been down there?" Aaron's voice sounded convincing to Megan. She hoped the rustler would buy the story.

"Somehow, you look more like ranch hands than day riders. If you don't come up with a better story, I'm gonna start shooting off body parts until one of you talks. Don't worry, I prefer extremities to privates," the rustler's rough voice chuckled with the reassurance.

"George, these guys are buying our outfits. You did good picking out cowboy clothes for us," Aaron sounded happy to be considered a real cowboy. Megan grinned. He knew how to lay it on thick.

"If you won't believe what we have to say. Go catch our horses. They're fat and lazy, unlike any cowpony I've ever seen. I'll bet by now those lazy things have headed back to their stalls at the R-bar-B, eating all the way. One of you boys should go catch them." The voice was familiar, but Megan couldn't name its owner. She didn't think George was his name, but she could be wrong. She knew he was an R-bar-M hand.

Megan listened for footsteps inside, but it seemed the rustlers weren't splitting up. Crap. She really needed to see into the room. She couldn't just look in the window. She'd be spotted in a heartbeat, and the old dry wood wouldn't slow a bullet down if they shot at her.

Old dry wood…logs with missing chinking. Megan's eyes and fingers began a search while she listened. There had to be a spot where she could see through the siding. To her right was the exterior of the lean-to. No hope there. However, her fingers found a crevice under the window to her left. Megan dropped silently to her knees, sliding over to the hole her fingers had found. Bingo!

She had a limited view of the room on the other side of the wall. Still, it was enough to see two men holding pistols pointed at Aaron and another cowboy. The prisoners had their hands tied to their bodies with what looked to be lariat rope. All Megan could see were their backs. She wasn't sure how secure the binding was when she saw Aaron's hand move. Maybe if she distracted the men, he'd be able to knock them off balance. Nah, that would be too dangerous. She needed to get one of them outside, where Tim could catch him.

A noise close behind her made her jump. Whirling around, she startled the horse, which had stepped into the lean-to. He jumped back, hitting the wall, knocking out a wall slat. The crashing of the horse, the wood, and the galloping as the horse took off caused the distraction Megan was hoping to create.

"What the fuck?"

Megan quickly ducked back against the wall as one of the rustlers stuck his head through the window to see what had happened. The man gave her a perfect presentation of his upper body. Using the stock of her rifle, she rammed it up against the exposed chin, pushing his head against the window frame. *Crack!*

Megan heard his body slump down against the other side of the wall.

"Jimmy! What's going on? Are you okay?" Footsteps hurried across the cabin floor.

Megan held her breath. She checked the peephole, waiting for the rustler to be close with his weapon no longer pointed at his prisoners. The man bent over his partner in crime, shaking her victim's shoulder.

"Jimmy. Wake up. What happened?" he asked.

Tucking her rifle into her shoulder, Megan stood, turning to face the man.

"I'm what happened to him. Put your gun down. You're under arrest!" Megan knew he had no chance with only ten feet or less between them. Obviously, the rustler didn't believe she would shoot. In slow motion, she watched his gun hand come up. Aiming upper right, she squeezed the trigger of her rifle.

Ka-Blam!

Megan cringed from the slam of her gun against her shoulder. Too many memories flooded her from her days in the army. The crack of the rifle deafened her for a moment to the sounds in the cabin. Her eyes only saw her comrades writhing in the sands after one horrific skirmish. She dropped her rifle, grabbing the window sill for support as her knees buckled. Suddenly, she wasn't in a wilderness cabin in Colorado but back in a deserted Afghani village. At least it had looked deserted when they entered to secure it. That day rivaled the day she was injured in her memories of war. In her mind, she could hear the rat-tat-tat of automatic weapons around her and the screams of the wounded in front of her.

Movement caught Megan's eye, drawing her back to the present. The wounded man was reaching for his pistol.

"I told you to drop your gun. I didn't mean for you to reach it again. Kick it toward the others," Megan ordered. She pulled her pistol from her belt, covering the rustler again. She was stuck waiting for either Aaron to get loose or Officer Perkins to get to the cabin. She couldn't take her gun off the two men until someone else had them covered. She looked at Aaron. He was almost free of his bonds, and the two rustlers were on the ground. The wounded one had given up trying to get his weapon. Instead, he was trying to staunch the bleeding from his shoulder.

"I'm going to bleed to death. Help me," the man ordered.

Aaron turned his chair so that the other prisoner could untie the remaining knots. A figure darkened the cabin's door, startling Megan and the prisoners. She heaved a sigh of relief when the sun reflected off Officer Perkins' badge.

"Work on the prisoner. Aaron will be loose in a moment. I'm on my way around," Megan said as she holstered her pistol, turned from the window, and collected her rifle. As she trotted around the cabin, she called for a medevac helicopter for the injured rustlers.

All she wanted now was for her hands to stop shaking. This was the first time since becoming sheriff that she'd had to draw down on a suspect and fire. The first time since her Army days that she fired at a human. She knew it wouldn't be the last. Did she want this job badly enough to face this kind of flashback? She needed to talk this out with Aaron. She felt like she was shattering into fragments and would collapse into a pile of fragile woman at any second. She stopped and leaned against the logs of the cabin. She bent over and vomited into the scrub next to the wall. The shaking subsided along with her urge to cry.

A hand massaged her shoulder, startling her. She hadn't heard anyone approach. "You did good. I'm proud of you," Aaron's voice calmed her further as he turned her into his arms.

"I had a flashback. I could have gotten us all killed because of it," Megan confessed.

"You reacted first and then had the flashback. You wouldn't have frozen if the man hadn't been down. I know that, and you do too."

"How can you be so sure?" Megan asked, needing Aaron's support more than ever.

"Because you're a soldier and a sheriff before anything else. Your subconscious knew the danger was past, allowing you to give in to your emotions. I have perfect faith in that. That ole' boy wasn't buying us as casual lost day riders. You saved John and me." With that, Aaron kissed Megan's forehead. "Let's get you some water. I wish I had some whiskey, but I don't carry it in my canteen like I did in my twenties," he laughed.

"I called for a chopper. Do Tim and John have everything under control in the cabin?" Megan inquired as Aaron led her toward his horse.

"Yep. I moved the rustlers' guns out of the room. They're on the porch, out of reach." Aaron reached for his canteen from his horse, opened it, and passed it to Megan. "Here. You're looking better, but take a drink; it'll help."

Megan did as ordered, swishing it around in her mouth before spitting it into the bushes. Then she took a deep drink to ease the dryness in her throat.

"What in the *hell* were you thinking? Why didn't you wait for us? I told you not to come! You not only jumped into this mess, but you also didn't bother to wait for me to get to the trailhead. I ought to arrest you for interfering with me. I'm sure there's a statute for that." Megan lectured Aaron. He'd scared the crap out of her and needed to understand his interference wouldn't ever be acceptable.

"I know. I'm sorry." Aaron ended his apology with a deep kiss. Off in the distance, they heard the *whop-whop-whop* of the approaching helicopter.

"Grab your horses. I'll round up Lucky and Radar. The animals won't like the big noisy thing in the sky." Megan broke away from Aaron's kiss, feeling more in control. She ran for the woods where she'd left Lucky, untied him, and followed the tracks left by Officer Perkins until she found Radar. She'd barely untied him when the helicopter approached to land in the pasture about thirty yards away.

"Easy, boys. You're okay. I know it's noisy. Easy. Easy," Megan murmured while stroking the neck and face of each horse. Both animals turned their butts to the chopper and buried their faces in her shirt. It soothed Megan's heart that they accepted her ability to protect them. Megan felt better by the minute between Aaron's faith in her skills and the trust of her horses. Yes. She was where she needed and wanted to be. Sheriff was her job, and soon she'd be a wife. Colorado was her home.

The helicopter took off with both wounded men about twenty minutes later, leaving Megan and her crew to investigate.

"Sheriff, what did you do to that one guy? He was still out cold when he was loaded into the medevac," John asked. "All we heard was a crash, and he was on the ground."

"Well, I hit him in the jaw with my rifle butt when he leaned out that window. He bounced back from that and slammed his head into the window frame. Guess he's got a concussion and maybe a broken jaw," Megan explained.

"Sheriff, if I had thought this cabin was occupied by rustlers, we would never have ridden up to it. We didn't see any smoke or signs of humans. We came out of the woods, looking for a vehicle, and the next thing we know, the one guy shot at us. I was pulling my rifle from the scabbard when a rope landed around me, and I was pulled from my horse," Aaron explained.

Megan was pleased he gave her the story without any "sweetheart" or "honey" comments. In this case, she was Sheriff first and his fiancée second.

"I told you why we were riding up here, not driving. You should have trusted that I had reason to believe rustlers could be hiding in one of the abandoned cabins. Next time, listen and do as I ask," Megan admonished. "Officer Perkins, look around in the cabin. See if our friends left anything behind that could be evidence. Grab the evidence kit off the back of your saddle before you go inside."

As she watched Tim approach Radar, she was pleased to see her horse stood without backing away. Ground tying only worked if the horse didn't feel threatened. Once Tim had the saddlebag and headed for the cabin, Megan turned back to the ranch hands.

"Did you get a chance to look for any loose cows? There must be a reason why those two were left up here when the others were hauling cows to buyers," she mused.

"There's a box canyon just beyond the trees on the far side of the cabin. Maybe they've got more cows stashed there. I didn't see any truck or car around. These two would need to walk out, or we're missing something." John replied.

"Catch your horses, and let's go look." Megan turned to Lucky, stroking his neck while looking for a rock or stump to use as a mounting block.

"Here, babe. Let me give you a leg up." Aaron bent over, offering her his laced hands as a step.

"Thanks." Megan stepped her boot into his hands, and he boosted her into the saddle.

"Here you go, boss." John handed Aaron the reins to a buckskin while he kept the reins of the bay Megan had used to sneak up on the rustlers.

Megan led the group around the cabin, looking for and finding a line of tracks leading to the woods. Cows, horses, and men had come this way. She stopped to examine the ground from horseback at the spot where it was apparent a corral had been set up and a vehicle backed to it.

"Well, this is where they loaded the cows into the trailers," Megan said. Both men nodded. "How far is the canyon?"

"About a quarter-mile. The settler and fur traders who used the cabin used the canyon for holding stock. They kept horses next to the hut, but everything else they kept at a distance. No sense luring predators close," Aaron explained.

"When I was here with Bethany, neither one of us was up to exploring more than just the building."

"I thoroughly explored the area when Roger leased this land from the Forestry Service. We needed to know what was here, especially if it could be hazardous to the cattle or the pack station clients." Aaron took the lead, picking up some speed. He seemed to know exactly where he was going and how to get there.

Megan followed, with John bringing up the rear. Aaron stopped, holding up his hand for silence. In the distance, Megan could hear a cow bellowing. Other cattle lowed, but one cow sounded highly distressed. Aaron kicked his horse into a gallop, never looking behind to see if Megan and John followed.

As the riders entered the clearing, they saw one cow in a pen alone while about a dozen other cows milled around in the box canyon corral. Aaron was off his horse and running to the distressed cow as Megan slid Lucky to a stop.

"Damn it!!" Aaron cussed, opening the pen and walking up to the cow. She had two gory legs extending from her back end while she labored to push the calf out. The cow circled the small pen, bellowing in pain.

"John, get a rope on her, give it to Megan. Megan, hold her head. John, I'm going to need your help pulling this calf. You don't see any chains laying around, do you?" Aaron asked as he took hold of the calf's legs.

Megan took the rope John had put around the cow's face and held her steady, stroking her to soothe her. "Easy girl. Easy lady. I know it hurts. It won't be long now, just easy...."

John walked around the cow, taking one of the calf's forelegs from Aaron and positioning himself shoulder to shoulder with his boss. "No chains. Guess we do this the old-fashioned way," John muttered.

"Okay, let's put one leg in front of the other to tweak the shoulders. Let's pray the nose is just out of sight. Let me see if I can feel it." He reached his hand up the calf's leg to the cow's vagina. Sliding his hand into the enlarged tissue, he extended his fingers until he touched the blunt nose of the stuck calf. Thank God.

"We're lucky. The nose is there. Let's get this calf born." Aaron brought his hand down the leg until he had a firm grip just above the knee. "Give your leg a light pull. Let's get this baby as small as we can. This has to be a first-year heifer. She's hardly full-grown enough to carry a calf, much less push it out."

John did as instructed, pulling the leg he gripped with both hands a few inches farther out of the cow than the leg Aaron held. They both saw the stretched vagina slacken with the movement. The cow bellowed again, instinctively pushing against the pain in her body. *"Pull!"* Aaron commanded, adding his strength to the pushing of the cow. Between the legs' repositioning and the extra help of the two men, the calf slid out of the cow onto the ground behind her.

Both men lost their balance and landed in the dirt beyond the wet, slick calf.

"Is it alive?" Megan asked as she comforted the cow.

Aaron jumped up, used his fingers to clear the calf's mouth and nostrils of the birth sack, and began to massage its chest. Nothing happened. He picked the calf up by its hind legs and swung it back and forth. He slapped the calf back down on the ground and massaged some more. This time, the chest expanded as the newborn took its first breath.

Aaron looked at Megan and John. "I think it might live. Bring the cow over to meet her baby."

Megan turned the cow around to face the wet pile of calf she'd just expelled from her body. The cow gently nudged the calf. The calf lifted its head and mooed at her. The sound seemed to stimulate the cow into caring for her baby. She began to lick off the afterbirth.

"Is the cow okay?" Megan asked John. He was one of the wranglers, more used to foalings than calvings, but he possibly could tell if a mother would recover from the birthing.

"I think so. What's the brand on that cow?" John asked Aaron.

"She's R-bar-M stock. One of ours. I knew we were missing some cows when we brought them from the far pasture for calving season. I put it down to a lousy year for predators. Seemed to me it was young heifers missing."

"You want me to call for a trailer to collect these cows? This heifer and calf should be able to travel within an hour or so." John offered.

"Yeah. Call Roger. We'll take this lot over to the R-bar-B pens where the others have been put until all the evidence is collected and ownership established," Aaron directed.

"I don't know if the brand inspector was done with that batch of animals. If he's still there, he can run ear tags and brands on this bunch too. I'll note that this calf is R-bar-B stock," Megan said, turning for her horse. "I'm going back to the cabin. You guys can handle the livestock. Now, we know why those two rustlers were still here. They weren't done with the heist. Every cow is likely going to calve, giving them more stolen animals to sell. The charges seem to be growing as fast as their herd."

Leaving the men behind her, Megan rode back to where Tim sat on the porch, waiting. "Well? Did you find anything we can use?"

"Boss, it's a one-room cabin. Not even a toilet. These guys were roughing it. There was no food left, just some wrappers and an empty container from Betty's. I don't know what they've been drinking, there isn't a well here, and I couldn't find any supplies at all." Perkins shook his head as he stood up.

"I didn't expect to find much. We found some more cows. Let's get back to town. We've got some paperwork to complete. Assault with a deadly weapon and kidnapping on both those men. At least they never fired on me. Would have added to the charges if they had." Megan watched Tim swing quickly into the saddle. "You get to lead going back to the rig. Radar knows the way."

Chapter Twenty

Megan was shocked to be back at her desk less than two hours later. She checked her watch, noticing it was almost one. No wonder her stomach was growling. She'd had a granola bar with her coffee on the way out this morning and nothing since then. She looked at the stack of paperwork needing her attention, put down her pen, and decided to go to lunch at Betty's Diner. It shouldn't be swamped at this time of day, and she could use the peace to think about all that had occurred this morning.

"Shirley! Hold any calls unless it's dire. I'm going to Betty's. I'll be back in an hour or so. I don't want *any* calls. Is that understood?" Megan asked as she passed Shirley's desk on her way out of the building.

"You got it. No one wants to talk to you with your mouth full, anyway. Not to mention that Betty's can get loud, though it shouldn't be at the moment." Shirley waved Megan out the door.

Megan counted eight men eating or sitting with coffee as she walked into Betty's. It must be the mid-afternoon break.

"Hi, Sheriff. Want your normal BLT and tots?" Betty called over the head of the man she was serving coffee.

"Sounds good, but I'm starving. Could you get me a strawberry shake while the food is cooking? I *need* something with sugar to replace the calories used this morning," Megan replied.

"Tim Perkins just left. He told me about the excitement up there in the woods. How did you know there would be rustlers hiding out on that old, defunct spread?" Shirley set down the coffee pot, scribbled on an order pad, and handed the page to the cook.

"It was the only explanation I could come up with for the rustlers having been on that road where we caught them. They must have been hiding up there to avoid being seen with the truck full of cows," Megan explained.

"That makes sense. Find yourself a seat, and I'll have this shake to you in a minute." Betty pointed to the tables by the window with her chin.

Megan set her hat down on the corner of her table and slid her suddenly tired body across the seat to lean her shoulders against the glass. A groan escaped her as she remembered her morning. From the rude wake-up to the woodland ride, the moments of terror as she worried about Aaron, and finally, the moments of the horrible flashback. Her hands shook as she scrubbed her face, knuckling the sand from her eyes. No, she didn't want this kind of excitement again, any time soon.

"Here's your shake, Sheriff. Are you okay? You look a little pale." Betty set the stainless steel tumbler down next to the tall, full drinking glass. "I gave you the entire thing. You need your energy."

"Thanks. I think I just ran out of gas. I only had a granola bar this morning, and it's been an exhausting five hours since then." Megan slipped her straw into the glass and sucked down the thick liquid. She gasped as she came up for air. "Brain freeze," Megan moaned.

"Serves you right. You know better than to guzzle one of my good milkshakes," Betty chided from behind the counter.

"I know, but my stomach is demanding sustenance, and this shake is not only handy, but it's also amazingly tasty." Megan took another long pull on the straw. She was setting down the icy glass when a siren began to wail.

All eyes in the diner turned to look at the volunteer station across the street. The doors rolled up, and the rescue truck rolled out to stop in front of the cafe. A heavyset man spun out of the driver's seat and trotted into the diner, arriving completely winded.

"Easy, Steve. Don't give yourself a heart attack. What's going on?" Megan jumped up and ran over to the man, whose face was an alarming shade of red.

"It's Oliver Grant," he panted, speaking so softly Megan had to bend over to hear his voice.

"What about Oliver Grant?"

"His mom can't find him. His dog is sitting in front of the hay barn. He refuses to move away from it. Samantha thinks Ollie went climbing in the bales again." Steve's color was returning to his normal florid complexion. His breathing was still ragged.

"*SHIT!* I gave that lecture last fall. The one about how dangerous it can be in the hay bales," Megan rationalized. "Why can't kids listen?"

"Beats me."

Megan looked around at the concerned faces of those sitting around whiling away their afternoon. Things were about to get serious. She looked out the window at the Rescue truck. People were gathering out there too. Lots of strong arms. They would be needed if Ollie was stuck in a hay tunnel collapse. Outside, she motioned the gawkers together with those from the diner. She explained the situation while Steve got back into the S&R truck.

"Everyone know where the Grant place is?" she finished. At all the nods, she continued, "Betty, you send anyone who shows up out to help us. Call the ranches. We can use as many hands as we can get. Let's go!"

Megan ran for her SUV, following the Rescue truck out to the Grant farm. A convoy of pickup trucks filled the road behind them. The Grant family had been dealing in hay for the past two generations. Buying hay, storing it, and selling hay by the bale or ton to people from Texas to Colorado and as far as Nevada and Arizona when the droughts were bad. Every available hand in the county would be at the farm within an hour. Megan prayed the boy was in a position where he could last that long. If he was in a pocket, he would be fine. If not, it could already be too late to save him. A ton of hay could crush a body or, worse yet, smother one within minutes. "Lord, please let us be in time," she prayed as she pulled her SUV up next to the largest barn.

Inside, men were talking, and a dog was pacing and whining. To the left side of the vast metal building were stacks of massive square bales. In the center of the barn was a baling machine used to create smaller bales from the half-ton monsters. The right side of the barn had neatly stacked smaller square bales. At sixty pounds each, they were more manageable for the hobby farmer to feed horses and smaller livestock. At the far end of the right side were stacks of banded bales. Each banded bundle filled a half-ton pickup bed. Megan guessed there would be twenty bales per bundle, but she'd never purchased a bundle and didn't know for sure. She knew that if the boy was caught in the bundled hay and trapped, things would be dicey getting him out safely.

With all the talking and dog whining, nothing was getting started. Megan put her fingers to her lips and let out an ear-piercing whistle.

"Quiet down!" She shouted. Sudden deathly silence followed. "Does anyone know what section he could be trapped in?" She looked at the hound, who still paced in front of the bales. "Come here, boy," Megan called, and the dog came to sit at her feet.

The dog twitched and whined, turning soulful eyes up to her. "Where is he? Can you find Oliver?" Megan asked as she scratched the dog's ears. "Show us, fella. Where's Oliver?" Megan lifted her hand, motioning the dog away.

The hound dropped his nose to the ground and began pacing again. This time, he appeared to be tracking. The dog ran to the far left, turned at the baling machine, and began working his way to where the growing crowd stood. The dog sat down and barked at the first row of smaller bales.

"I think this gives us a place to start. I want *no talking* other than calling Oliver's name and waiting one minute before calling again. We'll work front to back with those in the back calling first. Spread out in two's. Work your way up the bales. Watch your step. Move with caution; we don't need any broken legs or losing anyone down into a hole," Megan ordered. She walked to the wall at the end of the first stack of bales.

"OLIVER!" she screamed as loudly as she could. Then everyone waited. No response. Megan looked at the man three bales over and nodded for him to call.

"OLIVER!" his deep bass voice resonated around the barn. Again, no sound. Time passed, each minute an eon of

uncertainty. Next in line was the woman at the front corner of the stack.

"Oliver Kevin Grant! You hear me? If you don't call out, you're in such trouble, young man!" Samantha Grant used her loudest Mom voice. The one any child would respond to when his mom used it. Megan prayed this would get a response.

The hound jumped up from where he'd finally been sitting. Barking hysterically, the dog charged up the second stack of hay, jumping over bales. He climbed toward the back right corner of the multi-bale-wide rows. The dog came to a stop, dropping his nose between bales. He whined and began trying to dig.

"Samantha, I need you to move to a spot equal to the dog and talk to your son. He needs to tell us if he can breathe or if the hay is too tight," Megan ordered the distressed mother to a spot on the ground level equal to where the dog sat on the bales eight rows above.

"We may need a hose to get air down to Oliver. Find at least a twenty-footer and bring it."

"I've got an oxygen tank in the Rescue truck. Want me to bring it?" Steve was already hot-footing it out to his vehicle.

Aaron stepped to the front of the milling men. Megan didn't even know when he'd arrived. As foreman of the R-bar-M, he organized men every day into work crews. Megan was glad he could take over. Aaron would also know the inherent dangers of men climbing on the bales and moving them. Each row-level would need to be removed equally so that no row would collapse for lack of support as the surrounding bales were removed. The men formed a chain within minutes, and Steve pushed a hose down between bales. It was pretty useless, but it was a positive action that relieved some of the stress among the workers.

"Ollie can't see daylight. He says he can breathe, but it's really dark," Samantha relayed to the men on the hay above her. "He says he fell down a hole, and the bales fell after him. He's got one pinning him to another in front. He can't move," her voice cracked, and tears were streaming down her cheeks.

Samantha had been working hay since she was a teen, she knew the weight shifting as the bales were moved could kill her boy, but without them being removed, he wouldn't last. The only sounds in the open building were the men's grunts as they passed the heavy bales to the next in line. The momentary thrill at locating the child had evaporated in the worry of getting to him.

Megan walked over to give Samantha some emotional support. She slipped an arm around the woman's shoulders, and Samantha grabbed her hand. "It's going to be okay. The men know. They can get the hay moved without hurting Oliver. These guys have been humping hay since they could lift a bale. You just need to keep Oliver awake. Keep talking to him. Let us know if he sees light or feels extra weight pressing against him," Megan directed. Samantha's grip on Megan's hand tightened, but her tears lessened.

"Ollie, baby. You need to be brave. The men are throwing bales like hyped-up monkeys. I'll make a video for you," she offered.

A barely heard, muffled voice replied. "Okay, Mommy. I can be brave."

"Sweetie. If you see daylight, you need to tell me. Okay? Also, if the bale on your back gets heavier, you let me know," Samantha instructed her son. She turned to Megan, looking for support.

"He knows not to climb on the hay. We just got a shipment of those big one-ton bales from the coast last week, and these bales are the breakdown of those. Our bander broke, so they haven't been banded into truck bundles yet. The loose bales are the most dangerous. I've told him that. Shoot, he was told that in school too. Why do boys always need to explore?" Samantha's voice reflected her tears as she finally dropped Megan's hand to wring her own.

Megan rubbed her arm, pulling back before Samantha could recapture her hand. The blood flow was painful after the distressed woman's grip.

"I can only say that 'kids will be kids.' I can think of all kinds of dangerous things I did when I was a kid. I was just lucky Rescue never needed to be called. I did break my arm falling out of a tree, once." Megan tried to soothe Samantha by relating her experiences. It didn't seem to be working. The woman's tears flowed harder.

"Ollie, honey, how are you doing in there?" She punctuated her question with a massive sniff, trying to pull together her frazzled nerves.

"Mommy? Are you crying? I'm sorry. I love you." Oliver's voice seemed softer and more muffled.

Megan strained to hear his words. She prayed they were softer because his head turned, not because he was running out of air or energy. She stepped closer and hugged Samantha. Above them, the stack layers were disappearing as bales of hay were passed down or thrown over the side. A sense of urgency flowed among the men. Little talking, just one bale after another passed from person to person.

"Mommy! It hurts!" Oliver's squealed in pain.

"*FREEZE!*" Megan yelled, and all movement on the stack stopped. "Everyone take a step to a different bale," she ordered. She could hear Ollie crying. "Ollie, is that better? Can you see any daylight?"

"The hay bale pushed my face into the hay." Tears in his voice tore at everyone's heart who could hear him.

"Ollie. Can you push the hay bale on your back when I tell you to push?" Megan hoped he could move the bale, and the workers would see it move. This giant game of human Jenga had to end soon. Before Oliver sustained severe injury.

"Yes, ma'am. I can try. It seems a little looser," Olliver replied.

"Everyone up there on the bales. Stand where you are and watch the hay. Oliver is going to push at the bale on his back. If it moves, it may be visible and give you a place to dig. Ready? Oliver, are you ready?" Megan asked.

"Yes." Came from the muffled voice while all the men nodded.

"*PUSH!*" Megan shouted. She listened intently, hearing a grunt from the trapped child.

"*I SEE!*" John from the R-Bar-M shouted, pointing ahead of his feet. "Right here. The hay moved. Poor kid, I was standing on that bale a second ago," he explained as he reached down for the bale that had moved. He pulled, but it wouldn't come out. "*Shit!*" he exclaimed, then looked over at Megan and Samantha. "Sorry for the language. This bale is loose, but it's caught on the bale I'm standing on. Boss, come hold the strings while I move to get this bale out of the way."

There was shuffling of men right and left of John while he stepped aside one row to free the bale needed.

Below him, Steve held the oxygen tank, waiting for the child to be released from the stack of hay. Aaron leaned down to grasp the loose bale by its strings so that it wouldn't collapse onto Oliver. Megan could do nothing but watch the slow-motion action of each bale being removed and the shout of the men when they could see the child. She could feel tears on her cheeks, and she kept a tight hold on Samantha until Oliver had been handed down to Steve. At that point, nothing short of handcuffs could have held Samantha away from her child.

Grown men were cheering through tears as they watched Steve give Oliver oxygen while his mother held him close. Dr. Samuelson had arrived at some point in this rescue, and he stepped forward to check the boy over for injuries. Instead, he watched while Samantha ran her hands over every inch of her boy, looking for reactions that would indicate pain. This maternal inspection was as critical to Samantha's peace of mind as to Oliver's sense of being loved. The doctor would have his chance in a few minutes.

"Oliver Grant, don't you *ever, ever* scare me like this again! You *know* better than to climb in the hay, especially the small bales. I think I aged fifty years in the last hour. I hope you're ashamed of yourself." Samantha alternated hugging and shaking the boy. The shaking came from her hands when she held him out from her body to inspect him. She was shaking so severely that Megan stepped in to keep her from falling over.

Oliver dropped his head and then looked up at his mother with tears streaming down his cheeks. "I'm sorry. I saw something in a bale. It looked like Ralph's wallet that fell into the baler. I wanted to get it for him," Oliver's reason brought more tears to Samantha.

"Honey, Ralph is the last person who would want you crawling up to get his wallet. You should have thrown a stick as close as you could to the bale and let Ralph climb up there later," she reasoned with her boy.

"Okay. I won't ever climb up in the bales again. Unless another person needs me. I promise." Oliver crossed his heart with his fingers to show his mother he meant the vow.

The men in the massive building began restacking the hay that had landed helter-skelter during the search. They all had stacked hay for family, friends, or a summer job and knew the bales couldn't be left on the ground. Hay on the ground rotted from moisture in the soil. Dr. Samuelson finally got his chance to inspect the child and confirmed to Samantha that Oliver wasn't seriously injured. Bruised and scratched here and there, but nothing that wouldn't heal in a week or less. Oliver had been extremely fortunate today.

As the men finished, Megan began walking up to each one, shaking hands and thanking them for arriving so quickly. Her eyes had dried, but she felt the burn of tears again when she noticed Oliver beside her, following her example. He solemnly shook every man's hand and thanked each for saving his life. His mother was beside him, doing the same, her tears still wetting her cheeks.

Yes, this was right. This was the America she'd been born in, and here is where Megan wanted to live and raise a family. These were her people, men, and women who would drop anything when help was needed by a neighbor. People who helped each other and worked hard to provide a life for those they loved. Riverview was her kind of hometown.

The End

Made in the USA
Columbia, SC
15 March 2024